Birds in the Air

Also by Frances O'Roark Dowell

THE SECRET LANGUAGE OF GIRLS

THE KIND OF FRIENDS WE USED TO BE

THE SOUND OF YOUR VOICE, ONLY REALLY FAR AWAY

* * *

ANYBODY SHINING

CHICKEN BOY

DOVEY COE

FALLING IN

THE SECOND LIFE OF ABIGAIL WALKER

SHOOTING THE MOON

TEN MILES PAST NORMAL

TROUBLE THE WATER

WHERE I'D LIKE TO BE

* * *

PHINEAS L. MCGUIRE . . . BLASTS OFF!

PHINEAS L. MCGUIRE . . . ERUPTS!

PHINEAS L. MCGUIRE . . . GETS COOKING!

PHINEAS L. MCGUIRE . . . GETS SLIMED!

* * *

SAM THE MAN & THE CHICKEN PLAN

Birds *in the* Air

A NOVEL

FRANCES O'ROARK DOWELL

Milton Falls MEDIA

Milton Falls Media, Inc.
2608 Erwin Road, #148-152
Durham, N.C. 27705
www.miltonfallsmedia.com

For information about purchasing Milton Falls Media books, please write to the publisher at: sales@miltonfallsmedia.com.

This is a work of fiction. Names, characters, businesses, places, events and incidents are either the products of the author's imagination or used in a fictitious manner.

Cover Design: Jenny Zemanek
Seedlings Design Studio | www.seedlingsonline.com

Publisher's Cataloging-In-Publication Data
(The Donohue Group, Inc.)
Names: Dowell, Frances O'Roark.
Title: Birds in the air : a novel / Frances O'Roark Dowell.
Description: Durham, N.C. : Milton Falls Media, [2016]
Identifiers: LCCN 2016908960 |
ISBN 978-1-945354-00-7 | ISBN 978-1-945354-01-4 (ebook)
Subjects: LCSH: Women--North Carolina--Fiction. | Quilting--North Carolina--Fiction. | Country life--North Carolina--Fiction. | Moving, Household--North Carolina--Fiction. | Friendship--Fiction. | LCGFT: Humorous fiction.
Classification: LCC PS3604.O939 B57 2016 (print) | LCC PS3604.O939 (ebook) | DDC 813/.6--dc23

Library of Congress Control Number: 2016908960

For my mother and BQF (Best Quilty Friend), Jane O'Roark

1.

It's a midwinter Wednesday, a blustery, unforgiving sort of day, and Emma Byrd is talking to her house. She doesn't usually talk to houses, but here she is, stranded in an island of boxes, bundled up in her husband's blue and gold high school letterman's jacket and his thick, wool camping socks, and she wants to tell someone, anyone, how much she hates January. She wants to explain how January's blank days make her feel aimless and adrift, her mind unable to focus without December's long list of errands in front of her. But her husband's at work, her kids are at school, and her phone is in the other room, out of reach. So although she wants to talk, there's no one to listen. The house, she has decided, will have to do.

"I've always hated January," she explains to the fireplace, where flotillas of cobwebs float dreamily in the corners. Pulling a stack of folders from a box, she looks around for someplace to put it and settles for the top of another box. "When I was little, I stood at my window and begged it to go away. But it never listened to me. It just stayed January day after day until I thought I'd go crazy."

So what is she doing here, unpacking moving boxes three weeks after Christmas? What sane person would pack up and move house this time of year? The sky is a gray blanket outside her window, the morning light dim and unpromising. "It's all your fault," she grumbles at the wide-planked oak floors. She squints menacingly at the wainscoting, shoots a suspicious glance at the built-in shelves. "If it weren't for you," she says, glaring at the crown molding, "we would have moved in April, and I'd still be in a house that actually got warm when you turned on the heat."

A branch smacks the window, and Emma jumps, nearly falling backward over an unwieldy stack of books. On this particular January morning, the wind is having a field day, repeatedly blasting the north side of the house and causing all the windows to rattle like chattering teeth. Emma pulls the letter jacket tightly around her shoulders. *Call about insulation*, she adds to the running list in her head, which also includes *Call about leak in the upstairs toilet, Call about Sarah's bedroom door, which refuses to stay shut*, and *Call about weird smell in cellar.*

She'll call this afternoon. She'll sit down at the computer and do an Internet search for "Plumber, Sweet Anne's Gap, NC" and "Carpenter, Sweet Anne's Gap, NC." She doesn't know who to call about weird smells in the cellar, but maybe she can ask the plumber.

"Why don't you just go next door and get a recommendation?" Owen asked at dinner the night before. "They'll know who's good."

"I don't want be a bother," Emma replied. "Didn't the realtor say that Hannah Byers is really old? She might not appreciate visitors."

"She might have Alzheimer's," Sarah said matter-of-factly. Her best friend Sophie's grandmother had Alzheimer's, and

Sarah considered herself an expert on the subject in the way only a ten-year-old could. "She might give you the name of a plumber who isn't even alive anymore."

"Not everyone who's old has Alzheimer's, sweetie," Emma told her daughter. "It's probably not a good habit to make assumptions."

Sarah shrugged. "Well, if she does, we can call Sophie to get advice."

"Speaking of calls to Sophie, I don't even want to know what the phone bill's going to be this month," Owen said. "You guys need to be communicating via computer like everyone else in your generation."

Sarah brightened. "You'll get me a smart phone?"

Emma and Owen shook their heads in concert. "Not until you're thirteen," Emma told her.

"And maybe not even then," Owen added. "I meant email."

Sarah pouted into her pasta. Owen turned back to Emma. "All you do is go next-door, say, 'Hello, Mrs. Byers, I'm your friendly new neighbor, Emma, and I need the number of a good plumber.'"

"Mom's not really all that friendly, though." Ben, who had spent the last few minutes examining the stack of baseball cards hidden in his lap, looked up at Owen. "She's nice, but not friendly. She should probably let Mrs. Byers know that."

"I am too friendly," Emma protested. "I've always been friendly."

"No, you always wave and say, 'Hi,' in a really loud voice," Ben corrected her. "Friendly is stopping to talk, the way Dad does."

Emma thinks about their discussion now as she runs a utility knife across the top of a box and peels back the flaps.

It's true that as a rule she's more comfortable with books than with people, but it isn't like she doesn't have friends. Well, not here, of course, but they've only lived in Sweet Anne's Gap for a week, and she's been too busy unpacking boxes to get out and meet people. Besides, who could make friends in January? You survived January by lying on the couch in your flannel bathrobe with a mug of hot chocolate and watching the BBC production of *Pride and Prejudice*. Everybody knows that.

She looks up from the box she's unpacking and surveys the room around her. This, at least, is a room that needs no repairs. As long as she can remember, she's always wanted a room exactly like this, a room with a fireplace and a window seat, a room where Emily Dickinson might have felt at home. It's the sort of room that makes you lose your mind and move house in January, Emma decides. "I should have known better," she complains to the fireplace, but she doesn't mean it. The whole house is marvelous. Flawed, in need of serious repair, but marvelous nonetheless, and it cost a third of what it would have in Chapel Hill. And best of all, Emma finally has a room of her own.

"Now I have no excuses," she says in a firm voice to the crown molding. "I have the room, I have the time."

She reaches into the box and pulls out a book, *The Poisonwood Bible* by Barbara Kingsolver, one of her favorites. What would it be like, to be Barbara Kingsolver, sitting down at her desk every day, putting words on paper until a story spills off the page and into the imaginations of thousands of readers? It's what Emma has always dreamed of doing, ever since second grade when she wrote a one-page epic called *Oh, No! My Dog Ran Away!* "Wonderful!" her teacher had written next to three gold foil stars on the bottom of the page, and Emma had been hooked.

Yet here she is, forty, and it's been years since she's managed to write anything besides press releases and talking points. She knows it's an old story: You graduate college with all sorts of dreams, but you have to pay the rent, so you take the so-so job at the community newspaper, and that leads to a slightly better job writing PR copy at a small local firm, and that leads to another, better job, and suddenly you're a public relations specialist. You try to write at night, and some nights you do, but it gets harder after you get married and have kids and a mortgage. In fact, it becomes impossible.

But now, much to her surprise, Emma finds herself in a new story. She's happily unemployed, with all the time in the world to write, at least between the hours of 8 a.m. and 3 p.m. All she has to do is put the house in order, clear a space on her desk, and get started. She does her best to ignore the nagging worries that sneak up on her in the middle of the night, like what on earth is she going to write about and what if she doesn't have any talent? What if she's used it all up writing content marketing?

Overhead, a pipe begins to clank. Don't you have to flush a toilet or turn on a faucet for the pipes to clank? Emma stands and brushes off her hands. A plumber. She needs a plumber. How can she write novels if the pipes are making a racket all day long?

"I'm going to go next door and ask Mrs. Byers for the name of a good plumber," she tells the fireplace firmly. "And then I'm going to come back and finish unpacking my books, and then I'm going to — oh, I don't know — join the PTA or something and make lots and lots of friends. Oh, and find a carpenter."

Emma takes off the letter jacket, puts on her shoes, then finds her coat on the couch in the living room, where she left it that morning after walking Homer, their chocolate brown Lab now asleep on Ben's bed upstairs. The living room had been the first room after the kitchen they'd gotten unpacked and in working order, and she feels a surge of housewifely satisfaction as she looks around. The couch, newly spruced up with a white twill slipcover, faces a picture window that opens to a view of the mountains. Two overstuffed chairs cozy up to the wicker trunk that serves as the coffee table, and a rocking chair stands guard in front of the fireplace. The look is simple, elegant, and uncluttered. Emma knows that it's only a matter of days. Children, like nature, abhor a vacuum, and soon Sarah and Ben will fill the room with their markers and drawing pads, Ben's matchbox cars, Sarah's unending supply of Barbie paraphernalia. Maybe when she returns from visiting Mrs. Byers, she should take pictures; the room will never again look this composed.

She steps out onto the front porch and takes a deep breath. Fresh mountain air, she tells herself. Fresh, bitterly cold, possibly doing damage to her lungs, January mountain air. *What doesn't kill ya makes you stronger,* she can hear her father say, and she can't help giggling. Her dad has always been a fount of fatherly wisdom, and Emma and her sister Holly delight each other over the phone with their Big Ed imitations. "It's nice to be important, but it's more important to be nice," Holly might intone sagely if Emma complained that Owen wasn't getting the recognition at work she thought he deserved. "The only time success comes before work is in the dictionary," Emma liked to repeat to Holly, who usually replied, "It's not how far you fall, it's how high you bounce."

Still, sometimes her dad has a point. Pulling her scarf more tightly around her neck, she takes another breath, throws back her shoulders, and walks out into the late morning chill. She can be such a baby, complaining about things that bother everyone — long stretches of rainy weather, traffic delays, a bout with the common cold — as if she were the only person in the world affected by them. Everybody's cold in January, she scolds herself. You'd be cold back home, you're cold here, you'd probably be cold if you went to Disney World. Suck it up. Buy some long underwear. *Buy long underwear.* She adds that to her list.

The gravel drive spills out messily onto the road. "We'll need to get that paved," Owen had declared as soon as they'd gotten out of the realtor's sedan to see the house for the first time. He spoke like a man with one hand on his checkbook, ready to buy, and they hadn't even stepped inside yet. They didn't have to. One look at the wrap-around front porch, the multitude of gables, the oak tree in the front yard shedding red and yellow leaves, and they were hooked.

"Everyone here has a gravel driveway," Emma had said, looking up and down the road. "A paved driveway might look out of place."

"Maybe," Owen said, not believing it for a minute, his precise engineer's brain calculating the volume of concrete he would need to set the drive to rights. But paving a driveway is not a mid-winter job, and so Emma happily kicks little bits of gravel as she ambles along the road to her neighbor's, officially next-door, but in reality a few minutes' walk away.

Mrs. Byers' house sits back on its sloping lot like a squat Buddha. It appears to Emma to have started out as a one-story house that had another floor added on, and then some years later yet another. None of the house's layers quite match, and they seem to be sinking into each other. The first story is brick and traditional, the second wood and a bit rustic, and the top story is a gingerbread concoction covered in vinyl siding. "It's a real looker," Owen had commented dryly the first time they'd seen it, and Emma had to agree that houses didn't get much stranger than this one.

Halfway up the drive, Emma wonders if she should have brought something, a plate of cookies or a houseplant. But no, it's the other way around, isn't it? Mrs. Byers should make the cookies, preferably chocolate chip, and knock on Emma's door. Not that Emma minds the oversight. She imagines herself in the front hall, dutifully answering questions about their reasons for moving: Owen's new job with the Department of Transportation, the desire to slow their pace, back away from the demands of modern suburban life.

That's the problem with small talk — you were supposed to keep it small, vague, impersonal. But Emma likes personal details best. She likes to hear the stories behind scars — *Your sister hit you in the face with her Chatty Cathy doll?* — and interesting bits of family history. She likes to know how people fell in love with their spouses or chose their children's names. Wading through polite talk, unrevealing talk, she can feel herself grow heavy and dull. *Yes, the weather certainly has been beautiful, yes, we think the school has a wonderful music program.*

By the time she reaches the Byers' front porch, she feels winded from the climb. She stands at the screened door, waiting to catch her breath and practicing her lines in her head. "Hello! I'm Emma Byrd, your new neighbor, and I need a plumber!"

The front door opens before she has a chance to knock. Emma finds herself looking through the screen at a slightly bent figure with snow-white braids wrapped around her head and lovely, powdery cheeks etched with tiny lines.

"Hello! I'm Emma—" Emma begins, sticking out her hand, although she isn't sure what she intends to do with it. She can't exactly shake hands through a screen. What she really wants to do, she realizes, is touch her neighbor's face, which looks impossibly soft.

But before she can even finish her sentence, the woman cuts her off. "I'm sorry, honey," she says, shaking her head sadly. "But I just ain't got the heart for anybody new."

With that, the woman closes the door, leaving Emma with her hand still extended.

"You don't happen to know a good plumber, do you?" she asks the door. When the door doesn't reply, she sticks her hand in her pocket and walks back home.

2.

The coffee has just finished brewing when the doorbell rings. It doesn't ring, actually, it buzzes and rattles, and Emma nearly drops the carton of half and half she's delivering to the fridge when she hears it.

"Coming, coming!" she calls as she trots down the hallway, not exactly sure why she feels she has to hurry. It's something about the bell's tone, demanding and impatient, as though it's not convinced Emma is up to the task of answering the door.

The young woman standing on the front porch wears a bright yellow nurse's smock under a pink, puffy coat. Her thick brown hair is pulled back into a loose ponytail, a few strands escaping to curl sweetly around her heart-shaped face. "Hey!" she greets Emma, the "hey" stretching out into two syllables, sounding friendly and apologetic at the same time. "I'm Lettie, from next door? I believe you just met my grandmother?"

"Um, I guess I sort of met her," Emma says, not quite knowing how to describe her experience with the old woman. A drive-by rejection? An encounter with the unwelcome wagon? "She didn't seem like she wanted to talk to me. Was it a bad time?"

"Oh, no," the woman says, smiling as she shakes her head. She has a raggedy edge to her voice that Emma likes. She remembers screaming into her pillow as a teenager to get the same effect. "She really doesn't want to talk to you. Not just you, I don't mean that. She doesn't want to talk to anyone. Granny's feeling a little, well, antisocial these days."

"I'm sorry to hear that," Emma says, and then it occurs to her that maybe she should ask Lettie in. "Do you have time to visit? I just made some coffee. It wakes me up after lunch."

"Oh, I don't want to be a bother," Lettie says, shivering a little. "I just wanted to tell you not to take Granny personally." She takes a step forward and peers inside. "How's the house coming along? I bet you've got a whole lot of work to do. But it's a great old house, isn't it? I used to play here all the time with Miss Lydia's grandkids when I little."

"You want to come in and look around? It's a mess, and you might trip over some boxes, but you're welcome."

"Oh, no, I couldn't," Lettie insists even as she's crossing the threshold. "Well, maybe just a peek. It's been years since I've been inside this old place. Miss Lydia was sick for a long time before she passed, and they had her down at Pine Manor — the nursing home? Lord, I know she hated it there. She loved this house, though. Raised all her babies here and her grandbabies, too, after their mama died. Breast cancer — it was the saddest thing."

Emma follows Lettie inside. "Don't mind the dog," she says, pointing to Homer, who has wandered into the study and is now sniffing at some freshly opened boxes. "He's very sweet."

"Oh, I'm not scared of dogs," Lettie says. "My last boyfriend had a pit bull, and he didn't scare me the least bit. He scared my boyfriend though." She laughs. "That oughta tell you something right there, a man scared of his own dog. Bad sign. Very bad sign."

She walks into Emma's study, and Emma follows her, wondering if Lettie will want a tour of the entire house. The only presentable rooms are the kitchen and the living room. The children are making slow progress in their bedrooms; they can't unpack a box without examining every little thing, calling out their discoveries — "I found my Transformers! But Optimus Prime's arm fell off!" — and then abandoning their work to play until dinnertime, the rest of the box's contents left for another day. Emma hopes she closed the door to the master bedroom, because she's pretty sure the bed-making fairy hasn't shown up yet this morning.

"I always loved it in here especially," Lettie says, standing next to the fireplace and running her hand over the mantle. "Me and Dawna used to sit in that window seat and talk and talk. We were going to be, oh, fashion models and movie stars, and marry the most handsome men and build our mansions next door to each other."

"Where's Dawna now?"

Lettie laughs. "She's a missionary. Furthest thing in the world from a movie star."

Emma nods toward the kitchen. "Are you sure you wouldn't like some coffee?"

"Well, if it's truly not a bother. I just finished up a week on the overnight shift at the hospital, so this is still kind of morning for me. I'd of come over sooner to say hey, but when I work third shift, I sleep until lunch and run Granny's errands all afternoon, get her groceries and medicines and all that."

They walk to the kitchen, and Lettie takes a seat at the table. She rubs the edge of a roughly woven placemat between her fingers and says, "This is pretty. Did you make it?"

Emma laughs, setting two mugs on the table and taking a seat. She's famous in some parts for just how certifiably uncrafty she is. "I wouldn't know how. I got those at Target."

"I could tell you some stories about this house," Lettie says, taking a sip of coffee. "Have you been poking around in the attic? Are the trunks still there?"

"I haven't looked through them yet," Emma tells her. "I'm sort of saving them."

"For a treat?" Lettie asks.

Emma nods, pleased that Lettie understands. She'd noticed the three trunks in the corner of the attic the first time she and Owen had looked at the house and immediately began imagining what might be inside. Old Letters? Diaries? Yellowing christening gowns wrapped in tissue paper? When should she open them? Maybe the first day they moved in (she was already sure they would be moving in). Or should she wait?

Wait, she'd decided. She would wait for the right sort of day, a quiet day, a wood smoke and cedar-smelling sort of day. She would know the right day when it came, she told herself. It would announce itself to her.

"Well, I won't tell you what's in them," Lettie says. "Fact is, I probably don't remember half of it, it's been so long. But there are a few things I'd sure like to see again. Lord, I could tell you some stories. This one time — "

Lettie stops herself and covers her mouth. "I'm sorry — I know I'm talking a blue streak. It always happens after I've been on third shift. All your patients are sleeping and you don't hardly talk to anyone all week. And Granny doesn't talk any more, she's so upset about Mama, so everything gets bottled up inside. You'll have to excuse me."

"I've been talking to my house lately," Emma confesses. "I don't have a lot of people to talk to, either, at least not until my kids get home from school."

Lettie laughs. "I talk to my car sometimes, especially when the roads are bad going down the mountain. I like to keep its spirits up." She takes another sip of coffee, and then gives Emma a mischievous look. "You don't want to go up now and open one of those trunks, do you?" She raises a hand. "Now, you feel free to say no. I don't want to talk you into anything. But there's one I remember..."

"I guess it wouldn't hurt to look at just one," Emma says, a little reluctantly. "I've gotten all the bathroom stuff unpacked and put away. That's worth one trunk, right?"

"Oh, at the very least," Lettie assures her. "I want to see if what I'm thinking about is still there. I bet it is — Miss Lydia was so particular about us putting everything back in its place just the way we found it."

Emma follows Lettie up the stairs to the second floor landing. "I'm acting like I'm in charge, leading you around this way," Lettie laughs. "You'll have to excuse me. But I really did spend a good amount of time here."

"That's okay," Emma tells her. "The house is so big, I feel like I'm still finding my way around."

"It *is* big," Lettie says, opening the attic door and looking up the stairs. "But I bet you're just being polite and letting me boss you around. This is the sort of house you fall in love with the minute you walk inside." She turns to Emma and raises an eyebrow. "I mean, the way you'd fall in love with a man and want to know every square inch of him."

Emma feels herself color, but she laughs and nods her head. "Yeah, that about sums it up."

"How are your kids liking school?" Lettie asks as she climbs the steps. "Did they mind moving in the middle of the year?"

"Ben, my second-grader, minds more than Sarah. Sarah was in a mean girls class this year, full of queen bees. She was sad to leave her best friend, but happy as anything to get out of that classroom."

Lettie waits for her at the top of the steps. "When I was a kid, I use to wish girls would just be like boys, you know, using their fists to settle things. What girls do is a whole lot worse. And they're so sneaky about it."

"And now they use technology," Emma informs her. "I can't believe parents give ten-year-old girls smart phones, but they do. The girls text all sorts of awful things. In fifth grade!"

"We did the same thing with notes," Lettie says. "A pencil's a pretty vicious piece of technology in the wrong hands."

Emma sighs. "I guess so." Still, she can't help but hope that the fifth grade girls of Sweet Anne's Gap are a little less tech savvy and a lot kinder than the girls of Mrs. Kelly's homeroom class.

Emma follows Lettie into the attic, which is a large space, three-quarters finished, with windows at both ends, so that the room is flooded with natural light on sunny days. When she first saw it, she immediately thought about making a playroom for the kids, but right now they need the storage space. She's a little embarrassed for Lettie to see the dozen or so ransacked boxes where they've all gone searching at one time or another for a sweater or toy or pair of shoes they couldn't find downstairs. She tells herself that it's no big deal, just the overflow detritus of your average early 21st century American household, nothing to get excited about.

"Now, is that where the trunks are, under those blankets?" Lettie points to the south end of the attic. When Emma nods, she says, "Okay, well, I hope the keys are where they used to be."

She leans over a stack of boxes and strains to reach behind a post. "When we were kids, the fact that you had to get the keys from their hiding place was a big part of the fun. It made opening the trunks feel mysterious, even though we knew exactly what was inside."

"The realtor told me the keys were around here some- where, but she didn't know where," Emma says, following Lettie to where the trunks are stored under the eaves. "It's a good thing you came over. I probably never would have found them on my own."

"Hope I didn't spoil it for you, knowing where they were." Lettie waves a skeleton key at Emma. "But you might have been looking forever."

"I'll get over it," Emma says with a laugh. "I have to admit I'm disappointed that I'm not the first person to find the trunks. I've imagined them filled with secret documents from the original owners. You know, maps to where all the hidden passageways are, things like that."

"I hate to tell you this," Lettie says, "But the Buchan- ans — the people that built this house? — they didn't own those. According to Miss Lydia, the trunks belonged to her mother, who was a McKinney. Miss Lydia just happened to inherit them after she married Bob Buchanan and moved into his family home." Lettie cups her hand to her mouth and lowers her voice to a whisper, as if sharing a secret. "She was her mama's favorite, don't you know?"

Emma feels childishly disappointed. All along she's been thinking of the trunks as a kind of gift left to her from the original Mrs. Buchanan. She'd imagined packets of letters tied with ribbon, and genteel journals, their yellowing pages filled with Mrs. Buchanan's reminiscences and recipes for chokeberry preserves, all safely stored away for Emma to find eighty years later.

Really, she thinks, she's got to stop watching the Hallmark channel.

Kneeling down beside the largest of the three trunks, Lettie carefully inserts the key. "There's a trick to it, if I recall correctly." She jiggles the key a few times, turns it, then tugs. The lock clicks open.

Lettie stands up and turns to Emma. "I'll let you do the honors. I just hope something's still in there. I'll feel foolish if they're empty."

Emma's surprised to feel a flutter of nerves. It's just an old trunk, after all. What's left inside is probably moth-eaten or mouse-nibbled beyond recognition, if in fact there's anything left at all. She imagines the awkward moment she and Lettie are about to share as they stare at the remains of ancient newspapers and water-stained linens. Leaning down, she gingerly tugs at the side of the trunk's lid. It doesn't want to give immediately, and then suddenly it pops open like the top of a jack-in-the-box. Emma stumbles backward and instinctively holds her hands in front of her face.

"Oh, Lord!" Lettie exclaims, rapidly fanning her cheeks with both hands. "That about scared me to death!"

Emma is practically hyperventilating. "Good grief! I thought snakes were going to jump out at me."

"Well, go ahead, take a look," Lettie urges, moving a step closer. "Don't keep us in suspense."

Edging toward the trunk, Emma lifts her head to peer over the side without having to get too close. She gasps. Two sets of glassy eyes are peering back at her.

Lettie comes up behind her. "The dolls! They're still here. Sunny and Tuesday. That's real human hair, by the way."

The two dolls lie on their backs, one raven-haired, one blonde with a garish crack running down the side of her face. Their lips are parted to reveal tiny teeth yellowed with age. The dark-haired one is dressed in blue calico, the blonde in what appears to be a wedding dress, the lace ripped, the hem in tatters.

"Oh, we wore these girls out," Lettie says. "Took 'em everywhere. Everybody else had dolls that wet their pants and cried and grew their hair, but no one had anything as wonderful as Sunny and Tuesday."

"Sunny and Tuesday?" Emma asks as she eyes the dolls. The crack in Sunny's face gives her a judgmental expression, one that suggests she doesn't think much of Emma's outfit.

"Well, Dawna named that one Sunny — "Lettie points to the blonde — "but I thought she said Sunday. When she told me to name the other one, I didn't want to name it Monday, but I thought Tuesday sounded nice. Granny made Tuesday's dress. I wanted her to be like Laura, from *Little House*. She was always doing wild stuff and Sunny here was always giving tea parties."

"You should take them," Emma tells her now. She picks up Tuesday and hands her to Lettie. "I can tell they mean a lot to you."

Lettie shakes her head. "Oh, I couldn't. You should give them to your little girl."

Emma opens her mouth to insist, and then decides not to, even though she suspects Sarah will take one look at these dolls and run screaming back to her Barbies. She doesn't want to hurt Lettie's feelings by suggesting the dolls aren't every little girl's dream. "Well, thanks, but if you ever change your mind…"

"I'll let you know," Lettie says, grinning. "I just might. Now why don't you look and see what else is in there? I can't remember, other than the dolls. Might just be some old yearbooks, but there could be a treasure or two."

The dolls have been resting on a baby blue receiving blanket. Emma hands Sunny to Lettie, and then the blanket, which smells strongly of mothballs. Underneath is an assortment of yellowed front pages from the *Mountain Times*, which have been layered over a tissue-wrapped package. Emma looks at Lettie, to see if she knows what it is.

"No idea," Lettie tells her. "It doesn't look big enough for Miss Lydia's wedding dress. Maybe it's her lace tablecloth that she brought out for Thanksgiving."

Emma carefully lifts the package, as though it might break into pieces if she's rough with it. She pulls back the paper and sees that there are several layers. Carefully she removes each one until she comes to the last sheet, which is white and almost translucent, like onionskin.

"I think it's a quilt," Emma reports. The paper slips away to reveal the folded blanket inside. She carefully lifts it and lets it fall open. The colors are faded to grays and browns, each block of the quilt a series of carefully stitched triangles and squares.

Emma turns to Lettie. "Do you remember this?"

"I really don't," Lettie says, shaking her head, as though she's surprised the trunk contains something she's unfamiliar with. "It's a beauty."

"I don't know anything about quilts," Emma admits. "I guess this looks handmade."

"Oh, it's handmade for sure. Granny makes quilts, so I was raised around them. And this one's old, too — maybe even 19th century. I don't know about the pattern name, though. It could be an 'Ann and Andy,' but I'm not sure." Lettie reaches out and runs her hand along the quilt's border. "You could take it down to Ruth at the Sewing Room. She'd know."

Emma carefully refolds the quilt and places it on top of the pile of tissue paper next to the trunk. She reaches back in and feels around. Is that it? The dolls, the newspapers, the quilt? Her fingers brush against the hard corner of something. A frame.

"Who's this?" she asks, pulling out a photograph of a young girl. She squints to read the words scrawled on the lower right hand corner of the matting. "1906," is all she can make out. She looks up at Lettie. "Maybe Lydia's mother, or her grandmother? How would the math on that work?"

Lettie shrugs. "I guess it could be Miss Lydia's mother. Miss Lydia was born a few years after World War I ended, I'm pretty sure. Right before the Great Depression."

Emma examines the picture. The girl is posed sitting sideways, looking off into the distance, her coiled curls pulled back with a band. She's wearing a simple white dress, lace-up boots, white stockings. She might be Sarah's age, maybe a year younger. She's pretty despite her sour expression, her mouth set in a firm line, as if she's sitting for this picture against her will.

"A mystery," Emma proclaims, and she lays the photograph on top of the quilt. "Two mysteries, really."

"Take that quilt to Ruth," Lettie insists. "The shop's down on Trade Street, across from the old train station. She'll know something, I bet."

Emma closes the trunk lid, picks up the quilt and the photograph. Treasures, she thinks. She feels pleased, as though someone has left an unexpected gift at her door.

After Lettie leaves, Emma watches out the window as she walks down the road toward her grandmother's house and wonders if they will become friends. She's kind, Emma thinks. Then she holds out the photograph and looks at the girl, who appears on the verge of scolding someone — Emma, maybe, if she doesn't shape up.

"What's your story?" Emma asks the girl, who doesn't look kind at all, but scornful and inscrutable instead, stubbornly silent behind the dusty glass.

3.

"A mystery quilt!" Holly exclaims when Emma gives her the rundown on her visit with Lettie Byers. They're in the middle of their weekly Thursday afternoon phone call and Emma can just see her sister, done with her teaching duties for the day, sipping a cup of coffee from the student union, feet up on her desk. "What an amazing thing to find in your attic. When are you going to take it to have it looked at?"

"I don't know," Emma says. She's sitting at the kitchen table, doing her best to ignore the day's dishes piled in the sink. "I'm so busy right now, I haven't had time to think about it."

"You sound sort of hesitant," Holly observes, shifting into full psych professor mode. "What's going on inside that brain of yours?"

"I'm not hesitant," Emma says. "I told you — I'm busy. I've started volunteering in the library at the kids' school, where, by the way, I have met the world's shyest librarian, even though she wears these cool green glasses that I don't think she should wear if she's not willing to discuss them. So yes, I'm a school volunteer, and tomorrow afternoon I've got another shift, and then hopefully the guy's going to come see about the insulation in the attic. The quilt just isn't at the top of my to-do list right now."

Emma stands, stretches, and walks over to the sink to rinse out her coffee cup. The dishes give off a disparaging vibe, like they want to know what else she's been neglecting besides them and the attic quilt. The worst thing about not working in an office, Emma's discovered, is that you constantly have to explain to people that you are, in fact, using your time constructively. Just this morning she got an email from her mother with the greeting "Dear Lady of Leisure." As if.

"Okay, so you've been busy," Holly finally concedes. "Busy writing, by any chance?"

"Um, sort of, but not exactly, " Emma says, purposefully vague. She's not sure she wants to get into the subject of her so-called writing life.

"What do you mean 'not exactly'?" Holly asks. She's apparently not going to let Emma hem and haw her way out of this discussion, so Emma takes a deep breath and tries to explain.

"I mean, every time I sit down at the computer, my mind goes blank. There's all this how-to stuff online, and it's all the same: *write about what you know, write about what you know.* But what do I know? I know a lot about being a mother, but is that even interesting? It's really just a lot of peanut butter and jelly sandwiches when you get down to it."

"Of course motherhood is interesting!" Holly insists. "Motherhood is a defining experience for a lot of women. And peanut butter and jelly is only a small part of it."

"Oh, it's at least thirty percent of the entire mothering experience," Emma counters. "Maybe even thirty-five. The point is, if you're going to write a novel you need to have a story, and a story has to have a plot, and to have a plot you need to know what kind of book you're writing. Romance? Mystery? Chick lit? Romance is out, and chick lit is, too. That leaves me with mystery, but I don't know any good mysteries, other than the mystery of Sarah's lost winter jacket. She says she brought it home from school on Friday, but the evidence suggests otherwise."

"Maybe you need to give yourself more time to get settled in," Holly says sensibly. "You're barely unpacked; how are you supposed to write a novel? And maybe you should start small. Carry a notebook with you, take notes about what you see, get the juices flowing. You could go to that café you've told me about — what's it called?"

"Helen's," Emma tells her. She turns from the sink and walks down the hall to the study, where her lonely computer stares at her reproachfully from her desk. Quickly changing route, she heads for the living room. "I tried writing there once, but these old men were hanging out drinking coffee, and they stared at me the whole time."

"Be brave, little sister," Holly says. "And while you're being brave, I think you should take that quilt to get it appraised. Put that on your chore list, too."

"Why is it so important to you that I get this quilt checked out?" Emma asks. She flops on the couch, feeling irritated. Holly can be like a dog with a bone sometimes, refusing to drop a subject when Emma's more than ready.

"Why are you so resistant to the idea?"

"Quit talking to me like you're my therapist," Emma says, a common refrain, and Holly snorts in a very un-therapeutic-like way.

"I know you, Emma," she says. "There's a reason you haven't gone yet."

Emma leans back and looks at the ceiling. Okay, to be honest, maybe she *has* been resistant to the idea. She tells herself it's because she's busy, and also she feels shy about going somewhere she doesn't know anyone. But really, she can't understand why the idea of walking into a place where ostensibly she'll find brightly colored fabrics and cheerful — if most likely elderly — salespeople, makes her feel suddenly heavy and slightly depressed.

"It's Aunt Nora!" Holly exclaims suddenly, nearly causing Emma to drop the phone. "Remember when Aunt Nora came to live with us? It was only for a few months. I think I was in eighth grade."

"Dad's Aunt Nora?" Emma asks, calculating. If Holly had been in eighth grade, she would have been in sixth. They'd lived in northern Virginia, in the split-level their mother had hated for its suburban blandness but the sisters had loved because the downstairs family room where they watched TV was out of hearing distance of their parents' bedroom.

And then Emma sees it — the sunroom off the kitchen, a room she loved for its cool red ceramic tiles, for the flokati rug she liked to lie on while she read, her feet propped on the wicker couch. It was a room that felt like summer even in the middle of winter.

But a few weeks after the beginning of sixth grade, Aunt Nora moved into the sunroom with her rented hospital bed, her pharmacy's worth of medicine, her endless supply of cigarettes. Emma's father had explained that Aunt Nora was his mother's older sister, and she would be living with them until her room in the state-of-the-art nursing home they were building in Annandale was ready for her. "She's a little forgetful," Emma's father had told them in the car on the way to pick Aunt Nora up. "And she's not too happy about going into a nursing home, but she can't live alone anymore. Be nice to her, exactly the way you'd be if she were Grammy."

But Aunt Nora wasn't Grammy. Grammy wore knock-off Chanel suits and spectator pumps and White Shoulders perfume. Grammy had her hair done every Wednesday, and didn't leave the house without at least three coats of Revlon "Love that Red" lipstick on her lips. She treated Emma and Holly as if they were newly crowned royalty, their wishes her commands. She drove a Cadillac. Aunt Nora had never learned to drive, didn't wear lipstick, refused to dye her hair, and didn't much like children.

"Remember how Aunt Nora used to trash talk Grammy?" Holly asks Emma. "Seventy-five years worth of resentments."

"Oh, yeah," Emma says as it comes back to her. "She was the workhorse, Grammy was the clothes horse. Do you remember her saying that?"

Holly laughs. "How could I forget? She said it at least ten times a day. And remember how she put sheets up on the sunroom's windows, because the light hurt her eyes? It was like a cave in there, and it smelled awful. Like mothballs and Vicks VapoRub and cigarette smoke."

"Okay, yeah, I definitely remember," Emma says. "But what's the connection between Aunt Nora coming to live with us and me being totally unable to walk five minutes into town to show some woman a quilt?"

"What did you say the shop was called?" Holly asked. "The Sewing Room? Put it together, Em."

And there it is. Emma can see the old Singer in the corner of the sunroom. Sewing was Aunt Nora's one activity. She didn't read, didn't watch TV. According to her, all of her friends were dead, so there were no phone calls or visits. All Aunt Nora did was either lie on her bed and smoke Pall Mall cigarettes, an overflowing ashtray on either side of her, or else sit at her machine, stitching patchwork quilts out of ugly polyester fabric.

"When you think of Aunt Nora, you're thinking of that sewing machine," Holly spells it out for her now. "When you think of sewing machines, you think of Aunt Nora. Cigarettes, Vicks VapoRub, decay, death."

"The VapoRub smell wasn't that bad," Emma says. "The cigarettes were a lot, lot worse."

"Okay, sure," Holly says agreeably. "But you see what I'm getting at."

"I've just been busy," Emma insists again. "I don't think this has anything to do with Aunt Nora."

"The real problem is that you're introverted," Holly says, sounding clinical now. "You're an introvert who has unpleasant associations with sewing machines and quilts. Do you remember those awful quilts Aunt Nora made? She was inordinately fond of brown and yellow. Even when she finally went into the nursing home, she kept making them."

"I do have some unpleasant associations with sewing machines and quilts," Emma admits. "And it's also true that I'm an introvert. But mostly I think the problem is February. It's hard to meet new people in February."

"You know, Emma," her sister says, her voice lowering, a clear indication she's about to go into Big Ed mode, "if you want to make a friend, be a friend."

"The City of Happiness is in the State of Mind," Emma replies, giggling.

"Go to the quilt shop," Holly commands. "Face your demons head on."

Emma takes a deep breath, lets it out. "Okay. Tomorrow morning, I promise."

"I'm going to call you tomorrow night," Holly warns. "I want a good report."

Still bossy after all these years, Emma thinks, hanging up. But she gets the notepad from the kitchen counter, writes herself a note to stick on the fridge: *I am going to the Sewing Room on Friday morning.* At the bottom, she signs her name.

4.

On Friday Morning, after the kids have gone
to school and Owen has left for work, after she washes up
and puts in a load of laundry and feeds Homer and makes
the beds, after she glances in her study and feels a twinge
of guilt for not working on her nonexistent novel, Emma
gets ready to go out. She stands in front of the bathroom
mirror and runs a brush through her shoulder-length brown
hair, ignoring as best she can the few worrisome strands of
gray. She'd love to cut her hair short, something chic and
vaguely French, but Sarah and Ben shout her down every
time she mentions it. Worse, Owen tells her he thinks she'd
look cute with short hair. But she doesn't want to look cute;
she wants to look glamorous, mysterious. Emma scowls
at her reflection. Much to her regret, she's not really the
mysterious type.

She pulls on her coat and goes searching for her gloves,
finally finding them in the living room serving as sleeping
bags for Fashion Fever Barbie and Bandmate Barbie. She
sighs as she pulls each doll out and sets it naked on the
coffee table. Before she had children, Emma had vowed
no daughter of hers would grow up believing that normal
women looked like this, the torpedo breasts, the feet molded

to fit into high heels. Her daughter would play with Amelia Earhart dolls, Sojourner Truth action figures. To Emma's dismay, Barbie entered Sarah's life without warning via a Buzz Lightyear gift bag on her fifth birthday, a present from a preschool friend. Sarah has never looked back.

Slipping on the gloves, Emma flashes the Barbies a dirty look, grabs her purse and the tote bag that holds the quilt, and steps out the front door. It's cold, but not bitterly cold, and the sky is clear. Since moving to Sweet Anne's Gap, Emma has been told at least ten times that if she doesn't like the weather, all she has to do is wait ten minutes. As she turns toward town, she ducks her head against the steady wind and shoves her hands into her pockets, hoping that in ten minutes it will be a balmy seventy-five degrees.

The center of town is a five-minute walk past a stretch of houses that span a wide range of architectural styles, first Mrs. Byers' strange concoction, then three ranch houses, each with a camper parked in its side yard, two Victorians, a lovely Cape Cod, and finally a doublewide trailer. Right after the doublewide, an ancient Mobil station raises its head and Emma breathes in a deep whiff of gasoline, one of her favorite smells ever, even if she knows she's probably stripping her lungs of valuable lining with every inhalation. She passes the phone company, the Sweet Anne's Gap Historical Society, crosses over Route 15, the anemic two-lane highway that runs through the middle of town, and looks up at the courthouse clock. It is five minutes before ten.

The Sewing Room opens at ten, and Emma doesn't want to be waiting when the clock strikes, bombarded with offers of help by a cheerful store employee as soon as the door opens. She'd rather have a few minutes to wander around the shop on her own, admiring the fabric, mulling over the pattern catalogues as if she had any idea how to use a sewing machine. So she walks down Oak Street, stopping to peer in various windows, killing time. She's been to mountain towns that would rank higher on the quaintness scale than Sweet Anne's Gap, that's for sure, towns where there seems to be a concerted effort to make every building a monument to coziness or folksiness or just general nostalgia. The buildings that line Oak Street have a certain historic appeal — all red brick facades and corniced roofs — but they seem slightly neglected, the brick chipped and dirty, the paint peeling. Maybe it doesn't matter, Emma thinks, when all you have to do is lift your head and see the mountains that ring the town, beautiful even in the dead of winter.

Willa's Antiques & Such sits on the corner of Oak and Route 15, and Emma notes the high price tags on the pieces on display, a doll-house and a primitive-looking table. Tourists' prices. Emma can imagine her mother-in-law, Linda, cooing over the dollhouse, its tiny, precisely hewn furniture, the darling tea set laid out on the dining room table. She'd buy it, ostensibly for Sarah, then find an excuse to take it home with her. Linda has always been generous, especially with herself.

Next door to Willa's is a pottery shop with an uninspiring batch of cups and plates in its front window, all beiges and grays, inexpertly thrown. There's no listing of hours in the window, and Emma wonders if it's not a shop at all, but instead a studio. Or maybe like other businesses around town, its hours are erratic until the summer tourists and snowbirds return to the mountains in the early weeks of June and there's real money to be made.

The public library's display window houses a family of teddy bears in rocking chairs, each with its own copy of *Goldilocks and the Three Bears*. Scattered around their feet are other classic children's stories, *Little Red Hen*, *Snow White and the Seven Dwarves*, and much to Emma's delight, James Marshall's silly version of *Red Riding Hood*. To the side of the main entrance, beneath the outdoor book return, someone has put out a box with a sign reading "Free for the taking!!" taped to it. Emma peers in and finds a pile of *Reader's Digest* condensed books and a few back issues of *Popular Mechanics*.

Helen's Café sits across the street, and Emma considers going in for a cup of coffee. She wonders what the mid-morning crowd at Helen's is like. Maybe the old men who congregate inside every morning have wandered off to Jim's Amoco, the gas station and convenience store a few blocks down Route 15, and taken up their positions in the white plastic seats outside the door. No sooner does she think this than an octogenarian wanders out of the café, cigarette in hand, and lights up. He gives a tip of his baseball cap to Emma, and she waves a few limp fingers back.

After the library, Oak Street becomes less interesting — insurance agent, dentist's office, Community Bank & Trust. Past the bank, Emma turns right and walks down a steep hill that tees into Trade Street. Owen, a geology major in college, has taught Emma that downhill slopes like this more often than not lead to creeks and rivers, and sure enough, Emma can look over Trade Street and past the railroad tracks to where the Toe River runs, gray and listless.

Trade Street houses a mishmash of concerns. The *Mountain Times* office is here, as is The Rainbow's Attic, a secondhand store that supports the battered women's shelter, Beloved Books, a Christian bookstore, and a low-end antiques store that Emma has never once found open. The Sewing Room is the last shop on the corner, right before the street inclines sharply and circles up to meet Oak.

Emma checks her watch. 10:05. Go time, she thinks. Now or never.

A bell chimes as she pushes open the Sewing Room's door, and a clipped voice from somewhere in the back of the store calls out, "Make yourself at home, please! I'm watering the plants at the moment. At least, I'm watering the ones I haven't killed yet."

Whoever this Ruth is, she's not Aunt Nora. Looking around the store. Emma almost laughs as she realizes that Holly was right, she has been expecting the Sewing Room to be the sunroom, filled with an army of Aunt Noras, cigarettes dangling from their lips as they sew away on polyester quilts. If there is polyester here, it must be hiding. All Emma can see is row after row of crisp, bright cotton. The shop is large, well lit and has a lovely, fresh smell, lavender maybe, a hint of roses. In spite of its size, it has a cozy feel, helped in part by the armchairs positioned here and there, at the end of aisles and tucked into corners, each one with its own quilt, the better to warm you up on a rainy afternoon, Emma supposes.

"Is there anything I can help you with?" the voice calls, and Emma realizes it's an English accent she's hearing, or else the voice of someone from one of those clans hidden way up in the hills where outside influences haven't been able to infiltrate. Though, weren't they all found a hundred years ago by ballad hunters and cultural thrill seekers?

Doesn't everybody have cable and the Internet now?

"I'm just going to look around for a bit, if that's okay," Emma calls back. "This is my first time here."

"Please do," the voice says. "It's a bit of a mess. We had a class here last night, and I was too tired afterward to do anything but close up shop. So now everything's at sixes and sevens and, worse luck, my African Violets are wilting."

Emma moves through the store, finding it hard to focus on one thing. Bolts of fabric line the walls, sit on tables piled one on top of the other, and fill up aisle after aisle. She begins to feel a little drunk on all the color she's absorbing, the bright oranges and pinks, the deep blues, the chocolate browns.

"Now then, what can I do for you? I'm Ruth Holland, this is my shop, and as you can see I have loads of wonderful fabric just in. Makes February a little less gray, don't you agree?"

Ruth has come up behind her, and Emma twirls around, knocking into a row of fabric, causing a bolt printed with huge orange and blue flowers to tumble to the floor. She fumbles with it as she attempts to put it back in place.

"Never you mind that," Ruth says, taking the bolt from Emma and expertly gliding it into its spot. A tall woman wearing a pink shirtwaist dress, navy blue cardigan and penny loafers, her legs bare, she has a slightly military bearing, as though she never got the memo that she needed to slouch in order to appear more feminine. Her snow-white hair is pulled back into an elegant chignon, and there is a flush of pink powder across her high, broad cheekbones. "Tell me who you are, and then you can tell me how I can help you."

Emma gives her name, mentions that she's just moved to the area. "We bought the Buchanan house."

"Your husband works for the state highway department? I believe that's what I've been told."

Emma laughs. "Yes, but who did you hear it from? I've hardly met anyone since I've moved here. I know maybe five people. Did Shana Martin tell you? She's the realtor we worked with."

Ruth shakes her head, puts a finger to her lips, thinking. "No, not Shana. I believe it was Charlotte Stengle, the young librarian. She's in here three or four times a week, always has all sorts of interesting information to share. Of course, the children at school tell her everything, but Charlotte is very discreet. She never uses last names."

Charlotte of the green glasses? Emma is momentarily dumbstruck. "Really? She hardly ever says a word to me. She's so shy."

"She *is* terribly shy," Ruth agrees. "It's taken me ages to bring her out. Tea helps. She's homesick, you know."

"But I thought she was from this area."

"Not precisely. She grew up in Banner Elk. Are you familiar with it?"

Emma nods. "We had lunch there once. It's really not that far from here, is it?"

"Less than sixty miles as the crow flies, yet nearly a two-hour drive." Ruth leans past Emma and tucks in a swath of fabric that's come loose from its bolt. "It's a very different community. There's a college there, a resort. Sweet Anne's Gap is a bit more insular, rougher around the edges. I remember moving up here thirty years ago with my husband, who grew up in these parts, and it simply took me ages to figure things out. You'll learn after you've lived here awhile. Now, tell me if there's something I can help you with. I'm very good helping people choose fabrics."

"Actually, I need help with something I've found." Emma pulls the quilt from the bag, but doesn't unfold it. "It was in a trunk in my attic. My neighbor Lettie thought you might know when it was made."

Ruth claps her hands. "Ah, a mystery quilt! Follow me to the back room and we'll spread it out properly and take a look," she says, leading Emma toward the rear of the store. "I'm not a textiles expert by any means, but I can make a guess. I suppose you don't have any idea who made it, if you don't know when it was made."

"I'm afraid not. I know a little of the family history, but not much."

Ruth shows Emma into what appears to be a workroom of sorts, six long tables, three to a side, filling up most of the space. "Let's see," Ruth says, taking the quilt from Emma and laying it on the table closest to her. She steps back, then walks around it, stopping at each side of the table to lift the quilt's edges, examine what's underneath, run her fingers over the fabric. "Well, we really should have Barbara look at this," she says after a few minutes. "She'll know much more than I, but if I were to hazard a guess, I'd say it was made sometime during the Civil War era. The browns were most likely Turkey red in their prime, and the grays Prussian blue, very popular colors in the mid-nineteenth century. It's a well-preserved piece. The pattern is called Birds in the Air."

"Birds in the Air?" Emma echoes. "Really?"

"I'm quite sure," Ruth says, sounding stern, as though

she's not used to being second-guessed. "There's nothing else it could be."

"Oh, I'm sure you're right, it's not that," Emma stammers, not wanting to be misunderstood. "It's just that, well, I'm a bird. A B-Y-R-D. Emma Byrd?"

Ruth laughs. "Oh, so indeed you are! How lovely then that the quilt hiding in your attic is this particular sort. Very poetic." She begins to fold the quilt. "There's a guild meeting here next Monday night, and Barbara is sure to be in attendance. She never misses. Why don't you bring the quilt back then? She can take a look at it and give you an expert opinion."

Ruth hands the folded quilt back to Emma. "Now, shall we get you started on a quilt of your own?"

"Oh, I don't quilt," Emma tells her, almost embarrassed to admit it, though she's never considered her lack of quilting skills a shortcoming before now. "I don't even know how to sew."

"Ah, but I saw how you looked at the fabric," Ruth says, putting a hand on Emma's shoulder and steering her to a wall of pinks and oranges. "You like it, don't you?"

"Well, yes, of course," Emma admits. "Who wouldn't? It's beautiful. But I'm not very crafty. It doesn't seem to run in my family. Well, my mother did needlepoint, but nobody does that any — "

"Can you cut in a straight line?" Ruth asks, arching an eyebrow, and Emma nods mutely. "Then that's by far crafty enough. If you have an eye for beauty and can cut out fabric into squares, then you can make a quilt. You don't even need a machine, though I can loan you one if you'd like to give it a try. It's a bit like driving a race car, I've found, using a sewing machine. Very addictive when you start hitting the high speeds."

Emma can't think of a single thing to say. She can't just keep repeating the words *I'm not crafty* over and over, can she? And yet she feels this is one of the most definitively true things that she knows about herself. Does she believe in God? Maybe, mostly, but not always. Is she a Republican or a Democrat? A little bit of both. What's her favorite food? Too many favorites to count. Is she crafty? No, absolutely not.

"I'm left-handed," she offers to Ruth's back. Ruth is pulling out bolts of fabric from the wall, striped fabric, fabric printed with tiny florals, huge roses, polka dots, stripes. "I think that's why I'm not that good at making things. Also, I'm terrible at math."

"You'll get better as you go along," Ruth says, not turning around. "And now they make all sorts of quilting calculators. Simply amazing things. I'm assuming you like pink, but please stop me if it's really not for you. We'll need to pick out other colors as well, for contrast, and then fabric for the border and the binding. And the back, of course. I'm envisioning a very simple four-patch for your first quilt. Lap-sized, no triangles involved whatsoever."

"My mother tried to teach me to knit," Emma goes on, feeling a little desperate. "I couldn't even figure out how to cast on, and when she cast on for me, I dropped all the stitches. I'm not making that up."

Ruth pauses in her search to look at Emma. "The wonderful thing about making quilts is that they never come out the wrong size. They may be longer than you had intended, or wider, but they always fit. I gave up on knitting years ago, after my fourth or fifth sweater that sagged and bulged and pulled and finally sent me weeping to the sherry bottle."

It takes thirty minutes to choose all the fabrics. Once Emma realizes there is no way out of this, that she will be making a quilt whether she wants to or not, she joins Ruth in selecting the colors and prints. She could make Sarah a quilt for her new bed. And then maybe she could make a quilt for the couch in the living room, a quilt with lots of creams and reds. Suddenly her head is filled with visions of all the marvelous quilts she'll make.

"But I don't even know how to sew," she says aloud. "This is ridiculous."

Ruth looks at her watch. "I've got an appliqué class coming in at eleven, and another class this afternoon. But I'm absolutely free tomorrow morning before the shop opens. I know Saturdays are busy times for parents, but if you could come in around nine, we could spend an hour getting you up to speed on one of our machines in the back. I teach hand piecing, so that's something you can think about, but I find for the beginner that machine piecing is so much more satisfying. You can have a quilt top done in a week, sometimes a weekend."

Emma finds herself agreeing to come in Saturday morning. Ten minutes later she's back on Trade Street, several large bags with "The Sewing Room" printed on them dangling from her wrists. She has fabric, a rotary cutter, a green self-healing cutting mat, one long ruler, two different sizes of square rules, and a book called *First-Time Quiltmaking*. She also has a receipt that caused her to pale when she realized how much she'd just spent.

That woman did a number on me, Emma thinks, walking up the steep hill to Oak Street, the wind snapping at the back of her legs. She'd gone in hoping to get a few facts about a quilt, and now, somehow, she has become a quilter. That's some kind of magic Ruth has, she thinks, and suddenly she can't wait to get home and start cutting out fabric.

5.

Emma has never been to Helen's on a Saturday before, and she can't put her finger on it, but it feels different. It's as if the fluorescent lights are shining just a bit more brightly, the kitchen radio turned up just loud enough to make it seem like a party. The old men are nowhere to be seen, their seats taken over by teenagers and young families, elderly couples dressed in brightly colored sweatshirts and pressed blue jeans. Three waitresses work the room, stopping to chat at each table, their voices light and teasing.

Emma glances at her watch, then at the door. She's supposed to meet Christine McCrae at eleven, and it's almost five after. Christine is the mother of one of Sarah's new best friends, Brittany. Sarah, it turns out, has become part of a clique. Three girls pick her up every morning for the walk to school, standing shyly at the end of the driveway until Emma or Owen notices them and calls to Sarah that she needs to hurry up. They never knock, this Brittany and Tiffany and Amber, and shake their heads politely when Emma calls them into the house, where it's warm. "We're fine out here, Mrs. Byrd," one of them — Brittany, Emma thinks — calls up the walk. "We'll just wait."

When the phone rang at eight-thirty last night, Emma had been expecting Holly's call. She was all geared up to brag about her visit to the Sewing Room, the cut squares of fabric laid out on the card table in her study at that very minute, her new skills with the very scary rotary cutter. "Hey ya!" she trilled into the receiver. "What's up?"

There was a moment's silence, and then the voice on the other end of the line said, "Uh, I'm calling to speak to Sarah's mom? To Emma Byrd? This is Christine McCrae, Brittany's mom?"

"Oh, sure," Emma said. "This is she. I mean me. I'm Emma."

Another hesitation. "Is this a bad time? I could call back later. I don't want to be a bother."

How could this conversation be collapsing so fast? Emma wondered. "No! Not at all! How can I help you?"

"I was just wondering if we could get together for coffee," Christine said. "Our girls are spending so much time together, and I thought it would be good for us to get to know each other a little bit."

Christine's tone was bright, but Emma could hear a line of worry running beneath it. "Is there something you want to talk about now?" Emma asked. "Some question you have? Sarah's had all her shots, if that's what you're concerned about." Emma laughed, but Christine didn't.

"Oh, no, no!" Christine's voice went up an octave. "I just wanted to meet you, is all. Brittany is just so taken with that Sarah of yours."

Now Emma wonders if she over-reacted by assuming Christine had something on her mind. Brittany and Sarah are planning a sleepover at the McCrae's next week. Christine probably just wants to check Emma out and give Emma a chance to do the same with her. It's basic Child Safety 101: The Tween Years.

"You still waiting on your friend, ma'am?" the waitress, a sixteen-year-old with a *Sweet Anne's Gap Rockin' Ravens* sweatshirt on underneath her apron, asks. "I could go ahead and bring you a glass of tea 'til she gets here."

"Do you have unsweetened?" Emma asks, and can tell by the waitress's expression that she might as well have waved a sign over her head saying, *I Am Not From Here.*

"No, ma'am, we sure don't," the waitress says. "Only in the summer, when the tourists come through."

"Maybe just some coffee, then," Emma tells her, checking the door again, then her watch. She's eager to get home. After a run of bungled attempts this morning at the Sewing Room, she suddenly got the hang of sewing straight lines, which Ruth promised her was all that was necessary to make any quilt she wanted. Now she's ready to get home and sew some blocks together on the machine she's borrowed.

But first, this meeting with Christine.

The door opens, and a slender, middle-aged woman with dark red hair enters, looks around, and then tilts her head when she sees Emma, as if asking, "Is that you?" Emma nods and waves the woman over.

"I'm so sorry I'm late," the woman says, sliding into the booth across from Emma. "I'm Christine, by the way, but you probably guessed that."

"Well, you mentioned the red hair," Emma tells her. "Although there are a lot redheads around here, I've noticed."

"It's the Scots-Irish blood," Christine informs her. "There's a lot of that in Sweet Anne's Gap, even though everybody swears that they're at least half Cherokee. And all the McCraes and McKinneys have got red hair running through their lines. We're all cousins — Miss Lydia, whose house you bought, was kin to my granddaddy."

"So you're a McKinney, too?" Emma asks, trying to work out the bloodlines, and Christine nods.

"You can't get away from us in this town," she says, which sounds to Emma's ears a little bit like *Best not get on our bad side.* Duly noted, she thinks.

Their waitress arrives with Emma's coffee. "Hey, Miss Christine! How you doing? I saw that Brittany the other day, and, Lord, is she growing. She's near 'bout seven feet tall."

Christine smiles. She has bright, watery blue eyes, and when she smiles, they crinkle up nicely at the corners. "She can't wear a pair of jeans more than a month anymore, seems like. Just grows straight out of them."

"You want some coffee?"

"I'll take some tea, if it's made fresh this morning and y'all didn't go overboard with the sugar." Christine turns to Emma. "Sometimes the tea here's so sweet, you can feel the dental decay set in."

Emma picks up a tiny container of half and half and peels back the foil lid. "I didn't grow up drinking tea, which my husband thinks is a form of child abuse. He's from Gastonia, and they had it every meal."

"I knew a girl from Gastonia once," Christine says. "I worked with her over in Linville, at the Esseola Lodge, the summer right after I got out of high school. She was real nice."

"I bet she liked sweet tea, too," Emma says, and smiles in hopes of coming off as charming and light-hearted, the sort of out-of towner you're happy to see move in next door.

"I reckon so," Christine agrees. "Most folks do."

Emma looks at her coffee. Which is not sweet tea. She

hopes that Christine isn't making a point about Emma not being most folks. "I think it's really nice that Brittany and the other girls have made Sarah feel so welcome. She was sad about leaving Chapel Hill, but everyone's been so friendly here, it's made it an easy transition for her."

"Well, that's kind of what I wanted to talk to you about," Christine says, squeezing lemon into the glass of iced tea that the waitress has just delivered. "About Sarah's influence on the girls, I guess. You know, kids up here aren't as sophisticated as they are in other places. I guess you could say they're running a little bit behind, which is pretty much the way folks like it."

"I'm glad to hear it," Emma says. "I want Sarah to stay a kid for as long as possible."

Christine raises an eyebrow. "Really? Because if that's the case, do you mind me asking you something? Why do you let Sarah watch R-rated movies? I was shocked when I heard that."

Emma nearly spits out her coffee.

"What? Where in the world did you get the idea we let Sarah watch R-rated movies?"

"That's what she told Brittany and them," Christine says. "She said y'all let her watch *Panic Room*, since Kristen Stewart's her favorite actress in the world, and *Panic Room*'s an R. And also that you've let her read all the *Twilight* books, and all the *Harry Potters*."

"Well, she has read the *Harry Potter* books except for the last one," Emma says. "But to my knowledge she's never watched *Panic Room*, and we don't let her watch PG-13 movies, much less R. We're really pretty protective parents. Obnoxiously over-protective, according to Sarah."

Christine looks suspicious. "Brittany said Sarah told her y'all had given her — how'd she put it? — 'intellectual freedom.' She gets to choose whatever she wants to read and she can watch R-rated movies as long as you or your husband watch with her."

Emma cocks her head to one side and studies Christine. Really? Is it really possible that a ten-year-old believes this kind of malarkey, much less her mom?

"Listen," Christine continues before Emma has a chance to say anything. "I get it that y'all are from a much more — well, I guess you'd say *advanced* place than Sweet Anne's Gap. We must seem pretty backward to you. But I guess since y'all moved here and not the other way around, you're the ones who need to figure out how to fit in."

Emma stares into her coffee cup. It suddenly occurs to her that this is not a friendly mom-to-mom *let's make sure we're all on the same page* conversation. Christine McCrae is throwing down the gauntlet: Get in line or get out of town.

"I could be wrong," Emma says finally, making her words slow and precise. "But you seem to be taking what a ten-year-old girl says to impress her friends as the gospel truth. I'll talk to Sarah and make sure she straightens this out with Brittany. But we are very careful about what influences Sarah is exposed to, and believe me, she's not watching R-rated movies."

Christine is opening her mouth to reply when a voice calls from across the room, "I see you over there, Christine McCrae! You better not be hiding from me!"

A tall woman in a suede jacket and high heel boots makes her way to the table. "Pastor Riley says if you're not in charge of the overseas missions committee, then he's shutting it down. He doesn't trust anyone else to make it happen."

Christine laughs and shakes her head. "Good lord, Clarice, I missed one meeting last week because Travis had a doctor's appointment, and now Pastor Riley thinks I've jumped ship. I swear I'll be at Monday's meeting just like I said I would."

"I believe First Baptist would shut down if you weren't there to keep the ship sailing," her friend says, leaning down to give Christine a quick hug before turning to go back to her table. "I'll see you Monday then."

"Nice to meet you," Emma calls after Clarice, her cheeks burning. Just how many times can she be insulted in one morning? She should start keeping a tally sheet.

Clarice turns and looks at her as though she's only just now noticed Emma's existence. "Well, who on earth are you?"

Emma smiles her nicest smile. "I'm Emma Byrd. My family just moved here in January."

Christine leans her head toward her friend and half-whispers in an apologetic voice, "There's no reason you'd know her. It's that new girl Sarah's mom. They bought Lydia Buchanan's old place."

Clarice gives Emma a distracted smile. "That's so nice! Well, y'all, I've got to run — Casey has a youth group trip today!"

Emma watches as Clarice greets people at every table on her way out of the restaurant. "That was the mayor's wife, in case you're wondering," Christine says.

"Yeah," Emma replies. "I kind of was."

They settle into silence for a moment, Christine sipping her tea and Emma folding and refolding her napkin.

Suddenly, something in Christine's expression clicks on, as though she's just remembered an important point she needs to make.

"You said something about the gospel truth before and that reminds me," she says, sounding like a prosecuting attorney grilling an uncooperative witness, "Sarah also says y'all don't go church and never have."

Emma takes a deep breath. Owen has warned her that this would come up. They've always meant to go to church, but they could never find one that felt like a good fit. It didn't help that Owen had been raised Southern Baptist — church on Sunday mornings, Sunday evenings and Wednesday nights — and Emma's family had been lackadaisical Presbyterians. Where was the middle ground there? Not that Owen had much interest in returning to the Baptist church, but he thought it would be good to go to somewhere, and Emma agreed. But where? That's what they were still deciding, fifteen years into their marriage.

"We're going to look for a church," Emma tells Christine now. "Very soon."

"That's good," Christine says. She gives Emma a long look. "You should do that."

"Okay, then!" Emma says, pasting what she hopes passes for a halfway genuine smile on her face. "Well, I guess I ought to get home. Lots to do this afternoon." She digs through her purse, takes a couple of dollars out of her wallet, and puts them on the table. "I appreciate you letting me know what's going on with Sarah, and I'll have a talk with her."

Christine nods and smiles brightly. "Maybe Sarah could give Brittany a call later, clear a few things up?"

Emma stands and puts on her coat. "Sure. Yes, of course. Sarah will call."

She is all the way to the Mobil station before she realizes she drove into town this morning so she could bring home a machine from the Sewing Room. She turns around and crosses Route 15. The car is parked in front of the insurance agency. Emma stomps toward it, eyes on the sidewalk, hoping she doesn't run into Christine again.

The image of Christine's sour expression flashes in her mind, and she realizes it reminds her of someone. But who? Someone she's met recently, she thinks, but not Ruth, not Charlotte, not Lettie. Who could it be?

And then it comes to her. The girl in the picture she found in the trunk. So there's a clue, Emma thinks. No doubt about it, that girl's a McKinney.

6.

"**Mom, did you make the pizza** dough yet? I'm hungry."

Emma looks up from the table, where she has been laying out squares of fabric on the cutting mat and trying to pin them together so that their edges will match perfectly. She's had the crazy idea that she might be able to finish the quilt top, nine blocks in all, in time for the Mountain Counties Quilt Guild meeting a week from Monday. She imagines holding it up in front of a group of appreciative quilters, explaining how she made her design choices, giving credit to Ruth for helping her pick out the fabric, of course. But now Ben is standing in the doorway of her study, giving her his patented pathetic, starving kid look, and while she'd like to ignore him, she knows she can't.

"Couldn't we just order pizza?" she asks. "I'm sort of in the middle of a project."

"Mom, remember?" Ben whines. "There's no Domino's here. We'd have to drive all the way to Pine City and go to Pizza Hut, and the pizza gets all cold before we get home. That's why we make homemade pizza for pizza night, remember?"

"I keep forgetting that," Emma says. "But maybe you and Daddy could go pick up a pizza, and we could reheat it when you got home? Or the three of you could eat at Pizza Hut and bring me something back?"

"But we're supposed to watch a movie while we eat," Ben, a stickler for routine, reminds her. "We can't watch a movie at Pizza Hut."

Emma wonders if it's wrong to bribe children — maybe throw Ben a ten and hope that he moves on? "I'm really in the middle of something, honey," she repeats. "Why don't you talk to Dad and figure out a plan, okay?"

"You make me stop stuff in the middle all the time. You should have to stop in the middle, too."

"Except I'm the mom, and moms don't have to stop if they don't want to."

Ben leaves, muttering under his breath something about stupid, unfair grown-ups, which Emma decides to ignore. She wiggles her arms and hands, trying to relax. She's not used to claiming time for herself when the kids are home and there are mouths to be fed. But she wants to keep working on this quilt. She's already sewn together four blocks and can't stop herself from pausing every few minutes to admire her work. She did that? Just by sewing some squares of fabric together? Amazing!

She carries a length of fabric over to the ironing board and sprays it with a wonderful concoction Ruth gave her this morning called *Mary Ellen's Best Press*, which magically removes wrinkles while scenting the air with lavender. Her afternoon has been a dance from one station to another, from the cutting board to the sewing machine, from the sewing machine to the ironing board. And while she has had to rip out seams more times than she can count and has actually thrown her copy of *First Time Quiltmaking* across the room — but once, only once — she has found the process deeply satisfying in a way she can't explain.

Glancing up at the mantel, Emma catches the eye of the scowling girl, whose picture she has set next to a vase filled with dried grasses, something she saw in *Martha Stewart Living*, though in the magazine the grasses looked more like a miniature sheaf of wheat, less like a present picked by a three-year-old for her mother. She wishes she knew the girl's name. Clara, maybe? Or Annabelle? Something suitably old-fashioned, but not unbearable. How disappointing if her girl turned out to be a Henrietta or a Gertrude. She thinks about opening the other trunks in the attic in search of clues, but what if all they contain are Dawna's old dress-up clothes or plastic baggies of junk drawer fodder — grocery store trading stamps, Samsonite keys, crusty pennies? What Emma really wants to find is a diary and stacks of ancient photographs and crumbling-around-the-edges letters.

Maybe there are more quilts in those trunks. Emma brightens at this thought. She imagines showing up at the guild meeting with a box filled to the top with quilts, which she would hand over like a ticket, admission for one. She imagines Ruth and Charlotte the librarian and several other women with either British accents or interesting eyewear gathering around her, welcoming her into their club. Emma's never been much for clubs, but looking out the window at the darkening February sky, she's pretty sure she could use one.

In college, aspiring writer that she was, she had an E.M. Forster quote taped to the shelf over her desk: "Only connect." Everyone else in her family seems to be connecting like crazy. The dinner table talk is all about Ben's new classmate Jason, who can make milk come out of his nose, or the scenery that Sarah and Amber are designing for the fifth grade play. The children, six weeks into their new life, are in the thick of things, brimming over with news and plans and school gossip.

Owen, too, seems invigorated. His new job keeps him outside most of the day, as he and his team rethink how to keep boulders from pouring off the mountains and onto the roadways. And although the weather is often damp and cold, Owen seems impervious to it. He's learned from his co-workers how to dress to survive the elements, and some nights he and Ben spend a good hour poring over camping catalogs, looking for gear to keep Owen even warmer, ever dryer.

Emma is the only one who still seems to be finding her way, which isn't a huge surprise. She's always been the last person to dance at a party. But just think of all the people she'll meet at the guild meeting — there has to be one or two she'll connect with, right? Maybe someone who's also new to the area, new to quilting, in need of friends. She suddenly sees herself at Helen's, no longer intimidated by the old men staring at her from under their shaggy eyebrows. She'll be too busy talking with a girlfriend over a cup of coffee and a piece of pie — rhubarb pie, Emma thinks, although she's never eaten rhubarb pie in her life. Maybe her new friend will be trying rhubarb pie for the first time, too. Maybe like Emma, she'll have absolutely no idea what rhubarb is. After pie and coffee, they'll take a drive down to the Penland School of Crafts outside of Pine City and wander through the gallery, finding inspiration for all the marvelous quilts they're going to make.

Emma shakes her head. She should probably finish one quilt before she invests any more time in this fantasy world of hers. She holds up the piece of material she's just ironed and examines it. If there were a word that meant "the opposite of calico," it would apply to this lively polka-dotted print. "Come and look at my fabric," she calls over to Sarah, who's reading in the living room. "Come tell me if you love it."

Sarah appears in the doorway, her copy of *Misty of Chincoteague* in her hand. "Do you think I could get a horse now that we live in the country?"

"We live in town, honey, not the country. We don't have room for a horse." Emma holds up the fabric so Sarah can see it. "Isn't this amazing?"

Sarah comes closer, touches the fabric with a slightly grimy finger. "Can I do some sewing? I'll be really careful."

"Gosh, I don't know." Emma holds the fabric close to her chest as if to protect it. "I mean, I just learned how to use the sewing machine this morning. Maybe I should get some more practice before I try to teach you."

Sarah shrugs. "Whatever."

"No *whatever*," Emma scolds. "You're not a teenager yet."

"Well, you keep telling me to get off the computer and do some arts and crafts, but now that I want to do some arts and crafts, you say no," Sarah complains. "It's like you're a hypochondriac or something."

Emma knows she means *hypocrite*, but lets it go. If she corrects her, Sarah will argue that she knows the meaning of *hypochondriac*, thank you very much, and the discussion will go downhill from there. They've already weathered one rough patch this afternoon, when Emma informed Sarah she'd have to call Brittany and admit to lying about watching R movies, and that's all the drama Emma has the energy for right now.

"I've got a great idea," she says brightly to her sulking daughter. "How about I take you to the fabric store after school on Monday? We can pick out fabric for you to make your own quilt."

"Okay, I guess. If I'm not too tired. We have track and field in P.E. on Monday."

Emma can tell from Sarah's tone that she's already lost interest. "Okay, well, why don't you go check with Dad about the pizza situation?"

Sarah rubs her hands together, exclaims, "Pizza! Yum!" and scrambles down the hallway in search of her father. Emma knows it's only a matter of time before it will take more than the promise of food to improve Sarah's mood, only a year or two before Sarah greets her every utterance with a "whatever" and eyeball-rolling. Emma herself had been a champion eyeball-roller and knows not to expect that the fates will be any kinder to her than they were to her own mother, who had not one but two teenage girls to deal with. Hell, Emma thinks. It must have been hell.

She picks up the four squares of fabric she's decided will look nicest together, two pink prints, two solid grays, and holds them up to the picture of Annabelle/Gertrude. "Nice, huh?" she asks, but clearly nothing's going to impress this girl, so Emma proceeds to the sewing machine. Taking a seat, she pins a pink square and a solid square together and slides them under the presser foot. Once she's sure she has them in exactly the right spot, she gingerly presses the pedal. Nothing. She presses more firmly. Still nothing.

"I bet turning the power on will do the trick," Owen says

from behind her, laughing when Emma jumps in her chair. "Sorry, didn't mean to scare you."

Emma turns to look up at her husband standing in the doorway. He's wearing her favorite shirt of his, a faded denim button-down, the sleeves rolled up precisely, revealing muscular forearms sprinkled with ginger-colored freckles. He is, she thinks, still quite the catch, tall and broad-shouldered, with lovely green eyes and short sandy hair that's just now starting gray around the hairline. Of course it looks great on him, which drives Emma crazy, though not as crazy as the fact that whenever Owen wants to lose five pounds all he has to do is give up drinking beer for a week and — poof! — the weight is gone, just like that.

"I hear I'm on pizza duty tonight," Owen says, walking into the room. "Ben and I decided that the best idea is to run down to Walmart and buy some fancy frozen pizzas. As long as we're there, is there anything else you need?"

The Super Walmart in Pine City is the closest grocery store, a twenty-minute drive. Emma went for her weekly grocery run on Thursday, so she's stocked up on what she'll need for the next few days. She starts to shake her head no, but has a sudden inspiration. "Quilting magazines? I bet they have some. Would you mind picking up one or two?"

Owen grins. "Wow, you've really been bit by the bug. Sure, I'll get you some magazines. Anything else? Some needles and thread? A sewing machine?"

A sewing machine? Emma knows Owen is joking, but she's supposed to return this sewing machine to Ruth on Monday, and then what will she do?

"Would you mind?" she asks, as though she's asking him to grab a gallon of milk. "I mean, I bet they carry them.

Nothing too cheap, though. I don't want something that's going to fall apart on me after a couple of weeks."

Owen begins making an imaginary list. "Quilting magazines, check. Not-too-cheap sewing machine, check." He looks up at her. "Anything else?"

"I'm totally serious," Emma tells him, and she totally is. She stands up. "I better come with you, though. You might not get one that I want."

Owen shakes his head and laughs. "You can't go out and buy a sewing machine just like that. You have to do some research first. You'd probably do better ordering a machine online than buying one at Walmart."

"But I have to give this machine back on Monday," Emma says. "Even if I ordered a machine tonight, it wouldn't get here until late next week. That's too long to wait."

Owen rubs his temples, which is what he does when he's perplexed. "Correct me if I'm wrong, but before yesterday you had no interest in sewing whatsoever. Never mentioned wanting to make a quilt. And now you want to go spend two hundred dollars on a Walmart sewing machine?"

"It might be three hundred dollars, I don't know," Emma tells him. "The machines at the Sewing Room were over a thousand, but they were pretty fancy. I would think you could get something a lot cheaper but that still worked pretty well at Walmart."

"If you really want a sewing machine, I think you ought to get a good one, one that will last. Having the right tools is important. Quality tools."

"You think I should buy a thousand-dollar sewing machine? After sewing for less than twenty-four hours?"

"No, not really," Owen admits. "But I don't think you

should buy a two hundred-dollar machine, either. Maybe the owner of the fabric store will loan you this machine a little longer if you tell her you're thinking about buying one."

"So where am I going to get a thousand dollars?"

"We made money on the house sale," Owen offers. "And we got this house for a song. You never get anything for yourself, except for shoes. I'd rather see you spend a thousand dollars on a sewing machine, frankly. You've got enough shoes."

Emma sits down and leans back in her chair. She knows Owen is right; it's better to buy a good machine than a junker. And it's crazy to buy a machine at all until she knows whether or not this quilting thing will stick. Maybe it's just a phase she's going through. She's been through other phases. She and her co-workers got caught up in the yoga craze a few years ago, and now Emma has a box in the attic stuffed with her barely-used mat, several unwatched DVDs, and a fuchsia-colored yoga bolster she bought to support her neck. And after she saw *Julie and Julia* (hated Julie, adored Julia), she decided gourmet cooking was in her future and spent too much money on a set of expensive knives she used a total of three times. Maybe she'll make one quilt and be done with quilting forever. It could happen.

"Talk to the lady at the store," Owen urges her. "Ask her about renting. Maybe you could work out some sort of rent-to-own deal."

Emma nods. This is a sensible plan. She is married to a sensible man. "Would you mind getting me the magazines, though? I mean, at Walmart."

"I'll get you every quilting magazine I can find," Owen promises. He points to her four completed blocks, which are neatly laid out at the end of the table. "These look nice, by the way. I always did like quilts."

Emma smiles and repositions herself in front of the sewing machine. "Well, if you're nice to me, maybe I'll make you one." Then she flips on the power switch and begins to sew.

7.

A week later at the Sewing Room, Emma sits in a folding chair near the back, her finished quilt top and the attic quilt folded neatly in a canvas bag on her lap. She's chosen a seat in the back row in case she decides to leave the meeting before it's over. This morning she stood in the middle of her study — which she has started thinking of as her studio after reading all the quilting magazines Owen picked up for her — holding up her freshly-minted four-patch quilt top to an imaginary audience, but now she's not sure she wants to show it off. For one thing, she had no idea there would be so many people here. Taking a rough head count, she'd estimate at least sixty women (and several men) have crowded into the Sewing Room's meeting space. She'd thought there might be ten, twenty tops. And then there's the fact that everyone seems to know each other. Happy chatter fills the air, laughter erupting every few seconds from different parts of the room. Emma feels conspicuously alone.

So why exactly did she think coming to this meeting was a good idea? Well, there's the attic quilt, of course. Emma has almost forgotten that getting the attic quilt looked at was what brought her to the Sewing Room in the first place. Really, she's starting to get a little concerned about her mental health. How did she go from trying to get some information on a mystery quilt to being Suzy Sewer? Or is that Suzy Sewist? According to some of the quilting blogs she's read online, this is a matter of debate. In either case, Emma feels that she's quite possibly nuts.

She checks her watch. It's 7:04, and the meeting doesn't seem anywhere close to getting started. Maybe she should go. She could arrange to meet this Barbara woman another time. Everyone here has probably been quilting for years, they probably have all the friends they need, and as she studies the quilts hanging on the walls around her, she realizes her little four-patch isn't really all that much to look at. It's laughable, is what it is.

"Well, hey there, you must be new, 'cause I ain't never seen you before, and believe me, I know everybody for fifty miles around."

A heavyset woman falls into the chair next to Emma, huffing a bit with the effort of carrying two large bags that appear stuffed with fabric. She shoves them under her seat, and then offers Emma her hand. "I'm Mavis Abercrombie, I live over to Red Hill. What's your name, honey?"

Emma takes Mavis's hand, which is plump and slightly damp. "I'm Emma Byrd. We just moved here in January."

Mavis grins, revealing a small gap between her two front teeth. She has a broad, pleasant face with sympathetic brown eyes. "You picked quite a time to move up to the mountains; it stays bitter cold until at least mid-March. But you'll never see a prettier spring. My yard just comes alive with flowers and birds. That's when I make my best quilts — the flora and fauna inspire me, they really do. Now tell me who you know here," she says, waving an arm to indicate all of the room's inhabitants, "and I'll tell you if I'm related to 'em or not."

't know anybody really," Emma says. "Well, Ruth.
ner a week ago."

"Well, let me ask you this," Mavis says, smiling conspiratorially. "Was you a quilter before you met Ruth, or did she convert you?"

Emma laughs. "I just made my first quilt top this week. I'd never even used a sewing machine before."

Mavis looks delighted. "Half these folks in here could have said the same thing at one time or another, and not so long ago. Ruth opened up this shop eight years back, and since then I don't know how many people she's turned into quilters. First she got all the Baptists quilting, and then she got all the Episcopalians, and then the Church of God folks. Next, she started volunteering at the middle school, and so all the teachers was quilting. Same thing happened at the hospital. There are at least two doctors and five nurses I can see just looking around this room. I don't know how she does it. It's like she puts a spell on you."

"How about you?" Emma asks, warming to this friendly woman. "Did she convert you, too?"

"Naw, honey, I've been quilting all my life. My mama taught me, and her mama taught her, and so on, all the way back to Eve in the Garden. What Ruth's done is give me other folks who love it as much as I do. I don't know why it's such a blessing to talk to people who love what you love, but it is."

The noise around them suddenly dies down to a murmur, and both Emma and Mavis look toward the front of the room, where Ruth is now standing, her arms raised in welcome. "Hello, everyone! Find your seats!" She turns to a doorway which has a sign over it marked "Sale Fabrics — This Way" and calls, "Time to stop shopping, dears! Never fear, I'll keep the register open after the meeting."

"Is that a promise?" someone calls back, and several people laugh and applaud. A group of women file into the meeting room, and Emma sees Charlotte Stengle, a stack of folded fabric half a foot high in her hands, and, a few feet behind her, Brittany's mom, Christine. Seeing Christine makes Emma thankful the room is so crowded; she's not in the mood for a follow-up to their last conversation.

"Ruth runs a good meeting," Mavis whispers as the shoppers find their seats. "Keeps it moving at a fast trot. Back when my young'uns was still in school and I went to the PTA first Thursday of every month? Lord, I thought I'd like to die. Folks just went on and on about this and that, and nothing ever got done. But Ruth'll get us to show-and-tell in no time flat, just you wait and see."

"Show-and-tell—that's where you show your latest quilt, right?" Emma whispers back as though she hadn't spent the weekend rehearsing for it, yet another reason to question her sanity.

Mavis rubs her hands together as though anticipating a fine meal. "Oh, it's the best part of things."

"First on our agenda tonight: charity quilts," Ruth begins, and the room comes to order. As Mavis has promised, Ruth keeps a brisk pace. After charity quilts, she moves on to an upcoming road trip to Asheville in early April for the annual quilt show there—is there enough interest to rent a bus or shall they carpool?—and then reminds the group about the Quilts of Valor sew-day that will take place at the Methodist church in Pine City in mid-March. After a few more such reminders, she announces she is turning over the floor over to Barbara Tyson.

"Barbara will go over March's Block of the Month with you," Ruth tells them, "which you should already be familiar with if you've read your February newsletter." She raises her eyebrows and looks over the crowd with a steely glint in her eye. "You *have* read your February newsletter, haven't you?"

"Is there going to be a test?" someone calls out, and everyone laughs.

"Careful, or there just might be," Ruth replies, wagging a menacing finger at them. "Now, where is Barbara?"

"Here, here, here," calls a muffled voice from the back of the room. Emma turns to see tall a woman dressed in black frantically searching through a quilted tote bag. "I brought a ruler I wanted to show everyone, and now I can't find it."

"Perhaps you could look for it later, dear?" Ruth suggests, consulting her watch. "We do want to have plenty of time for show-and-tell tonight."

The woman straightens. "Of course," she says, brushing some threads from her slacks. "So sorry. And sorry to be late! My hospital rounds this afternoon took longer than I thought they would."

This is when Emma realizes the woman is wearing a white collar, and that her black pants and top aren't a fashion statement; they are, in fact, clerical garb. She must be one of the Episcopalians Ruth converted to quilting, Emma thinks, wondering if she's the same Barbara who will be examining the attic quilt after the meeting.

"Hello," the woman says when she reaches the podium. She runs a hand through her messy, silvery-blonde bob. "My name is Barbara, and I'm a quilter."

"Hi, Barbara!" the crowd choruses back.

"First, if you brought the appliqué block for February and haven't put it up on the design wall in the classroom, please do so after the meeting adjourns," Barbara begins. "We need twenty blocks altogether — in fact, can I see a show of hands of who brought a block tonight?"

At least half of the room raises hands. Barbara looks relieved. "Wonderful!" she exclaims. "As you know, we'll be auctioning all the quilts we make from our blocks at St. Stephen's Christmas Bazaar in November, and it would be great to have at least eight. Okay then — this month's block. This month we're going to practice some very basic paper piecing — "

There are a few groans, but Barbara waves them away. "With a little practice, paper piecing is a breeze. And I noticed the other day that the Pine City library has a Carol Doak DVD in its collection. I highly recommend it."

"Who's Carol Doak?" Emma whispers to Mavis, who is busy taking notes on a steno pad.

"She's the queen of paper piecing," Mavis informs her, and then seeing Emma's confused look, says, "I'll explain it to you later. You probably ought to focus on the basics for now."

Emma nods and turns back to Barbara, who is pulling something out of her tote bag. "This block is called The Twist," Barbara tells them, holding up a piece of fabric, "but it's a play on the more typical Twist block you might have seen in books or online. This one is considerably twistier."

The block Barbara shows them looks to Emma like a series of squares, one set on top of the other, each one slightly smaller than the one before, each turned at a slight angle to the square beneath it, so that it does in fact look as though it's been twisted.

"The complete instructions for this block are in this month's newsletter. If you get the email version, print out the page with the block diagram at a percentage that will produce eight-and-a-half inch blocks. I'll be available at the end of tonight's meeting if you have questions, and I'll be here next Monday at the Quilter's Lunch Bunch and can help you then."

Mavis taps Emma on the arm. "You ought to come to the Lunch Bunch. It's a real good way to get to know folks. You bring whatever quilt you're working on and your machine, and if you've got a problem or a question, there's always somebody who can help you out."

Emma nods, and thinks that maybe she'll find new friends at the smaller lunch meeting; it's hard to get to know anyone in a crowd like this. Looking over the sea of faces, she tries to pick out someone who resembles her fantasy pie-eating friend, but no one quite matches the image Emma holds in her mind. She'd guess the average age here is fifty-five, maybe sixty. Most of the heads are gray, though there are a few dramatic redheads Emma feels sure came from a bottle. Sprinkled here and there she sees a woman her own age, and of course there's the much younger Charlotte Stengle.

You're not looking for a prom date, Emma scolds herself. Her friends don't have to be her exact age or look like her or wear the same sort of clothes. Glancing down at her black V-neck sweater worn over a white tee shirt and jeans — what Owen calls her uniform — she thinks that in fact it would do her good to find a friend who actually cared about clothes; maybe then Emma would finally learn how to accessorize.

Mavis, who has been scribbling rapidly in her steno pad, now rips out a piece of paper and hands it to Emma. "That's my cell number. You got any questions or just need someone to talk to, you give a call or shoot me a text. I'd give you my home phone, but I'm always out and about. I got three daughters-in-law and seven grandbabies, and they keep me busy."

Emma takes the piece of paper and carefully deposits it in her purse. "Thanks," she says, and is surprised to find herself suddenly teary-eyed. She wipes her face with her sleeve. "Allergies," she explains when Mavis looks at her with concern. "I always get them this time of year."

Mavis pats her on the knee. "I know, honey. I know."

In the front of the room, Ruth once again takes the podium. "Very well, then. I believe it's time for show-and-tell. Please form a line to the left of the podium if you have work you'd like to share. I'll need two volunteers to be holders. Who's up for the job?"

A roly-poly man in the front row, whose bald head gleams as though it's been polished with floor wax and buffed to a high shine, stands and nods to the woman next to him. The two go to the front of the room and take a place at Ruth's right.

"Them's the Widows," Mavis informs Emma. "Too bad neither of 'em brought something to show tonight. Hamish makes art quilts, and Wanda's a lot more traditional, but both of them do topnotch work."

"That's an interesting last name," Emma says as she watches the first woman in line struggle to pull her quilt out of a large Walmart bag. "I've never heard it before."

"Oh, that ain't their last name. They's just both widows, and after they got to be widows, they moved in together. Not like man and wife or anything, of course. They became real good friends at the hospital when — "

Before Mavis can go on, the couple in question unfurls a quilt, and the quilt's maker, a tiny woman in a pink sweat-shirt that reads *Ask Me About My Grandchildren* begins to speak.

"Well, y'all know I've been working on this quilt for an age and a half, and now it's finally done. We had a bee the last two weekends up in Ledger, in the back room of the Elks Lodge, and I need to thank Catherine, Layla, Shirleen and Annie for their help. Couldn't have done it without you, girls."

"What a simply marvelous quilt, Dorothy! I believe it's the most glorious Dear Jane I've ever seen!" Ruth exclaims, clapping her hands. "Can you tell us about it?"

As Dorothy explains what went into the making of her quilt, Emma quietly puts her bag on the floor and nudges it under the chair with her foot. What on earth was she thinking, bringing her pathetic little quilt top to the guild meeting? From her blog reading, Emma knows that the Dear Jane is made with over two hundred small, intricate blocks, and is considered a milestone quilt, the mark of a true artisan.

Mavis leans down and tugs at the two bags stuffed under her chair. "Once Dorothy's done talking, let's go get in line. I just wanted to get a good view of that quilt before I went up."

"I'm not going," Emma says, trying to sound casual. She knows she could take up the attic quilt, but then someone might ask her if she made her own quilts and Ruth might say that Emma has started a four-patch… it all just seems too embarrassing for words. "I don't have anything to show."

"Then what's in that bag you've been pushing under your seat?"

"Nothing," Emma replies limply, sounding like Ben when she's caught him taking contraband cookies from the jar. "Just some stuff."

Before she can stop her, Mavis swoops down and grabs Emma's bag. "I know you got your quilt top in here. Ain't a quilter alive who's made herself a quilt that didn't want to show it off." Mavis peers inside. "In fact, I'd say you got two quilts in here."

"One's from my attic," Emma warily explains. "I found it up there in a trunk."

"Show that one, too, then. Folks like an old quilt." Mavis grabs Emma's hand. "Come on. Let's get moving."

Reluctantly, Emma follows her to the line. Maybe they'll run out of time before it's her turn, she thinks. Maybe she'll faint and have to be carried out. She tries to enjoy the quilts being displayed, but they only serve to emphasize how unworthy Emma's little quilt-top is, how unfit to be in the same room.

When Mavis's turn comes, instead of pulling out the quilts from her bag, she points to Emma and says, "I want y'all to meet somebody new. This is Emma, and she just moved up here in January. She's a quilter."

"Hi, Emma!" the crowd calls out in unison.

"Now, she's a new quilter, mind you," Mavis continues, "and she's feeling a little shy about showing you her quilt. It's your first one, ain't it, honey?"

Emma nods mutely. When she finds her voice she says, "It's just the top, actually. It's not a finished quilt yet."

"That's alright," Mavis tells her. "You ain't the first one to bring an unfinished object up here." She turns to the audience. "Is she?"

Several voices call out, "Where's Minnie?" and another voice answers, "Now, don't you go giving me grief. I just like to get feedback while I'm still working. Keeps me from making too many mistakes."

Mavis carefully pries Emma's bag from her and hands the four-patch to Hamish and Wanda, who unveil it with touching care.

"How lovely," Ruth says, having stepped from behind her podium to get a better look. "Quite nice for a first effort!"

There is applause and exclamations of "Beautiful!" and "Great job, honey!" and Emma feels herself blushing. She can't believe how generous everyone is, and feels this doubly when Wanda, from behind the quilt top, says, "Honey, your seams are just as straight and even as they can be. I believe you're a natural."

There is more applause, and then Mavis leans over and whispers, "You want to show them that other one?" When Emma nods, Mavis pulls out the attic quilt. "Now, she didn't make this one, she found it in her house. Where'd you say you live?"

"In the old Buchanan place?" Emma half-says, half-asks, as though looking for confirmation from the group. "We bought the house from Lydia Buchanan."

There are murmurs of acknowledgment, and someone says, "Bet you spent a pretty penny fixing that old place up," and Emma laughs, feeling better now that the four-patch is tucked back in its bag. Mavis gives Hamish the attic quilt, and Wanda takes an end. The two step apart, shaking the quilt out to its full length. The response is immediate.

"Looks like Birds in the Air," someone calls out. "That, or — no, it's Birds in the Air alright."

"You think Miss Lydia made it?" someone else asks. "I don't recall her ever making a quilt."

And then from the very center of the room, a voice cries out, "That quilt's mine! You stole my quilt!"

8.

Christine McCrae storms to the front of the room and yanks the quilt out of Hamish and Wanda's hands. There is an audible gasp from the audience, and Ruth says, "Christine, that's a very old quilt. It must be handled with care."

"What I'd like to know is how you got it?" Christine turns to Emma with a look of such anger that Emma takes a step back. "Because last time I saw it, it was in my granny's hope chest."

"It — it came with the house," Emma stammers. "It was in the attic. In a trunk. It was there when I moved in. I — I don't even know where your grandmother lives."

Mavis steps between them. "Now, come on, Christine. Don't tell me you believe that somehow this woman moved into town, went to your granny's house all the way up on Roan Mountain, stolt a quilt out of her hope chest, and then brought it here to show all of us? That's crazy in about five hundred ways."

Christine's shoulders sag. "Well, no, I don't really believe she did that. But that quilt belongs to my family."

Barbara moves over to Christine and puts a hand on her back. "I wonder if we can talk about this after the meeting? Let's you and I go put some water on for tea while we wait for the others."

"There's nothing to talk about," Christine says, but she allows Barbara to lead her away. As soon as they're gone, the room explodes with excited chatter, and Emma falls into a chair in the front row, feeling as though she's been struck. Her face is hot to the touch.

Mavis sits down beside her. "Why don't you give them a few minutes?" she says in a low voice. "Then we'll go on back, and you two can settle things."

"I'm — I'm sorry," Emma says, though she doesn't know what she's saying sorry about, or why.

"Don't you worry none about Christine, honey; she's all bark, no bite. In fact, I'm going to go on back and make sure she's calmed down enough to be reasonable."

Emma smiles gratefully, feeling close to tears. So much for not having another run-in with Christine McCrae, she thinks. So much for joining a quilt guild to make lots of new friends, or getting the attic quilt looked at by an expert, for that matter.

"Here's some tea for you, dearie."

Hamish is suddenly in front of her, holding out a steaming ceramic mug. "It's chamomile, very soothing." He leans in closer as he hands her the tea and whispers, "Christine is famously difficult. Believe me, we've all suffered her wrath at one time or another."

Stepping back, he continues in a louder voice, "I love the fabrics you chose for your quilt. You have an eye for color, which some people do, but many people don't."

"You're saying some people are just born that way, Hammy?" a woman with a head full of steel gray curls asks with a grin from a few rows back.

Hamish waggles his eyebrows at her. "Yes, indeed, Irene,

I am. I'm sure one day they'll discover a gene for it. Emma here clearly has the color gene, and Miss Dorothy as well." He nods toward Wanda. "I'm working on her."

"It's just so overwhelming at times," Wanda complains. "I'll think I've picked out the most perfect colors for a quilt, and then Hamish will show me where I've got it all wrong."

"You're getting better," Hamish comforts her. "It can be learned."

Ruth appears and gently takes Emma's arm. "Why don't you come back to my office, dear. I'll show you how I've revived my African Violets. It's a miracle, really."

The store's office is barely large enough for two occupants, and there are already three people crammed inside when Emma and Ruth arrive. Christine is seated in the room's only chair, with Barbara standing next to her emanating waves of calm while Mavis stands behind the chair and glares down at the top of Christine's head. The attic quilt sits on Ruth's desk amid piles of fabric samples, books and several very perky violets in pink pots.

Emma finds a place to stand next to the door. She feels like a child waiting to see the principal, though she's not sure why. She hasn't done anything wrong. The quilt came with the house. Now, if it's somebody else's family heirloom, of course she'll give it back, but it's not her fault that it ended up in her attic.

Barbara smiles at Emma, and Emma relaxes. Barbara seems to possess the soothing instincts of a mother combined with a no-nonsense, let's-get-to-the-bottom-of-this attitude. Emma finds the combination comforting. Her own mother, Janice, was good at soothing, not so good at problem solving. Once, when Emma and Holly were fighting over a doll, her mother, unable to come up with a way for the sisters to compromise, gave the doll to the little girl next door. Emma and Holly had been scandalized, but their mother just shrugged, seemingly helpless to come up with a better solution.

"I think maybe the best place to start here — and Christine agrees with me — is an apology," Barbara begins, and for one scary second Emma thinks *she's* the one who's supposed to apologize, but no, Barbara puts a hand on Christine's shoulder and gives it a brief squeeze.

Christine looks at Emma, then to the ground. "I'm sorry about that," she says, barely audible. "I mean, about what happened out there. It's just — well, I've been looking for that quilt. It belonged to my great grandmother — Daddy's mother's mother — and one day it just up and disappeared."

"Around the time of your parents' separation?" Barbara prompts her.

Christine nods glumly. Then she looks at Emma. "They just got separated six months ago. Two days after I turned thirty-six, Mama calls me up on the phone and says, 'Christine, your daddy's leaving me for another woman.' Can you imagine that? He left Mama for the church secretary, which is so embarrassing. I mean, good Lord, man, show a little imagination!"

Emma laughs and then quickly covers her mouth with her hand.

Christine gives a rueful shake of the head. "No, it's laughable alright. Not that things would have been any better if he'd left Mama for a movie star."

Barbara gives Christine's shoulder another squeeze and turns to Emma. "Christine's father has been living at his mother's house during this difficult period and has his things stored there. Somehow or another, a number of valuable items belonging to both him and his mother have disappeared. There was no sign of a break-in, and the items were such that no one realized they were missing right away. In fact, it's just been in the last few weeks that it was discovered things had been taken."

"Including that quilt," Christine says, nodding toward the desk. "I used to sleep under that quilt when I stayed at Granny's when I was little, and she would tell me the stories she remembered her mother telling her about how it was made during Civil War times."

Emma notices Barbara give Ruth a brief nod, and is sure that Barbara must be the quilt expert. So her quilt is a Civil War quilt, she thinks, feeling excited until she remembers that it isn't her quilt anymore. Her disappointment is quickly replaced by a sense of unease — who was up in her attic? Who opened up the trunk and slipped the quilt in under Sunny and Tuesday? Who besides Lettie knew where the keys were?

She turns to Christine. "You could talk to Lettie Byers. She was there when I opened the trunk and was surprised as I was to find the quilt, but she might know who else had keys to the house before we moved in."

Christine's eyes narrow. "Oh, I've thought all along that Angie had something to do with it. I just haven't been able to pin anything on her."

"Angie?"

"Lettie's mama. You haven't met her yet?" Christine's expression is a sneer of disgust. "She's one of those crystal meth addicts that's ruining everything around here, lives up in some hollow in a trailer now."

Emma feels confused. "Why would she steal a quilt?"

"That quilt's worth a lot of money! She probably hid it up in your attic until she could figure out how to sell it to get money for drugs."

"But now we have the quilt," Barbara interjects. "And we have to decide what to do with it. I have an idea, at least for a temporary solution. As you may know, we have a contemplation space at St. Stephen's, a room for prayer and meditation, and I've been making plans to help celebrate the town's centennial by hanging an exhibit of local quilts on the walls and telling the stories behind them. This quilt would make a marvelous addition to the show. It would be a way for Christine to share her family history with the entire community."

"But what about when the exhibit's over?" Christine asks suspiciously. "What happens to the quilt after that?"

Everyone in the room turns to Emma. "I guess you take it home with you," she tells Christine. "It belongs to your family, not mine."

"But it was in your attic when you bought the house," Mavis points out, Emma's dogged protector. "Or probably was, anyway. Unless Angie snuck in while you were out at the store."

"If it was Angie, she probably got in the house after Mrs. Buchanan moved out and before we moved in," Emma tells her. "At least that's what I hope."

"Speaking of hopes," Barbara says to Emma, "It's my hope that you might help me with the exhibit. I hear you have a background in public relations. I'll want to do a lot of publicity for this. We're raising funds for missions."

Mavis's eyes widen. "Episcopalians do missions? I never knew that."

Barbara grins. "Oh, we Anglicans are full of surprises."

"How did you know I had a background in PR?" Emma asks, amazed by how much of her life story has leaked out into the community without her having to say a word.

"I have my sources," Barbara says mysteriously.

"Shana Martin, everybody's favorite realtor," Christine says flatly. "That woman knows everything about everybody, and she does *not* have a reputation for being discreet."

"So what do you say?" Barbara asks. "I can pay you a little from our grant, though not much, and it should be fun. We'll be collecting quilts from every nook and cranny around these parts. And Jesus will love you better than everybody else if you do it."

Well, then, how can she refuse?

Twenty minutes later Emma is in her car and driving toward home. She feels exhausted, elated, and also strangely nervous. What is it? The idea of helping Barbara publicize the quilt show? No, that sounds like the perfect job, amazing, as a matter of fact. So is she nervous about next week's Quilter's Lunch Bunch? But Mavis will be there, and Barbara and Ruth — she practically has a clique now, Emma thinks, laughing to herself — why would that make her nervous?

It's not until she's pulling into the driveway and glances up at her next-door neighbor's house with a single light shining from an upstairs window that she realizes what has her feeling so unsettled.

Was it Angie Byers who was in her house? And would she be coming back?

9.

Something changes for Emma after the guild meeting. It seems to her as though for the last month she's been sitting in the audience waiting for a play to begin. The curtain has been drawn back so she can look at the scenery, but no actual players have been on the stage. Now, suddenly, the cast has appeared, groups of two and three here and there, chattering, working out bits of business, and, from time to time, waving to Emma and calling out hello.

She first notices the change on Wednesday morning, when she decides to take a notebook to Helen's and, over a cup of coffee, make a list of things she wants to do with the house now that everything's unpacked and put away, and the house has been visited by both a plumber and an electrician. Next comes the fun part, or at least what Emma hopes will be the fun part — the painting and restoring, maybe even a little remodeling. She's decided to take Holly's advice not to worry about getting started on her novel. The novel will come when it's ready to come, she tells herself, feeling like she's channeling Oprah. But the fact is, as soon as she makes the decision to stop worrying about writing, she feels calmer than she has in weeks. Besides, there are lots of ways to be creative, including doing home renovations, right? Right.

She could do her list making at the kitchen table, of course, music streaming softly from the radio as she writes and nibbles on a pumpkin muffin. In fact, it would be useful to have her laptop on the table in front of her so she can do Internet searches for phone numbers and addresses. But it's a gray and gloomy morning — February has been full of them — and she's afraid if she stays inside all day, her energy will slowly seep out of her until she ends up in a limp ball on the couch, thumbing through last month's issue of *Cooking Light* and wishing they could get take-out for dinner.

And even more than that, she feels buoyed by the guild meeting. She texted Mavis when she got home Monday night, just to say how much she'd enjoyed meeting her, and has gotten an email and three text messages in reply. Barbara has emailed her as well, to make a date to discuss the quilt project early next week. And much to Emma's amazement, Charlotte Stengle called Tuesday afternoon to issue a shy invitation for lunch on Friday before Emma's volunteer period. "We'd have to eat in the cafeteria," Charlotte told her, "but I get an employee discount, and it's pizza day, which is always good."

So why shouldn't she pull on her red toboggan, wrap a scarf around her neck, and head over to Helen's? Isn't that the point of small-town life — you don't have a Target, but you do have a place to get a cup of coffee and chat about the weather with your neighbors?

Walking into the cafe, Emma realizes with a start that she actually recognizes two of the old men seated at a round table in the middle of the room. She's never met them, of course, but she's seen them in various spots around town, at the gas station, waiting in line at the bank, checking out books at the library. One of them, the taller of the two men, has cropped white hair and very small ears; Emma remembers noticing them one day in the post office when she'd gone to buy stamps for Sarah's Christmas thank you notes. The other man she recognizes has an impressive potbelly and bright blue eyes above ruddy cheeks. He nods at Emma as she takes a seat in a booth, and she smiles back, pleased. They're not so scary, she thinks.

She takes out her notebook and pen, writes *To Do* at the top of a page before turning to look out the window. Across the street, a young woman is leading a gaggle of preschoolers into the library. The children are dressed in brightly colored coats and several of the girls are wearing Dora the Explorer rubber boots although the weather is clear. Emma remembers wearing red galoshes on snow days when she was little; she had to tug them on over her regular shoes, and then buckle the two straps at the top. What she wouldn't have done for a pair of boots you could slip a socked foot into.

"You want some coffee, hon'?" The waitress has materialized at her side, pencil and pad ready. Emma nods, and the waitress asks, "How about some coffee cake with that? Helen made it fresh this morning."

Emma ponders this. Now, of course, she really shouldn't have coffee cake; her jeans are feeling a little tight as it is. But the idea that Helen is back in the kitchen right now, cutting squares of her homemade coffee cake and setting them onto dessert plates is almost too much to resist.

"Does she make it from scratch?" Emma asks, imagining Helen sprinkling brown sugar and walnuts over the yellow batter. Better yet, she imagines Helen in a

red-and-white-striped broadcloth apron, her graying straw-
berry blonde hair pulled back in a messy bun, peering at
her batter through cat's eye glasses.

"Well, she pre-mixes the dry ingredients for the cake, if
you know what I mean," the waitress informs her. "It's like
her own personal cake mix. And then in the mornings she
decides what cakes she's going to make. Today it's coffee
cake and Mocha Surprise cake — the surprise is that it's got
vanilla pudding inside. She thought about making angel
food cake, only you can't use the mix for that, plus you've got
to separate eggs. Helen hates separating eggs, but nobody
else who works in the kitchen can do it other than Julio,
and today's his day off."

"I'll take the coffee cake," Emma decides. "And coffee."

The waitress peers over her pad at Emma's notebook.
"Oh, are you making a to-do list? I love making to-do lists!
Do you ever do that thing where you'll have a list, and then
do something that's not on your list and add it on later, so
you can scratch it out?"

Emma nods. "All the time."

The waitress laughs. "Me, too! In fact, I have made entire
lists of things I've already done, just to have the satisfaction
of crossing them off."

"Cindy, you're talking that woman's ear off, and all she
wants is a cup of coffee," the man with the little ears calls out.
"While you're at it, why don't you bring a pot over here, too?"

"Are you going to leave me a tip today?" Cindy asks him
with a hand on her hip. "Because yesterday you failed to
leave me one."

The third man at the table, whose jacket is zipped all the
way up so that he looks like a turtle with its head halfway

out of its shell, says, "That's Ron's fault. It was his turn to leave the tip yesterday."

The potbellied man says, "I just plumb forgot. We'll leave you double today, and that's a promise."

"I'll believe it when I see it," Cindy says and marches off toward the kitchen.

Emma returns happily to her notebook. She feels like she's in a play starring a friendly waitress and three slightly grumpy but charming old men. When the front door chimes, she doesn't look up. She wants to imagine who it might be. The drama is about to unfold, she tells herself, something's going to happen. Maybe the preschool teacher got her charges settled in with some good books and now has five minutes for a cup of coffee and a chat with Cindy, who as it turns out, is her sister. Her long-lost sister. Or her estranged sister. Or her sister who owes her fifty bucks, which the teacher needs desperately, because she's spent all her money on a new tattoo and can't afford to pay her electric bill.

"Hey, there!" Lettie Byers greets Emma with her husky voice, sliding into the seat across from her. "I haven't seen you in ages!"

Lettie's cheeks are rosy, her hair a mess of curls spilling from under a *Rockin' Ravens* baseball cap. "How are you getting settled in? I feel like such a bad neighbor, but I swear, girl, I spend all my time running around from this place to that one. If it's not the grocery store, it's the pharmacy, and if it's not the pharmacy I've got to go pay the cable bill."

Emma has to take a moment to readjust. This is not the turn she expected the play to take. To be honest, she wishes Lettie were the preschool teacher with the new tattoo. Still, she does her best to be neighborly. "Are you still on third shift?"

Lettie nods. "Yep. It really works out best for Granny. That way I'm home during the day, even if I'm sleeping for part of it. She sleeps a lot, too, so that helps."

"So she's okay by herself at night?" Emma asks. "I mean, if she ever needed someone while you're at work, she could call us."

"That's so sweet," Lettie says. "But Granny's good, you know. Her health and all's good, and for a woman her age, she sleeps real solid. Sometimes Mama'll show up and pound on the door at some godforsaken hour, but that doesn't happen too often, thank goodness."

There's a pause. Lettie seems to be studying her hands. She looks up at Emma and says, "You know about my mama, right?"

Just then Cindy appears with the coffee and the coffee cake. "Hey, there, Lettie! You want some coffee?"

"Extra strong," Lettie says with a grin. "I just got off work, and Granny's got a list a mile long of things she wants me to do this afternoon."

"How's Miss Hannah doing?"

"She's alright. The damp weather doesn't help her arthritis any, but other than that, she don't have too much to complain about."

After Cindy leaves, Lettie says, "Well, I know you know about my mama, because Christine McCrae called me and told me all about Mama stealing her granny's quilt. Now whether or not Mama stole that quilt, I don't know. But the fact is, she could've gotten into your house easy, and she knows about the trunks in the attic because she used to do some cleaning for Miss Lydia."

"She could have gotten into my house *easy*?" Emma sits back in her seat. "You mean, while we've been living there?" Lettie nods. "Sure. Everybody's got everybody else's keys around here, or knows where the keys are hid. Now, don't panic. Mama's not dangerous. She's not as bad as Christine makes out. For one thing, she's not a meth addict; she's addicted to painkillers. That's a whole different ballgame."

"I see," Emma says, taking a shaky sip of her coffee. "How long has she — how long has she been this way?"

"Oh, Lord, I reckon it's been about three years. Well, she's always been a little bit of a wild child, but she wasn't ever an addict. She kept things under control. How the thing with the painkillers started was she got injured at work — broke her back falling down some stairs — and the doctor prescribed her codeine for the pain. Mama got hooked, and when the prescription ran out, she went looking for more, and that's when she got tangled up with Ray Blount. He sells used cars over in Yancey County, and deals drugs on the side. It's just the saddest thing in the world, Mama being with him. I've tried like the devil to get her into rehab, but Ray keeps getting in the way. He likes Mama all cool and chilled out, sitting right by his side. She's a real good cook, Mama is. Pretty, too."

"So — so you don't think she stole the quilt to sell it later, to get money for drugs?"

"She gets all the drugs she needs from Ray. No, if Mama stole that quilt, it's got more to do with Christine McCrae's daddy than it does with any kind of criminal activity. There's some pretty complicated entanglements between Mama and Dallas McKinney."

Emma pours more half and half into her coffee cup. She's

starting to understand why Christine McCrae might be such difficult person. Her father seems like a man with a lot of complicated entanglements.

Lettie looks left, then right, then leans toward Emma and says in a barely audible voice, "It's been my suspicion for many years that Dallas McKinney is my daddy."

Emma's eyes widen. "You don't know for sure?"

"Not for sure," Lettie concedes. "Mama's never said, but they were real tight growing up. And I remember for a long time when I was little, Dallas would just drop by the house unannounced. One year he gave me a bike for Christmas, and when I said something to Christine about it at school, man, she got mad. I mean she started wailing on me. Teachers had to break us apart. It didn't occur to me 'til a long time later to ask why Dallas was giving me presents, and when I did, Mama just said he liked me, was all."

"What did she say when you asked who your father was?"

Lettie swallowed hard. "She said my father was a mistake. She said he was none of my business."

Emma can't help herself. "You're kidding? Who would say that to a child?"

"Mama would," Lettie says with a shrug. "She's hard-headed. That's why I think if I could just get her into treatment, she'd have a chance. Anything Mama puts her mind to, she can do it."

Chairs scrape on the floor behind them, and Emma turns to see the three men getting up to leave. "Tip's under Ron's coffee cup," Turtlehead calls over to Cindy, who's refilling ketchup bottles at a table at the back of the room. "Come and check if you don't believe me."

"Oh, I believe you," Cindy says. "It just better be double."

The man with the small ears comes up to Emma and Lettie's table. "Hey, there, Lettie-girl," he says. "We sure do appreciate you stopping by my brother's place to give him his insulin. Carl never did like giving himself a shot."

"I'm glad to do it," Lettie tells him. "You know of anybody else who needs home care, give me a holler. I'm looking for more work."

The man nods and turns toward Emma. "I don't rightly think I've met you, but my wife Dorothy says you're the ones who bought Lydia Buchanan's house. Well, my daddy was good friends with Lydia and Bob Buchanan, and my granddaddy helped build that house back in the day. If you ever have any questions about it, you just let me know. I'm Trace Brown. I live over on Apple Orchard Road, Ledger Community."

He doesn't wait for Emma to answer, just tips his cap and turns to his friends. "Come on, boys. Let's go and see what's shaking at the gas station."

Emma and Lettie watch the three men leave, the bell chiming in their wake. "That's all they do, sunrise to sundown," Lettie tells Emma. "Go on their rounds and make sure the town's all locked up at the end of the day."

Emma clears her throat. "So, this might sound weird, but could you make sure your mother knows the quilt's not at our house anymore? I mean, if she took the quilt, for whatever reason, she probably has plans for it."

"Oh, I think if she took it, she did it to get a rise out of Dallas. Maybe send him a message. What that message says, I don't rightly know."

"Okay," Emma says, nodding. "That's fine. But go ahead and tell her, would you? Because I really don't like the idea of somebody I don't know rummaging around in my attic, even if she is a neighbor. I hope that doesn't sound awful."

Lettie drains her coffee cup and smiles tightly. "No, I completely get what you're saying. And I was thinking about driving over to see Mama this weekend. Sort of breaks my heart to do it, if you want to know the truth, but I like to check in with her from time to time. Keeps her from pounding on Granny's door in the middle of the night because she thinks we've been neglecting her."

After Lettie leaves, Emma walks over to the coffee pot and pours herself another cup. When she returns to her table, she looks at her pad of paper, which she thought she'd have filled up by now. With a sigh, she picks up her pen.

"*Number one,*" she writes at the top of the page. "*Change the locks.*"

10.

Back in September, after Owen and Emma had decided to move to the mountains, Emma had called Holly to give her the news. "The fates have intervened!" she announced grandly. "I'm finally going to live the life I'm meant to live!"

Holly laughed, and Emma could practically hear her roll her eyes. "Oh boy, I can't wait to hear this. Go on."

So Emma had explained how the highway department had offered Owen a job in Morgan County, an opportunity for him to finally get away from a desk and eight hours a day in front of a computer screen. Everything about the idea of moving appealed to Emma. She imagined a simpler life in the mountains — the pace slower, the pressure to be successful less pressing. They'd have more time to just *be*. And between the lower cost of living and the bump in salary Owen's new job would bring, Emma wouldn't have to work. She could finally chart her own course.

Naturally, the first thing they'd done after deciding Owen should take the job was look at houses online. They couldn't believe how cheap they were compared to houses in Chapel Hill. "There's this one that looks absolutely perfect," Emma told Holly. "It has *gables*. You know how I feel about gables."

"Gables have always been important to you," Holly agreed. "So maybe you'll finally get the house of your dreams. That would be a nice change of pace."

Poor Holly, Emma thought, having to listen to her complain about her house all these years. But the house was just so — *something*. So bland. So dominated by its garage. So *not* Emma. She and Owen had chosen the neighborhood for its schools and its easy access to both of their jobs, and they'd chosen the house because it had been at the right place at the right price at the right time, with no need of repairs or remodeling. Some day, they promised themselves, they'd buy the house they'd always wanted, one with a wrap-around porch, crown molding and wavy glass in the windows — and yes, gables. Emma was very serious about gables.

And now here she is on Saturday morning, standing in the kitchen of her marvelous house with its gables and attic trunks and mysterious quilts, feeling a little bit exhausted by her to-do list, which has increased in length by leaps and bounds since her trip to Helen's on Wednesday. The problem, she's realized, is that if you want to transform your house into your dream house, you have to do a lot of painting and tearing up of shabby indoor-outdoor carpet. The means aren't half as romantic as the ends.

Emma takes a sip of coffee and turns to Owen, who's finishing his breakfast and reading *Sports Illustrated*. "Have you ever thought we might need to paint the paneling in the living room?"

Owen's eyes widen with alarm. At heart, her husband is a conservative. He doesn't believe in change unless it's absolutely warranted. "You want to paint the paneling? Are you sure that's a good idea?"

Owen's tone of voice suggests he thinks this may be Emma's worst idea ever, but Emma is prepared. After fifteen years of marriage, she's learned that supporting materials are always a good idea when she wants Owen to get on board with a new plan.

"Let me show you my Pinterest page, and you'll see." She walks over to the table and moves her chair so she's sitting next to her skeptical husband. Opening up her laptop, she says, "I found all these pictures of painted paneling and a bunch of articles and tips on how to do it right. For instance, the paint can peel if you don't use the right kind of primer."

"And what kind of primer is that?" asks Owen. "Do you know?"

"Um, I don't remember," Emma says, grabbing her notebook and riffling through the pages. "I've got it written down here somewhere."

Owen nods slowly. "Okay, how about this. Let me do some research, and then we can go to Walmart together after lunch to buy paint."

"I could email you some links," Emma offers. "That might speed your research up for you."

"That would be great, honey," Owen says, sounding very much like a man who's humoring his wife. "Really helpful."

While Owen researches, Emma revisits her to-do list, which is closely aligned with her to-buy list, a list she vastly prefers to one that has her putting on coveralls and getting paint in her hair. Her current plans for the house come in two flavors — big stuff and little stuff. The kitchen features prominently on the big stuff side of the ledger. She loves her white farmhouse sink, though she'd love it even more if it had an apron drawer beneath it, and she desperately wants to replace the fake oak cabinets with white, glass-door cabinets. She envisions dark gray granite counters, broad-planked hardwood floors, and a bead board ceiling. She has yet to envision how she's going to talk Owen into this remodeling job, so for now she's focusing on the little stuff list, which includes prying up the green indoor-outdoor carpet in the living room (she's pulled up a corner and seen the scruffy hardwoods beneath), painting the downstairs bathroom and putting in a new mirror and new fixtures, and painting the children's rooms. And she's starting to imagine the quilts she might make, now that she's bought a used Bernina from Ruth — quilts for the children's beds, for the king-sized bed in the master bedroom, for the living room couch... This is becoming her longest to-do list of all, and Emma's not sure if it qualifies as big stuff or little stuff. A little bit of both, maybe.

After lunch, the whole family loads into the car and heads for Walmart. Given that it's Saturday, the parking lot is crowded. Given that it's Pine City, "crowded" is a relative term. They easily find a parking spot fifty yards from the store.

"So I get to carry Mom's phone, right?" Sarah asks as they get out of the car. "And I'm in charge of Ben?"

"That's right." Emma digs her phone out of her purse and hands it to her daughter. "Keep us updated about where you guys are in the store. If the phone buzzes, that's us texting you from Dad's phone, so be sure to check."

"I know how texting works," Sarah replies in an imperious tone. She nonchalantly tucks the phone into her back pocket, like it's no big deal, but Emma notices her patting it every five seconds as they walk toward the store.

"She has to let me look at Lego, right, Dad?" Ben asks.

"That's right," Owen says. "Sarah's going to be fair." He glances at Emma, who rolls her eyes. Sarah will boss Ben around and make him give his opinions on whether she should spend her allowance money on Barbie accessories or Barbie clothes, and there's nothing Ben can do about it. Fortunately, the excitement of being parent-free in Walmart will be enough to keep him temporarily docile.

After grabbing a cart and directing Sarah and Ben to the toy section, Emma and Owen head for the Home section. "We're looking for a solvent-based primer," Owen tells Emma. "And we're going to want to clean the paneling before we paint. And sand it — scuff it up, really, to help the primer adhere."

He continues on in this vein, and Emma realizes that he plans on doing the job. She smiles to herself, guessing how it will go. They'll buy all of their supplies and when they get home, Emma will take steps toward getting started. She'll put down drop cloths, lay out the brushes and paint stirrers and paint trays, wonder aloud what she did with the painter's tape. Owen will come stand in the doorway, arms folded across his chest, and after a few moments of watching, he'll begin to wince and take deep breaths. Finally, when Emma makes a move that suggests now she's about to begin — by prying open the primer can, for instance — he'll hem and haw and finally blurt out, "You know what, why don't you let me do this?"

And Emma will be happy to let him, even though she'd also be happy to do it herself. But before he gets going, she'll have to demand a verbal contract in which Owen acknowledges that *A*, Emma had every intention of doing this job without his help, and *B*, Owen, upon finishing the job, is not allowed to make any remarks about how Emma starts projects with every intention of Owen finishing them.

He'll break the contract before the paint dries, but that's fine. The fact is, Owen is so much better than Emma at priming and painting and scraping and applying that they'll both be happier with the end result if Owen's in charge. Emma's talent is for coming up with an idea, researching it, planting seeds ("The paneling makes the living room awfully dark, don't you think?"), and getting the ball rolling. She's also good at praising Owen for his stellar work and complimenting him on his biceps. Really, she thinks, they make a good team.

They find the primer and paint, and then go off in search of sandpaper. "Do you think you should text Sarah?" Emma asks as they round the corner of an aisle. "I know they're fine…"

"But it's good to be sure," Owen agrees, pulling his phone out of his pocket and tapping at the screen with his thumbs. Emma reaches into her purse for her own phone and has a panicked moment when she can't find it before she remembers her phone is currently residing in Sarah's back pocket. Laughing, she's about to tell Owen about her mental glitch when someone grabs her by the shoulder.

"Emma Byrd! I was just thinking about you not twenty minutes ago! Is this your husband? You got yourself a handsome one!"

Mavis Abercrombie pulls Emma into a hug and then peers over her shoulder into the shopping cart. "You all doing some painting today?"

"We're going to paint the paneling in the living room," Emma tells her. "I want to lighten it up a bit."

"Oh, I love painted paneling!" Mavis declares, finally releasing Emma from her embrace. "It's got that nice cottage-y feel to it. When the grandbabies get older, I want to do my entire front room in white — white couch, white rug, white walls. But ain't no use doing it while they're still little and spilling Kool-Aid all over the place."

She turns to Owen. "How'd you get yourself such a nice wife? I just love Emma to death."

Owen grins. "I bet you're Mavis."

"You'd win that bet," Mavis says. "Now I'll tell you what. Why don't you let me steal your wife and take her down to the flea market? I saw the perfect thing for her not an hour ago."

Owen is still holding his phone, which suddenly buzzes. He checks it and says, "I think I need to go save Ben. Sarah's complaining that he won't help her pick out new clothes for school. Emma, if you go to the flea market, how are we going to get you home?"

"Oh, I'll give her a ride home," Mavis assures him. "And the good news is I have my truck."

Owen's forehead creases with concern. "And the truck is important *why*?"

Mavis laughs. "Oh, I don't want to spoil the surprise. I'll bring this lady back to you by four o'clock. I hope you're home, because we'll need us a big strong man."

Emma looks helplessly at Owen and shrugs. She has no idea what Mavis is going on about. Of course she can't wait to find out, while the expression on Owen's face suggests that he could wait a very long time.

He waves her away anyway. "Go on and have fun. I'll get the kids and take them home. You wouldn't mind if I got started on the paneling, would you?"

"Don't feel like you have to," Emma tells him, knowing he'll put down drop cloths within five minutes of walking through the front door.

Mavis watches as Owen pushes the cart toward the toy section. "You got yourself a good one, honey," she tells Emma, leading her toward the exit. "Hold on to him."

"I plan to," Emma says. "He's good with paint."

According to Mavis, the flea market is held every Saturday on the fairgrounds just north of Pine City and is an all-day affair. When they arrive, dozens of people are wandering through the booths, stopping here and there to examine the merchandise or chat with a seller. Emma wants to look at everything, but Mavis pulls her past the tables bearing stacks of plates and crates of silver spoons, shoeboxes filled with baseball cards and postcards and crumbling playing cards, racks of old dresses, trunks containing hats and shoes and musty leather-bound books.

"Leonard came over from Mars Hill this morning, and he always brings something good with him. Him and his boys hauled up three truckload's worth today," Mavis explains as she leads Emma into an enormous canvas tent at the end of the grounds. "I could spend my life savings in here."

When Emma's eyes adjust, she sees that the tent is home to a wide array of furniture, not all of it functional. She sees plenty of old chairs lacking one or more legs, some decidedly slanting tables, and at least two chests of drawers without any drawers.

"There's a lot of junk in here," Mavis says. "But there's treasures, too. Now come look at this and tell me what you think."

Emma follows her to the far side of the tent. There, sitting in the corner, is a farmhouse table, probably six feet long with butcher-block legs, its white paint chipped, the top deeply scratched in several places.

"You sand it, you paint it, you put your Bernina on it," Mavis says trailing her hand along the tabletop. "I see it right in the middle of that parlor room of yours, don't you? Can you imagine sitting there on a winter's day, a fire burning in the fire place, while you work on a quilt?"

Emma can imagine it. She starts looking around for the price tag. When she finds it, it's not a tag at all, but a piece of painter's tape with *$45* written on it in a shaky script.

"Forty-five dollars?" she exclaims to Mavis. "That's it?"

"Hush now!" Mavis holds a finger to her lips, then whispers, "You've got to barter for it. Tell him you won't pay a dime over twenty dollars, and then agree to twenty-five."

"I'd pay a hundred," Emma whispers back. "Besides, I hate to barter."

"Then let me handle it."

Mavis goes off in search of Leonard, and Emma investigates the immediate area. If she were in the market for a wardrobe, two serviceable specimens are available, and there's a lovely washstand and matching mirror she wishes she had a place for in the front hallway. But the truth is, Emma can't think of any furniture they need; in fact, there are a few pieces she'd like to get rid of. Even a table for her machine isn't a necessity. Really, it's just a nice idea that she happens to be able to afford.

She's struck by the realization that once she finishes her various remodeling projects, she's done. The dream house that has taken up most of her mental space since they moved to Sweet Anne's Gap will have been dreamed into reality, more or less. A sudden wave of panic washes over her as she considers that without the house to focus on, it might be time to get serious about starting her novel. She can't keep putting it off forever — can she? No, of course not. She doesn't *want* to put it off forever. But when she thinks about working on something — a novel, a short story, even a magazine piece — she freezes. Maybe she's been wrong all these years. Maybe she's really not meant to be a writer after all.

Mavis waves at her from across the tent. "Sold for $33.25!" she calls. "Leonard's waiting for you to pay at the register, and his boys are going to carry the table out to my truck."

When Emma looks in her wallet, she finds she has exactly three ten-dollar bills, three one-dollar bills, and a quarter. Nothing else, not even a few loose pennies.

"You're gonna make some beautiful quilts on that table," Mavis tells her when they meet at the cash register, and Emma decides that having the exact change for the table isn't a coincidence, it's a sign. Here's what she's going to do next, and by next she means this afternoon, she means every day until she comes up with something else that makes her happier than cutting out squares of fabric and sewing them back together in miraculous, aesthetically pleasing ways: she's going to make beautiful quilts in her beautiful room on her beautiful, battered table.

11.

But first, before Emma makes beautiful quilts, she has to figure out exactly what she's doing. On Sunday afternoon she tried to make her first half-square triangle and nearly tore her hair out in the process. She'd bought two more quilting books from Ruth — *The Better Homes and Gardens Complete Guide to Quilting* and *How to Piece Perfect Quilts* by Leah Day — and they offered clear, straightforward directions and multiple photographs. But no matter how closely Emma tried to follow directions, her half-square triangles never came out square. She's starting to wonder if she should take up embroidery instead of quilting, make some nice throw pillows, stitch up a few samplers and frame them.

Come to lunch bunch, Mavis texts Sunday night in response to Emma's email about her failure to launch as a quilter. *Bring a sandwich, a machine, and a project. We'll help you.*

So a few minutes before noon on Monday, Emma packs her Bernina into the back of the minivan, shoves a foil-wrapped sandwich and a bottle of water into her purse, and heads to the Sewing Room. She doesn't have a project, just a tote filled with fabric, a small cutting mat, her rotary cutter, and a 12.5-inch ruler.

Lunch bunch takes place in the classroom, and when Emma gets there, there are only a few spots left to set up her machine. Barbara waves her over. "Come sit with me!" she calls. "I've got all the good gossip."

Emma lugs her machine across the room and sets it down on the table next to Barbara's. "The problem is, I hardly know anybody in town, so I won't be able to enjoy it. Maybe you should save your best gossip until I've lived here a few months."

"Believe me," Barbara confides loudly, "I could spend the next three weeks filling you in on Ruth alone."

"I heard that!" Ruth calls from the front of the room, where she's bent over a machine. "And as soon as I finish this Y-seam, I'm going to come straighten you out."

"Better straighten out that seam first!" Barbara yells back, and everyone around them laughs. Barbara turns to Emma. "Now, is there anything I can straighten you out on?"

Emma grimaces. "How are you with half-square triangles?"

"Terrible," Barbara admits, "but I can teach you how to do them."

"Those who can't do, teach?"

"Those who can't do, know how to cheat," Barbara revises. "At least when it comes to half-square triangles. Let me introduce you to my friend, the Thangle." She reaches into a large tote bag and pulls out a plastic bag containing strips of printed paper. "You align the pattern over your fabric, pin it, sew along the diagonal lines, and you end up with perfect half-square triangles. A miracle of the highest order!"

A miracle indeed, Emma thinks a few minutes later as she examines the almost perfectly constructed half-square triangle in her hand. "It must be magic," she says, shaking her head in disbelief.

"It's Thangles," Barbara corrects her. "Whoever came up with the idea of drawing dotted diagonal lines on tracing paper and selling them for lots of money is a genius."

"Mrs. Thangle, I presume," Emma says, and Barbara laughs.

"I can tell I'm going to like working with you," she says. "You *are* going to work on the quilt show with me, aren't you?"

"I'd like to," Emma says, although what she'd like to do right now is make a dozen more nearly perfect half-square triangles, just because she can. What she's going to do with them, she's not sure, but she'll figure it out.

"Make fifteen more of those and I'll show you a really cool block you can do," Barbara says, as if reading Emma's mind. "And when lunch bunch is over we'll go to Helen's and grab a piece of pie and I'll tell you about the job."

Emma spends the rest of lunch making half-square triangles, the hum of her sewing machine joining the chorus of machines all around her. To her right, Mavis is machine-quilting a twin-size quilt, and Emma keeps glancing over at her, curious to see how she can keep all that fabric under control. Dorothy Brown, sitting directly in front of her, works on an appliqué quilt for her teenage granddaughter, who lives in Charlotte. "Her mama don't hardly let us see her, now that she and Kenny are divorced," Dorothy complains to the room. "Like she wants to punish us for the marriage ending." Other conversations bloom out of this one — difficult daughters-in-law, sons that have moved off the mountain to find work, elderly parents who need tending. It's not long before pictures of children and grandchildren are being passed around along with bags of miniature chocolate bars.

At 1:30, Ruth stands and claps her hands to get everyone's attention. "All right my dears, the machine embroidery girls are coming in today at 1:45 for an emergency meeting, so let's start getting packed up, shall we?"

Emma wonders what constitutes an embroidery emergency. She wishes she could stay and sew a little longer, and from the light grumbles of complaint all around her, she knows that others feel the same way. After finishing up the last half-square triangle, she takes a quick trip to the ironing board, then lays all sixteen half-square triangles out on her cutting mat. They're not perfect; in fact, even with the help of the Thangles paper, a few are downright wonky. But with just over an hour's practice, she's gotten better. How satisfying is that?

"Bring those with you to Helen's and I'll show you how to make a Star and Pinwheels block," Barbara says as she pulls a cover over her machine. "It's super easy, but looks complicated. My favorite kind of block!"

As Emma finishes packing up, Mavis comes over and rests her things on the table. "You get them triangles figured out?"

"Almost," Emma tells her. "I'm getting better at them anyway."

"Just keep practicing," Mavis instructs her, "and every day you'll get a little bit better yet. The problem is, we look at beautiful quilts and think we ought to be able to make them right off the bat. But it don't work that way. First, you got to mess up all over the place. Then you need someone to show you the right way to do things, and then you got to practice and mess up some more. It's a process. But you got natural talent — I could see it the minute you pulled out your quilt top last week. By the way, what are you going to do with that? Quilt it yourself or quilt by check?"

"Quilt by check?"

"She means pay someone with a long-arm quilting machine to quilt it," Barbara clarifies. "There are several good long-armers in the area. Ruth will give you a list if you'd like."

"I'd sort of like to do it myself," Emma says. "Or is that crazy?"

"Not crazy at all!" Mavis exclaims.

"Sort of crazy," Barbara says at the same time, then claps her hand over her mouth. "Sorry, I should be more encouraging. It's just that I find machine quilting frustrating. I watched Mavis here flinging that quilt around under her machine today and I could just feel the muscles in my neck tighten up."

"You've got to do it right, now that's the truth," Mavis agrees cheerfully. "Plenty of chiropractors have profited from the advent of home machine quilting. But I can teach you the tricks if you're interested. Otherwise, there ain't nothing wrong with writing a check to help a long-arm quilter make her living. Of course if you find out you like machine quilting well enough, you might become a long-armer yourself."

Emma laughs. "I appreciate your faith in me. But I guess I should stick to one thing at a time."

"Me, I'm more of a three things at a time girl," Mavis says, picking up her bags and turning to go. "But I take your point. Well, text me when you're ready for a quilting lesson. I'm off to pick up some babies from preschool."

Emma and Barbara watch as Mavis makes her slow exit from the store. She stops every few steps to give someone a hug or exclaim over a quilt. "She's good people," Barbara says. "Be glad she adopted you."

"I have the feeling she adopts everyone," Emma says, gathering her things. "I've never heard someone's phone buzz as often as hers."

"She's got a big heart for sure," Barbara says. "Me, I've got a big rear-end and to maintain it properly I need to eat pie on a daily basis. Shall we head to Helen's?"

Fifteen minutes later, having deposited their sewing machines and bags in their cars, Emma and Barbara are sitting in a booth at Helen's, their empty pie plates in front of them. "If I could choose my own death," Barbara says, leaning back with a sigh, "it would be from lying down in a giant graham cracker piecrust and having chocolate filling dumped over me. Doesn't that sound heavenly?"

Emma grins. "It sounds coma-inducing, I'll say that much."

"Speaking of sugar comas — " Barbara rummages in her purse and pulls out a crumpled piece of paper with a list of names and addresses on it — "we will be making a number of visits to a number of households where sweet tea and baked delights will be offered. It's considered rude to decline either."

Barbara scans her list. "Yep, we've got both Louellen Walls, who serves Christmas cookies all year round, and Becca Timmons, who doesn't bake but feels like she's mistreated her guests if she doesn't offer them a choice of chocolate-covered peanuts or Ho-Hos. Me, I go for the Ho-Hos — it's a nostalgia thing."

"What about Hannah Byers?" Emma asks, thinking of her reticent, white-haired neighbor. "Lettie mentioned that she makes quilts. Will she have one in the show?"

Barbara shakes her head sadly. "She's been asked to contribute, but I don't think she even bothered to reply to our invitation. Which is a shame, because she's one of the best quilters in the area. Maybe *the* best. She's had quilts at Quilt Week in Paducah and the International Quilt Festival in Houston. But she stopped quilting a few years ago, stopped showing up for meetings."

"Do you know why?"

"It's a mystery," Barbara says. "There aren't a lot of secrets around here, but why Hannah Byers stopped quilting is one of them."

Emma wouldn't mind pursuing this topic — the other night she saw a woman smoking on Hannah Byer's front porch and wondered if it was Angie Byers; she'd like to know more about who her neighbors really are — but Barbara's expression suggests she's ready to move on. "So what's my purpose on these quilt collection missions?" Emma asks, taking a sip of her coffee. "Other than gaining ten pounds?"

"You're the note-taker, the biographer," Barbara says. "We need a program for the show with brief bios of the quilters and some background on their quilts. And we need press releases, of course. I was thinking you could do some canned pieces — is that what they're called? — you know, essentially write articles about the show and some of the contributing quilters, and then send those pieces to area papers and the regional travel mags. They love prepackaged stuff; it makes their jobs easier."

"I don't know anything about quilts or very much about this region," Emma points out. "Are you sure I'm the best person for this job?"

Barbara leans forward, a serious expression on her face. "I've known you for a whole week, so I have no idea if you're the best person for the job. What I do know is that you're the only person for this job. In all the years I've lived here, God's never sent me a PR professional before."

"It doesn't sound like I have much of a choice then," Emma says, not quite sure how she feels about being God's chosen publicist, but knowing she wants the job, whether it's divinely ordained or not.

Barbara straightens and smiles. "You have no choice whatsoever. So what do you say? Should we order some more pie?"

12.

Barbara has told Emma to dress casually for their quilt-collecting trip Monday, but she doesn't know what *casual* means around here. Saturday morning, she stands in front of her closet wondering what on earth a person wears to ride around the countryside with an Episcopal priest. She doesn't want to overdress — she's afraid the people they visit might think she's snobby, or, as Aunt Nora would have put it, *hoity-toity* — but she doesn't want to look like she doesn't care, either.

Her real problem is that none of her casual work clothes fit her anymore. The dress code at the hospital had been fairly relaxed, a lot of the employees showing up in jeans, and while Emma dressed more professionally, she almost never wore anything tailored. Yet she has to tug at the zipper of her black slacks and can barely button the waistband. When did this happen? Her jeans have been a little tight, it's true, but they're fine after she's worn them for a day, and downright comfortable after two.

"I'm fat!" she wails to Holly on the phone twenty minutes later, after she's confirmed that it's not just the black pants, but all of her work clothes that are too snug for comfort. She's forced to confront the fact that she's gained at least ten pounds since they've moved, maybe more — she'd know for sure if she weren't too scared to step on the scale.

"You're forty," Holly reminds her. "It's time to accept it: you've got to choose between your face and your — well, I'd say it, but I'm at a junior gymnastics meet. Where nobody has rear ends, by the way, including the moms. And you know what? They don't look great."

"Well, I'm going to work on Monday, and what am I supposed to wear? Sweats?"

"You must have a wrap-around skirt, don't you? Doesn't every suburban mom have a wrap-around skirt? Wear that and a nice long-sleeve tee shirt. Casual, yes, but nice enough to wear into people's houses."

"What shoes?" Emma asks, pinning the phone to her ear with her shoulder as she rifles through her closet in search of a skirt. She finds an elastic-waistband black-and-white print skirt that was not quite nice enough for work but fine for parent-teacher conferences and yanks it from its hanger.

"I heard that," Holly says. "You just tore a skirt off its hanger, didn't you?"

"I yanked it," Emma clarifies. "That's different."

Her sister sighs into the receiver. "When are you going to learn to take care of your clothes? Really, Em', you're pathetic. Anyway, if you've got low wedges with a closed toe, that would be nice. And if you're worried about the weight, don't diet, just cut out white foods. Except for fish. Fish is fine. Wait a sec, Caitlyn is about to do her beam routine."

Emma lies back on the bed as Holly narrates her daughter's progress up and down the balance beam. Her stomach hurts. Why can't she be like Holly, who has the metabolism of a hummingbird? Holly, who has never had to diet in her life while Emma loses and regains the same twenty pounds over and over again? It's not fair.

But you have a good marriage, she reminds herself, which Holly doesn't — or didn't; she divorced two years ago — and a very nice house, which Holly does, too, but Holly's house doesn't have a single gable. And Holly has problem hair.

"I've got to go," Emma tells her sister after listening to the blow-by-blow of Caitlyn's dismount. "Thanks for the skirt advice. Now I just need to figure out what to wear on Tuesday."

"Same skirt, different shirt," Holly advises. "And buy some more clothes online this afternoon. Maybe they'll get there by Wednesday. And call me to let me know how it goes! I bet you'll meet some amazing people."

After they hang up, Emma rolls to the side of the bed and places the phone back on its charger. Maybe she should order two more skirts, one black, one tan, and a variety of scoop-necked tee shirts. And look just like her mother, she thinks with a grimace as she heads downstairs. But what are her options? When she'd been a teenager, she'd accused Janice of having no fashion sense, but now she knows that when you're a parent, the easiest thing is to find clothes you like and buy them in multiples. Who has time for putting together stylish outfits?

When she reaches the doorway to her sewing room, she stands for a moment, admiring the view. The farm table, which has been sanded and painted, takes up the center of the room, very *shabby chic*, Emma thinks, or *country classic*, or whatever phrase currently means *fabulous in a secondhand kind of way*. Most of the table is taken up by her four-patch quilt, the victim of her early machine-quilting efforts. Thank goodness Mavis made her invest in a high-quality seam ripper; her Ultra Pro Surgical tool has been getting a workout these last few days. Mavis has counseled her to not get overinvested in perfection — "Ain't nobody gonna look at those stitches as close as you do, so cut yourself some slack," she's advised on more than one occasion — but Emma can't help herself. She wants to learn to do things right.

And she's getting there. Watching online videos on machine quilting yesterday, she discovered pebbling, which as far as Emma can tell is just sewing dime- and quarter-size circles over and over until your quilt is covered with them. It's not fancy, but it looks good. Mavis has promised to come over and help with the binding the minute Emma finishes.

Looking at her partially-quilted quilt, Emma finds herself thinking of Aunt Nora. She has thought more about her Aunt Nora in the last six weeks than she has in the thirty years since the woman was shipped off to the nursing home in Annandale. If only Aunt Nora had had a Mavis — or a Ruth and a Barbara. If only she'd had shy little Charlotte Stengle emailing her links to quilting blogs and websites and making copies of articles from quilting magazines to tuck into Sarah's backpack for Emma to read. Maybe Aunt Nora would have quit smoking, opened a few windows and stopped complaining so much about Grammy, if she'd been part of a community of people who loved making quilts as much as she did.

Or quite possibly she would have remained the cranky old biddy she'd always been, Emma thinks, picking up a book from the window seat. *Layer Cake, Jelly Roll and Charm Quilts* by Pam and Nicky Lintott arrived yesterday via UPS and she's already leafed through it several times, noting six or seven quilts she'd like to make. She's trying to remember where she put the pad of sticky notes so she can mark the pages when Sarah appears in the doorway, her eyes red and puffy.

"I just thought you should know I officially hate it here," her daughter announces. "I wish we had never left Chapel Hill."

"What? Why?" Emma pats the window seat cushion. "Come over here and talk to me, honey. Tell me what's going on."

Sarah crosses the room and plops down next to Emma. Her lower lip sticks out, to further emphasize her unhappiness. "Brittany says she can't be friends with me anymore," she whimpers, curling into Emma's side. "She says we live next door to nasty people, which makes us nasty people, too."

"Oh, honey, that's a terrible thing for her to say. And totally untrue. The Byers are very nice people, and so are we. And even if the Byers weren't nice people, that has nothing to do with what kind of people we are."

Sarah looks up at her. "So are they nice people or not?"

Emma doesn't quite know how to answer this. Finally she says, "Lettie Byers is a nurse, which means she's a very caring person. I don't know her grandmother very well, but she seems nice, too."

"Brittany says they all take drugs."

"That's not true." Emma stops herself from telling Sarah that only Angie takes drugs. Sarah doesn't need to know about Angie. "What it is, honey, is gossip, and gossiping is wrong."

Sarah sits up straight and crosses her arms over her chest. "Well, who cares? Brittany's turning everyone against me. I just called Amber, and she said she had to spend all afternoon cleaning her room, but I could hear a bunch of laughing behind her, so I know Brittany and Tiffany were over there."

"Girls can be mean," Emma says slowly, searching for the right words to comfort Sarah. "There were mean girls in Chapel Hill, too. The good news is they grow out of it. And the even better news is, you can find nice girls to hang out with right now if Brittany and her friends are being mean to you."

This, it turns out, is not the right thing to say. "You don't even know what you're talking about!" Sarah's cheeks are flushed, and the tears are flowing again. "If Brittany doesn't like me, then nobody likes me. I'm doomed."

She jumps up and stomps out of the room. "This town sucks!"

"Give it time," Emma calls lamely, but Sarah's already halfway up the stairs. Sighing, Emma gives her new book a longing look and then stands up. Whatever plans she has for quilting this afternoon are tabled.

"Honey, do you want to make some chocolate chip cookies?" she calls up the stairs, ignoring the thought that the last thing her waistline needs is cookies. "We can make them with extra nuts, just the way you like them!"

"In a minute," Sarah calls back, still sniffling. "I need to email Sophie."

Well, she'll get the kitchen cleaned up from lunch, Emma thinks as she walks down the hall, and make sure they have all the ingredients. If they don't, a trip to Walmart might cheer Sarah up. But what if it takes more than just cookies and a shopping spree to get Sarah out of this funk? What if, in spite of everything that's going well in Emma's life, this move was a bad idea?

You're overreacting, she tells herself. Everything's fine. It's just a rule of family life: at least one person has to be in crisis at any given time. She takes a deep breath and goes into the kitchen, where Owen is leaning against the counter, the phone nestled against his ear. He's nodding, but not actually saying anything. "They can't hear you nod, honey," Emma whispers. "You have to say 'yes' out loud."

"Yes, Mom," Owen says into the receiver. He looks up at Emma and winks. "Yes, we'd love to have you and Dad up for a visit next week. Yes, Emma's right here. You two can make plans."

Emma sinks into a chair. *Thanks a lot*, she mouths at her husband as she takes the phone. "Linda? Is that you?" she chirps into the receiver, trying to sound as pleased as possible at the sound of her mother-in-law's voice; Linda can sniff out lack of enthusiasm from a hundred paces. "We'd love to see you! The dog? Yes, of course, bring the dog. What's that? *Dogs?* Well, sure, of course, bring all three of them."

You will pay for this, she mouths at Owen, who smiles, kisses the top of her head, and leaves her to his mother.

13.

Much to Emma's surprise, Barbara drives a pick-up truck, a 1965 red Ford F-100. When Emma saw it in the mostly empty St. Stephen's lot on Monday morning, she'd assumed the truck belonged to a janitor, or else that it had been abandoned by someone who figured the church secretary wouldn't call a tow truck to have it hauled away.

"It's my husband's old truck," Barbara explains as she jiggles the passenger door handle. "Ah! Here we go! Doesn't always want to open. Ty bought it for four hundred dollars from his dad and drove it until he finally got a new one last September. But he couldn't bear to sell old Sally here, so now she's mine. I think people relate to a truck better than they did to my Saab."

Emma climbs into the front seat. The air inside the truck is rich with the smell of pipe smoke, Turtle Wax, and something sharply sweet that Emma can't quite put a name to. "What kind of work does your husband do?" she asks when Barbara gets in.

"He has an apple orchard. It's been in his family for generations, but Ty's only been running the business hands-on for about ten years now. He used to be a mortgage banker, but it wasn't good for his soul. So now he and our two sons grow apples. Grab that notebook out of the glove compartment, would you? It's got our directions."

Barbara pulls out of the St. Stephen's parking lot and takes a left onto Highway 15. "Our first two stops will be to pick up a quilt from Louellen Walls up in Loafer's Glory, and then one from Peggy Weaver who lives close to Sugar Mountain. Oh, she'll be interesting for you to meet. Well, quite honestly, everybody you meet around here is interesting once you get them talking."

Emma leafs through the notebook until she finds the page with the directions. "Are you from here? You don't sound it."

Barbara shakes her head. "No, I'm from Cleveland originally. I met Ty in college — Wake Forest University; we were both econ majors. Which, I know, is a long way from the priesthood, but it's always a crooked path, isn't it?"

"To the priesthood?"

"Well, that and wherever you end up in life in general, I suppose," Barbara says, reaching over to turn on the radio. Suddenly the cab fills with country music. "Nice speakers, huh? Ty gave them to me for my birthday. The fact is, I always knew I wanted to be a priest, but I was raised Catholic. I mentioned that to a friend one day — oh, gosh, it's been fifteen years ago now — and she said, and I quote, 'So why don't you kiss the Pope's butt goodbye and march on over to the Church of England?' Nice, huh? Oh, let me turn this up — it's Taylor Swift. I think she's marvelous."

Barbara begins to sing along with the radio, slapping out the beat on the dashboard. Emma has to bite her lip. Barbara knows all the words, but her singing is off-key by a mile. "Sing with me!" Barbara shouts as the music builds to the chorus. "If you don't know the words, make some up!"

Emma gamely hums along. She's heard this song before, but she has no idea what the lyrics are, and it's impossible to make up lyrics when the person next to you is belting out, "*You should've said no, you should've gone home, you should've thought twice 'fore you let it all go!*" After two choruses, she's tired of humming, but she bobs her head to show Barbara she's still in the spirit of things.

"When I first came to St. Stephen's, I thought I was going to change everyone to my way of thinking," Barbara says after the song ends and a commercial comes on. "If folks didn't like Vivaldi, well, I'd make them like Vivaldi. I'd make them see that Vivaldi was so much better than Vince Gill. But you know what? I started listening to Vince Gill, and I realized he was a genius.

"And this Taylor Swift?" She points to the radio, as though a tiny Taylor Swift were perched on the volume dial. "Amazing! So young, and such a talent. All the youth group girls just adore her."

Emma tries to imagine what the girls in the St. Stephen's youth group look like. Sweet Anne's Gap doesn't really strike her as an Episcopalian sort of town. She's been to Episcopal churches for weddings and baptisms, and there's always been a kind of reserve over everything, a little whiff of country club. There's a golf course in Pine City, so clearly someone around here plays, but if she had to put money on it, she'd bet that most men spent their weekends hunting or fishing. At least that's what the bumper stickers on pickup trucks all over town would have her believe.

She's curious about who in Sweet Anne's Gap might attend Barbara's services, but it's probably rude to ask. Maybe there are only five people who show up on Sunday mornings, all of them little old ladies wearing pearls and clutching handkerchiefs perfumed with Chanel No. 5 to their breasts. But that would hardly explain the church's prayer room, a separate wing out back with lots of blonde wood and huge plate glass windows. When Barbara gave her the tour of the church on Wednesday, Emma felt blanketed in calm as soon as she stepped foot inside. It's not the sort of space that a repressed congregation would allow, or that a tiny one could afford.

Barbara turns left onto Highway 221, and the view opens up to bottomland, rolling hills and sturdy brick houses, the land behind them spotted here and there with cows and horses and craggy rocks poking out of the dirt like overlarge teeth.

How weird, Emma thinks, that this is where she lives. Other than a college semester spent in London, she's never lived anywhere but the suburbs. Who would have ever guessed that she'd end up in a place so haphazard in its planning? No two houses alike, some houses pressed back against the woods on the far end of their lots, others just a few yards from the road. She's never lived in any neighborhood that would have even entertained allowing livestock to roam through the front yards, that's for sure.

Louellen Walls lives in a stone house at the top of a frightfully steep driveway. On their way up, Emma starts to worry that the truck will flip backwards and finds herself pulling on her shoulder strap, as though somehow she can keep the wheels anchored to the ground. She tries to take in the view, which is mostly trees, but nice trees, she thinks, which is fortunate, since they may be the last thing she sees before she dies.

"Whew! That was quite a ride!" Barbara exclaims when they pull in next to the garage at the top of the hill. "When we first moved up here, I didn't know enough to downshift on steep hills like that, and I'd find myself rolling backwards. Terrifying!"

"What happened?" Emma asks, feeling like she needs to catch her breath.

Barbara shrugs. "I rolled back into a guy one day, and he explained to me about downshifting. Changed my life. I just wish I hadn't totaled his car."

They're halfway up the front steps to the house when a woman bursts out onto the porch, her face lit brightly with expectation. She has the wrinkled, brown skin of a dried apple, and a toothless grin. "Hope you don't mind — I didn't put my bridge in today. It's been aggravating me lately. I'm wondering if something ain't changed in there, like my gums have swolled up. My girl Suzy says it's 'cause I talk so much and my jaw muscles have gotten too big for their own good. Now what do you think about that?"

"I think I could listen to you talk all day, Louellen," Barbara says, joining the woman on the porch and kissing her cheek. "Have you met Emma Byrd? She's my communications specialist on this project."

Louellen laughs. "How you doing, honey? That sounds like a mighty important job you got there. You from off the mountain?"

Emma doesn't understand the question, but Barbara smiles and says, "Emma and her husband bought the Buchanan house in town."

"I heard Lydia had finally passed," Louellen says, nodding. "Shame they had to put her in a home that way. When it's my time, just set me out on an ice block like them Eskimos do. They got the right idea."

Louellen leads Barbara and Emma into her house, which, as it turns out, is decorated for Christmas. Not just the hallway, where Emma counts three Christmas trees alone, each with its own theme (gingerbread men, cats, and Carolina football), but every room she can see. Green and red lights flash on and off in the hallway and bathroom while white lights chase each other around the kitchen and into the pantry. The main room hosts several strands of blue lights, plus one white and two red, lending a Fourth-of-July feel to the Christmas celebration. At the center of the room sits a long, low table covered with green felt that showcases an elaborate Christmas village. Louellen picks up a small building and holds it out to Emma and Barbara.

"It's my new post office, just come yesterday via the UPS man," she explains, and Emma wonders how on earth a UPS truck could get up that hill. "It's a Thomas Kinkade. Ain't it pretty?"

She hands the post office to Emma. "I was a Christmas baby. Can you tell?"

Emma nods, the overwhelming décor suddenly making sense to her. "It's like December 25th here, everywhere you look."

"Ain't that the truth?" Louellen says with a satisfied nod. "Well, I'll tell you something, it wasn't always this way. I'd dreamed of having a Christmas house all my life, but I had to wait for Fred to die. He didn't like the idea of a Christmas house. Said we was to focus on Jesus on the cross who died for our sins, not Jesus to the manger born. He was a sour old thing, Fred."

She turns to Barbara. "Now, I'd offer you some coffee, but I can't remember if your kind drinks coffee."

"I believe it's the Mormons who refrain from coffee-drinking," Barbara informs her. "I personally drink it by the gallon."

"Well, good then. I'll get you some, and then I'll go fetch the quilt. Stayed up until midnight sewing on the hanging sleeve."

After Louellen gets them their coffee and goes to retrieve the quilt from her bedroom, Emma and Barbara squeeze onto a love seat festooned with *Frosty the Snowman* pillows. "How long do you think this coffee has been on the burner?" Barbara asks after taking a sip. "Seven hours? Eight?"

Emma takes her own sip. "Months," she says, her lip curling from the coffee's bitterness. "Possibly years."

Barbara hoots. "Exactly! Well, fortunately, as a long-time veteran of coffee-hour coffee, I've got a steel gut and no pride. You, on the other hand, might want to take it easy."

Louellen returns a few minutes later with a large paper bag in her hands. "Now, I don't reckon this is the prettiest tote you ever seen, but it's all I could find."

Barbara sets her coffee mug down and takes the bag from Louellen. "May I show this to Emma?" When Louellen nods, Barbara stands and carries the bag to the center of the room, next to the Christmas village table. "Louellen is what I would call an occasional quilter," she tells Emma, carefully pulling the quilt from the bag. "She's not one of those quilters who makes a quilt for any old reason or no reason at all. Her quilts commemorate events, important days, special times in a life."

Emma nods, expecting Barbara to reveal a quilt covered with Santa Claus appliqué, or a full-sized Rudolph the Red-Nosed Reindeer. So she is practically knocked out of her seat when Barbara unfurls a quilt with an embroidered banner running along the top that reads *MIA or RIP? Their Mothers Want to Know!*

Beneath the banner is a portrait rendered completely in fabric of a young GI in camouflage fatigues smiling out at the viewer. Beneath it are the words "John T. Walls, Gone Missing May 18, 1971. Still in Our Hearts."

"Do you see the ghost?" Louellen asks Emma, who feels a chill run through her. "It's right there, don't you see?" Louellen points to a spot over the GI's left shoulder. "That's the ghost of the part of me that died when I realized Johnny weren't never coming home."

And Emma can see it, a gauzy, ethereal image hovering above the soldier. Haunting is the word for it, she thinks, and not just for the ghost, but for the entire quilt. "It's amazing," she tells Louellen. "How did you do the portrait?"

"It's a process, I'll tell you that," Louellen says. "But it's not that hard once you know how."

"We're trying to get Louellen to teach a class at the Sewing Room," Barbara says, beginning to roll the quilt back up. "There are a lot of us who would love to do portrait quilts if we just had some instruction."

"Maybe I will one day," says Louellen, sounding doubtful. "But not until I get some teeth that fit me right."

Louellen sends them off with the quilt and a baggie filled with Christmas cookies from her freezer. On the ride down the mountain, Emma nibbles on a cold green-frosted wreath and imagines describing the scene she's just stepped out of to

Holly or Owen. She doesn't know if she could. She wouldn't want anyone to laugh at Louellen, which they might do if Emma told them about her Christmas-themed house, or mentioned her missing bridge. If you hadn't sat in the same room with Louellen, if you hadn't seen that quilt, the entire situation might sound ridiculous. And, okay, some of it was funny. The Santa figurine that belted out "Jingle Bell Rock" in the bathroom when Emma flushed the toilet had been downright hilarious.

But Emma knows there is nothing laughable about Louellen Walls. She thinks of everything she's just seen — the Christmas decorations, the missing dentures, the bad coffee — and still there's no denying one essential fact: Louellen Walls is an artist.

14.

As she makes dinner that night, Emma listens to the news on the Chapel Hill NPR station she streams through her computer. She finds herself waiting for a story, as though she'd heard a teaser earlier for something that sounded interesting. Finally she realizes she is waiting to hear the story of Louellen Walls' son or of Peggy Weaver, the young quilter they visited after saying goodbye to Louellen. She's waiting to hear the news of her day, as though everyone would be interested in these women's lives. As though anyone outside of Morgan County knew that they existed.

Chopping carrots for salad, Emma thinks about the quilts she's seen that day — Louellen's MIA ghost quilt and Peggy Weaver's Lone Star made entirely from fabrics she'd dyed herself, as well as the quilts they picked up on their way back down the mountain, Irish Chain quilts spotted and stained from use, a perfectly preserved Tulip quilt with "1886" embroidered in the lower left-hand corner, two Baltimore Album quilts, and four crazy quilts.

"We're really lucky," Barbara told Emma as they were driving away from Peggy Weaver's house. "A few years ago a group of folklorists from the university in Asheville came over to do a fieldwork project. They held quilt documentation days at area churches and went house to house to inventory every quilt they could find. They documented more than 200 quilts, which is especially notable since people up here aren't always welcoming to strangers. But I guess everyone likes to show off Granny's quilt. When I decided to do a show in conjunction with the centennial, I sent letters to everyone who'd shared a quilt with the folklorists."

"How many people replied?" Emma asked, wondering if people willing to show a quilt to a fieldworker knocking at their door would be equally as willing to let that quilt out of the house.

"Our response rate was around 35 percent, which isn't too bad. I suspect now that we're in the process of collecting the quilts, we may hear from folks who were initially hesitant to contribute. You know — you think you don't want to do it, and then you hear that your sister-in-law's getting involved, or Mary Kate down the road is going to put a quilt in the show, and suddenly having your grandmother's quilt on display sounds like a good idea."

Twenty-five minutes later, pulling into the St. Stephen's parking lot, Barbara turned to Emma and asked, "So, are you ready to do some research, get yourself primed for writing?"

Of course she'd said yes, but she might have thought twice if she could have foreseen Barbara carting out the huge box of books from her office a few minutes later. "I'd start with the Orlofsky book — *Quilts in America* — to get a good background," Barbara instructed, depositing the box into the back of Emma's minivan, "and then maybe move on to the Barbara Brackman books on Civil War quilts, because we're going to see a bunch of those. Oh, and I've put *North Carolina Quilts* in here — it's a great introduction to quiltmaking in this state. Well, admittedly, there's not much about African-American or Native quilts, but there are some decent articles online I can send you the links to."

Emma tips the cutting board and spills the carrots into the large wooden salad bowl. She's nervous about being in charge of writing all the bios, mostly because she doesn't want to get anything wrong — or really, if she's being honest, she doesn't want to get on anybody's bad side. What if she gets family histories mixed up, attributes a quilt to somebody's mother-in-law when it was their mother who made it? Just from driving around she knows that local surnames have a variety of spellings — there's Buchanan and Buchannon and Buchannen — how is she supposed to know which is which?

You fact-check, she tells herself. You double-check, you make phone calls. Calm down.

Suddenly Emma realizes that she's tired. Three hours spent roaming the countryside and socializing is a lot for one day, especially since she's gotten used to having hours at a stretch when she doesn't talk to anyone at all. But not for long. Linda and Mike will be here on Thursday, and Emma will have a full week of socializing. The very thought sends her to the fridge, where she pulls out a bottle of Pinot Grigio. She loves her in-laws, knows from stories her friends tell her that they could be so much worse than they are, and really, they're lovely people — but a week?

She pours herself a glass of wine and sits down at the table. She can hear Sarah and Ben chatting in the living room as they work on their homework. They're thrilled about their grandparents' visit, and why shouldn't they be? Presents! Ice cream! Unconditional love 24/7!

For Emma, her in-laws' visit will mean work. Cooking, cleaning, playing tour guide, and smiling. Lots and lots of smiling. Linda and Mike have a tendency to worry, and once they start worrying about something, they're hard-pressed to let it go. Several years ago, Emma offhandedly mentioned a strange looking mole on her arm she was thinking about having checked out, and Linda still refers to it as Emma's "cancer scare," always in a dramatic whisper, even though Emma has patiently explained dozens of times that the mole was benign. If Emma were to mention the leak they'd fixed in the attic a few weeks ago, Linda would ask if the patch was still holding for years to come. And Mike? Mike would go around pounding on the walls listening for rotten wood, wondering if this house really had been a wise investment. Had they had it checked for mold? Mold could kill you, you know.

Emma takes a healthy sip of wine. Okay, she tells herself, so remember: We have no problems. Everything is hunky-dory. Don't mention Sarah's mean girl crisis or the lice outbreak in Ben's class. Just smile and keep things happy and light.

And have a plan, Emma reminds herself. Mike especially needs to be kept moving. He's an amiable houseguest, but without sufficient programming, he tends to gravitate toward the TV, cranking up the volume on Fox News so that Bill O'Reilly can be heard in every room of the house. Maybe Emma can send Linda and Mike off to school with the kids one morning, a sort of an impromptu Grandparents' Day. And she could make a map of area antiques dealers, pack a picnic basket and shove Gram and Gramps out the door if she gets to the point where she just has to have a few hours of alone time. Speaking of which, what about quilting time? Lately Emma finds that if she doesn't get at least an hour behind her Bernina every day, she feels weirdly off-center, as though she's left something important undone.

She reaches across the table and grabs her trusty notebook and a pen. Time for a new list — *How to Keep Linda and Mike Occupied For One Whole Week*. She writes down "Grandparents Day" and "Antiques/Picnic (check 10-Day weather forecast)," and then her pen comes to a halt. What else? Would Linda enjoy a trip to the Sewing Room? Maybe Mike would like to see Owen's office, go out with the crew for a morning.

Of course, Linda might like the idea of helping Emma with her redecorating schemes. According to Owen, his mother spent almost all of her free time during his childhood refinishing furniture, re-upholstering chairs and putting up new wallpaper, so much so that he never knew what his bedroom would look like from one day to the next. So yes, Linda might come in handy during her visit. Now that the living room paneling is painted, Emma wants to focus on floors. There's the living room's indoor-outdoor carpet and the horrible shag carpeting in the upstairs bedrooms. From hopping around home decorating forums online, she's learned that mid-20th century Americans saw carpeting as a status symbol, a sign that you could afford to cover up your hardwoods. The good news is that the carpeting protected the floors. While the floors in the living room look like they got their fair share of wear and tear before being covered over, the upstairs floors were dirty but beautiful when Emma peeked underneath a corner of the brown shag.

Could she convince Linda to help her pull up the carpets and get the hardwoods back into shape? Maybe Mike, handy like his son, could help re-tile the downstairs bathroom floor. And then the three of them might take a good look at the ancient linoleum in the kitchen. Can they tear it up and put down a new floor themselves?

Emma adds these projects to her notepad and leans back, satisfied. Why has it never occurred to her before to put her in-laws to work? And while she's at it, maybe Linda, a retired librarian, could help with her research for the quilt show. Brilliant idea! Emma writes it down. The fact is, she doesn't quite know where to start when it comes to putting together a program. Does she really need to cover a hundred years of quilt history? Or she should just focus on the quilts in the show? Maybe she should go to Barbara's office in the morning and take pictures of the quilts collected so far. Also, she needs to get a link to the folklorists' field study. That could prove useful when she's writing descriptions for the program.

The phone rings just as Emma is getting up to resume her dinner preparations. She checks the caller ID and sees that it's Barbara, saving Emma a call to find out if she'll be in the office tomorrow morning.

"Please don't tell me you've found more books for me," Emma says as soon as she answers the phone. "It's going to take me a year to get through the first box."

"There are always more books," Barbara replies. "But you're safe for now. Sort of."

Emma doesn't know if she likes the sound of that. "I'm sort of safe?"

"How would you like a raise?" Barbara asks. "I could

double your stipend. Think about how much fabric you could buy with all of that extra money."

"That would be nice," Emma agrees. "But where's the money for these extra hours coming from?"

"From my salary, I'm afraid," Barbara says with a sigh. "The thing is, in the four hours since we last spoke, I've managed to break my ankle, which hurts, by the way. A lot. I should have known better than to walk down to the orchard wearing street shoes. One minute I'm waving to Ty, the next I'm sliding down a hill with one leg in front of me and one leg twisted behind. I'm lucky I only broke my ankle."

"Barbara! Oh, no! How are you going to —?"

"Get around? I'm not," Barbara says. "In fact, the diocese is sending up some junior priest from Morganton to help out until I'm back on my feet, which could be a couple of months. The good news is, it's my right ankle."

"Why is that good news?"

"I push my sewing machine pedal with my left foot. So I'm still in business when it comes to making quilts. But when it comes to driving around to collect quilts? Not so much. In fact, I'm going to have to hand the whole show over to you."

Emma takes a step back, as though there's a scaly hand grasping for her through the receiver. "I don't even know what that would entail," she says. "And I don't have any experience with quilt shows. I mean, none whatsoever."

"I'll still help some," Barbara says. "And a lot of the work has been done — I've already ordered the pipe and drape backdrops —"

"Pipe and drape backdrops?"

"To display the quilts. They'll be delivered three days

before the show. So that's a biggie that's already checked off the list. And let's see — the entire guild has essentially signed up to volunteer at the show, so *that's* taken care of … Really, you just need to collect quilts, write the program and make a few phone calls. Well, a dozen or so. It's simple — oh, listen, I've got another call and I think it's the pharmacist about my prescription. We'll talk more soon!"

There's a bright beep and then nothing. Emma stares at the phone. What just happened? "A dozen or so phone calls?" she asks the silent kitchen. "What does that mean?"

The only response is the whir of the refrigerator icemaker filling up with water. Emma sits down and picks up her list, looks it over, admires its neat, optimistic entries. Then she slowly tears the sheet of paper off the pad and rips it into tiny pieces.

She's pretty sure the floors will have to wait.

15.

By ten the next morning, Emma is dressed
and at her desk, drinking chamomile tea and occasionally
remembering to take deep, healing breaths. She's just printed
out an email from Barbara detailing all the quilts that need
to be collected when the doorbell rings. Can she ignore it?
Hide under her desk until the unwelcome guest goes away?

But maybe it's Mavis again — Mavis, her comrade and
support staff. She stopped by earlier this morning on her
way to drop off two grandchildren at preschool, responding
in person to Emma's texted cry for help.

"We got this covered, honey, don't you worry," Mavis
promised. "I called Barbara and told her I'll collect quilts
from all my relations, which means I've got half the
county covered. Now what you need to do is get in touch
with Lettie and get her to help you do the rest. That girl
knows about quilts and she knows everybody from here
to Roan Mountain."

"I don't know," Emma said. "She's awfully busy."

"She's busy, but she likes to do a good turn, and she'd
surely be an asset. Before Lettie started working third shift,
she used to run the Medical Mobile all over the place. If
nothing else, she'll keep you from getting lost. But she knows
a lot of the folks around here and could make introductions,

kinda ease your way through the front door. Fact is, there's a few folks who are pretty quick to pull out a shotgun if they've never seen your face before."

Emma leaned against the doorframe, suddenly feeling faint. Shotguns? Barbara never said anything about shotguns.

Mavis didn't seem to notice Emma's concern. "Just as soon as I drop off my babies at school, I'm going to text you Lettie's number. And don't you worry none about getting shot. I don't think anyone would actually shoot you per se. Now if you've got Lettie with you, you're good as gold."

That had been two hours ago. Maybe Mavis had texted Lettie, and Lettie was here to help. But when Emma opens the door, it's not her young neighbor waiting on the other side. The woman on the front porch is in her fifties, maybe early sixties — she's wearing sunglasses despite an overcast sky, so it's hard to tell — her blonde hair streaked through with gray. She's dressed in jeans and a denim jacket over a black tee shirt with silver lettering that reads *Foxy Mama*. Emma smells cigarette smoke the second she steps through the doorway, though the woman isn't smoking.

"Well, hey there, girl, I'm your new neighbor," the woman says in a husky voice. "Or maybe I should say your new former neighbor." She sticks out a hand. "I'm Angie Byers, and I'm sure you've heard all about me."

Emma offers a limp handshake. Is she about to be robbed? Beat up? Hit up for money? Really, how much worse can her morning get? "I'm Emma," she says after she realizes she's been standing there for several seconds with her mouth hanging open. "It's, uh, nice to meet you. Would you like to come in?"

"I'll tell you what," Angie says, grinning like she's about

to tell a good joke. "It's tolerably warm out here, and I need a smoke. I know you've got little 'uns, so I don't want to smoke inside, not that you'd probably let me. Why don't you grab a sweater, and let's you and me talk out on the porch." Emma nods mutely. She goes inside and grabs Owen's gray sweat jacket off the back of the kitchen chair and throws it over her shoulders. When she reaches the porch again, Angie has taken a seat on the top step and is tapping a pack of Marlboro Reds against her thigh. "I always said I'd quit when these things reached five dollars a pack," she says, looking up at Emma. "But you know what?"

Emma takes a seat on the other side of the step from Angie. "What?"

"I never do a damned thing I say I'm gonna do," Angie tells her with a regretful laugh. "I'm a fool and a liar. I keep telling myself that maybe one day when Lettie has a baby I'll get my act together. I'd like to be a better granny than I was a mom. But Lettie ain't settled down yet. She's too picky about men. She don't want a man unless he's got a job and health insurance and a car that starts up every morning."

"That doesn't sound too demanding," Emma says. "It sounds smart."

"The girl's twenty-seven. She needs to get down to business." Angie sticks a cigarette in her mouth and flicks a blue plastic lighter at it. "She won't have her looks much longer, especially the way she likes that tanning booth. I told her a million times, 'You're gonna wrinkle up and get cancer doing that.'" Angie inhales deeply, then laughs out a plume of smoke. "Funny, coming from me, right?"

Emma nods, not knowing what to say, or if Angie expects her to say anything at all.

"Well," Angie continues after a minute. "That's neither here nor there. Now that I'm living over here with Mama, I thought I'd stop by and say to you that you've got no worries. I put that quilt in your attic before y'all had even moved in. Wanted to get a rise out of Dallas McKinney, is all. And then you know what? I went and forgot all about it. Forgot I'd even done it. It wasn't until Lettie brought it up that it came back to me."

"What were you going to do with it? I mean, if you'd remembered that you'd taken it?"

Angie shrugs. "I didn't have much of a plan beyond the taking of it. I don't even know what I was thinking, to tell you the truth. I mean, what does Dallas care about some old quilt that ain't even his?"

"It's probably worth a lot of money," Emma points out. "Not to mention that it was made by his great-grandmother."

Angie waves this suggestion away. "Dallas don't care about none of that. He's got plenty of money, and he ain't senti-mental. Oh, I could tell you a thing or two about his lack of sentimentality." She pauses for a long moment, staring off into the distance. Shaking her head as if to disperse any lingering thoughts about Dallas McKinney, she says, "Won't be long before the flowers start to bloom. I bet you we'll see some narcissus poking their heads up in a week or two."

"That'll be nice," Emma says. "I'm ready for winter to be over."

"Me, too. I'm starting to feel it in my bones. Or maybe that's just from sitting here on this cold step. My butt's about froze."

Angie grabs hold of the railing and carefully pulls herself up. "There's one more thing I was wondering about," she says, stubbing out her cigarette on the bottom of her shoe and shoving the butt into the pocket of her denim jacket. "I heard that you make quilts, and I was wondering if you might make one for my mama. I'd pay you and everything, like for the fabric and for your time and all that. Her birthday's coming up in May, and I wanted to give her something she'd really appreciate, maybe even lift her spirits some. Mama always did like a quilt."

Emma stands, too, brushing off the back of her jeans. "Doesn't your mother make quilts?"

"She used to, but then Mr. Arthur came to live with her."

"Mr. Arthur?"

Angie laughs. "Arthur-itis. She's got it bad in her hands. Has for a long time now. Oh, she used to be big in that quilting group they got in town, and up to a few years ago she was always heading out to some quilt show or festival. But she don't do that no more. Mama's been a little down the last few years. I guess it's just old age taking its toll. So do you think maybe you could do that for me? Make a quilt, I mean?"

"I'm a pretty new quilter," Emma tells her. "There are all sorts of people around here who could do a better job than I could. You should go talk to Ruth at the Sewing Room. She could find someone a lot more qualified for the job."

"Nah, that wouldn't work. Mama's mad at Ruth and all them. Once she stopped making quilts, they dropped her pretty quick. Nobody's got time for an old lady who can't do nothing."

Emma finds this hard to believe. In fact, she's pretty sure there's a whole lot more to that story. "Let me think about it," she tells Angie. "I'm working on a bunch of different stuff right now, and like I said, I'm pretty new at this. I don't know if I could get a quilt finished by May."

Angie lights up a fresh cigarette. "It sure would make Mama happy. I'd do it myself, but I don't have the first idea how."

"I could teach you," Emma says, the words coming out of her mouth before she can stop them. "It's not that hard, really. And it would probably mean more to your mother if you made the quilt."

Angie stands very still. "I don't know," she says finally. "I never was much good at making things. Mama was always trying to get me to make quilts with her, and I'd get as far as picking out some material, you know? And then some boy'd come by the house in his car, and I'd go running outside and not look back."

"Okay, well, that's fine," Emma says, relieved. "Who knows if I could teach you to quilt in the first place."

"Mama's still got her machine up at the house …" Angie sounds as though she's thinking out loud. "I guess it still works." She looks at Emma. "Maybe you could come over to Mama's and we could work on something together? I mean, I don't reckon you want someone like me in your house, with your children and all. I'm sort of bad news."

"Your mother's house is fine," Emma says, figuring that Angie will forget all about learning how to make a quilt by the end of the day. "Maybe we could start next week."

"Yeah, I know your folks are coming later this week," Angie says, taking a drag off her cigarette. "Lettie told me."

"I don't remember telling Lettie they were coming," Emma says. She shakes her head in disbelief. "Is there anything anybody doesn't know in this town?"

Angie grins. "It all gets around. You ain't used to that yet?"

After Angie leaves, Emma goes inside and washes her hands and face, trying to get the stink of cigarette smoke off her skin. If the children come home to find her smelling like the Marlboro Man, she'll never hear the end of it. They've never known anyone who smokes, but they're ardently anti-smoking all the same.

When she's done cleaning herself up, she finds her phone and texts Mavis. *What's up with Hannah Byers? Why did she stop making quilts?* she writes, and two minutes later her phone pings with Mavis's reply.

To tell you the truth, I never figured that one out, reads the return text. *But I'm pretty sure Angie Byers has something to do with it.*

16.

Trudy Nidiffer is having a hard time understanding who Emma is. "You ain't that preacher lady, I know that much," she says when Emma knocks on her door and explains why she's there. "I know that's Lettie Byers behind you, but I can't figure out why she's here neither. Lettie ain't brought me my medications since I don't know when. Dorcas Blevins brings 'em now."

Lettie leans past Emma and says, "Hey there, Miss Trudy. Emma here is working for Barbara — that pastor you talked to awhile back about lending out your quilt for that big quilt show at the church. Only Barbara's gone and broken her ankle, so Emma is doing the quilt collecting."

"Broke her ankle?" Trudy shakes her head. "That's no good. An ankle never heals up the way it's supposed to. She's going to have trouble the rest of her life. Well, I reckon y'all ought to come on in. I'll get Mason to fetch the quilt."

Emma squeezes Lettie's arm and mouths *thank you*. And sends a silent thank you to Mavis as well, for suggesting that Lettie come along on some of these collecting trips. This is their second day collecting quilts together and having Lettie with her is like having her own personal ambassador. Emma has been greeted warily at most of the doors they've knocked at until Lettie's voice calls out, "Hey, there!" Immediately recognition melts the steel of suspicion. "What're you doing up this way, girl?" the person peeking out through the cracked-open door will exclaim. "I ain't seen you in a dog's age!"

Not only is Lettie a familiar figure, she also knows an impressive amount about quilts. Back in the car after a pick-up, Lettie drives while helping Emma with her notes, pointing out pattern names — "She called that her Widow's Walk quilt, but I'm fairly sure that's a Dutchman's Puzzle block" — and describing the prints of the various fabrics she's noted in the quilt blocks, the florals, shirtings, stripes and geometrics.

Emma's embarrassed to admit that she didn't know that prints had names. Well, sure, she knew about paisleys and calicos, but bead and reel? Vermicular? It's all news to her. And pattern names? She's been trying to study Barbara Brackman's encyclopedia of pieced block patterns, but there's just too much information to absorb quickly.

"So there's something I've been wondering," she said to Lettie on the way home the day before. "How is it that you know so much about quilt patterns, but you didn't know that attic quilt was a Birds in the Air?"

Lettie just grinned. "Maybe I did, maybe I didn't. But it was good for you to meet Ruth, now wasn't it?"

Emma laughed. "So did you get all your quilt knowledge from your grandmother?" she asked. "I mean, they don't teach that stuff in nursing school, right?"

"No, nursing school definitely had a different vocabulary list — you know, sutures and apical-radial pulses, that sort of thing. The fabric patterns and quilt patterns I got from Granny. She kept a scrapbook of every fabric she ever used, and I used to just pore over it for hours. She more or less raised me, what with Mama working all the time. Funny thing is, I never got interested in making quilts, but I liked knowing about them. I think it pleased Granny when I could look at a quilt and name the pattern. It's like she'd passed something down to me that had skipped right over Mama."

They were quiet for a moment, and then Emma said, "So I guess your mom is living with you guys now? She stopped by the other day."

"Yeah, I heard about that," Lettie said, her voice tighter now. "I wish you luck in that endeavor."

"It's too bad your grandmother stopped making quilts, or else she could teach your mom," Emma said, trying not to sound too interested, in case it was a touchy subject. But she desperately wanted to know why Hannah Byers had stopped quilting. After she'd talked to Angie, she'd gone online to see if she could find pictures of Hannah's quilts, and there'd been at least a dozen, including two that had been honorable mentions at the Houston Quilt Festival in the early '90s. When you could make quilts that beautiful, why stop doing it? "Do you know why she quit?"

Lettie shrugged, her expression relaxing now that they'd gotten off the subject of Angie moving back home. "Nobody's got that one figured out. It's like Granny just dropped out of life when Mama broke her back and moved home to recover." She glanced over at Emma, eyebrow raised. "My mama takes up a lot of the oxygen in a room."

"It'll be interesting to help her make a quilt," Emma said. "Especially since I really don't have a whole lot of experience myself."

"Well, we appreciate you giving it a try!" Lettie said, full of forced cheer. "Now, tell me again who we're going to see next?"

That was yesterday, when they'd collected six quilts in some of the remotest parts of the county. Tuesday's schedule was lighter and easier, with three quilts to be picked in town and only this one — Trudy Nidiffer's — a little further out. The quilt Trudy's teenaged grandson brings down from the attic appears to be some sort of crazy quilt. "My mother-in-law's mother made that," Trudy informs them as she folds the quilt and stuffs into a pillowcase. "Now what that makes her to me, I surely don't know, but that quilt's a piece of work."

"It's a beauty," Lettie says, and then she takes a sheet of paper out of the satchel she's carrying. "Now, Miss Trudy, we need you to sign a release saying it's okay for us to hang your quilt in the show come May. It's just sort of a permission slip, in case any of your relatives come around saying, 'Who said you could put up that quilt?'"

Emma stays silent, even though she knows the release is asking more of the signer than that. It's asking them to acknowledge that there's a risk in lending their quilt to the Centennial Celebration Quilt Show and to agree not to sue if the quilt gets stolen or the building burns down. It's just one more reason why she's glad Lettie is here. Emma suspects she'd have a much harder time getting the releases signed, but everyone is happy to oblige their former nurse.

"I'll tell you what, some of my relatives would do just that, and they'd probably snatch the quilt right off the wall while they were at it," Trudy says, taking the paper and a pen from Lettie. "My husband's people, really. They're a prickly bunch through and through."

On the way home, after she's written down all of Lettie's observations about Trudy's crazy quilt, Emma wonders if she should bring up Hannah Byers' early retirement from quilting one more time, but decides against it. If Lettie had more to say on the subject, she'd have said it. Maybe there was nothing more to be known. Emma had asked Mavis about it at Helen's the week before, but while Mavis had some theories, she didn't have any hard answers, either.

"For a long time, Hannah was probably the most renowned quilter of this area — her and Dorothy Brown," Mavis told Emma as she signaled Cindy for coffee. "This was back even before Ruth opened the Sewing Room and everyone got so crazy about quilting. They had quilts in shows all over the country. Hannah did such interesting work, just had an eye for color, you know? Anyway, her and Dorothy were best friends, always running off to shows and festivals. I think they made some pretty good prize money, too. But a few years ago Hannah disappeared into her house, and no one can say why."

Mavis had glanced behind her, as though she was worried someone might overhear what she was about to say next. Then she leaned across the table toward Emma and whispered, "A lot of folks think it has to do with Dorothy's son, Kenny."

"The one whose ex-wife won't let Dorothy see the grandchildren?" Emma whispered back.

"That's the one," Mavis said with a nod. "Him and Angie were friendly growing up, and when Angie broke her back and Hannah was taking care of her, Kenny would come by a lot. He's a physical therapist, so that might be the reason why, but rumors started spreading that him and Angie were more than friends. And it wasn't long after that Kenny's wife left him and a lot of folks were saying it was because of Angie. You can imagine how that might get in between Hannah's friendship with Dorothy, but here's the funny thing — Dorothy says she's gone to Hannah's many a time over the years, but Hannah won't open the door. So if there's a problem, it's on Hannah's side. Well, it's all a mystery, and it's a shame, too. Lord that woman made beautiful quilts."

It *is* a shame, Emma thinks, climbing out of Lettie's truck. She waves as Lettie backs out of the driveway. If Angie had had an affair with Kenny Brown, it wasn't Hannah's fault. Why stop doing what you love best of all because you have a problem child?

Sarah and Ben — who so far have not been problem children, only children with occasional problems — are doing their homework on the living room couch when Emma walks inside. The room has been recently tidied, and Emma thinks she just might miss her in-laws when they leave. Since their arrival, Linda has completely taken over the cooking and childcare, and Mike promises the downstairs bathroom will be remodeled by Wednesday afternoon. She can hear him chipping away at something now and hopes it's the awful green tiling around the sink.

"Where's Gram?" Emma asks, and Linda calls out, "I'm in here, darling!" When Emma crosses the hallway, she finds her mother-in-law bent over her laptop, a notebook and pen by her side.

"I'm finding out so many interesting things about quilting in this region!" she exclaims to Emma. "And moreover, I'm learning where all the good antique shops are. Tomorrow let's go out and look around. There's two over in Pine

City, and three over in Mars Hill. I bet we can find some wonderful quilts."

Emma holds up the bags she's carried in, including Trudy's pillowcase. "I'm drowning in antique quilts at the moment."

"Oh, not for you, honey. For me!" Linda's expression is bright. "I think I've caught the quilt bug. Oh, and I've ordered you a book — *Antique Quilts and Textiles* by Bobbie A. Aug and Gerald Roy. It should be here Friday."

"It sounds like you've had a productive afternoon," Emma says. "And by the smell of things, I'd say you have dinner cooking, too."

"Mike's making chili," Linda informs her. "Would you mind stirring it? I'm reading a fascinating article about how to haggle with antiques dealers."

Emma sets down the quilts and shrugs off her coat. "Do you want a glass of wine?"

"I'd love one, dear. Oh, and before I forget — this was slipped under the door this afternoon. Found it when I got home with the kids from school."

Linda holds out a piece of notebook paper, and Emma takes it from her. *4pm Friday, Angie B* is scrawled mid-page in a surprisingly girlish script. Emma finds the note disarmingly charming, as though she and Angie are back in third grade arranging a play date.

"Friend of yours?" Linda asks, sounding only halfway interested as she scrolls down the computer screen.

"Not really," Emma says, and then wonders if that sounds too harsh. "At least, not exactly."

Yet stranger things have happened, she tells herself as she walks down the hallway to the kitchen. And then pauses to worry — just how strange might things get?

17.

As Emma walks over to meet Angie Byers on Friday, she wonders if Angie will actually be there. Just because she had confirmed a date and time doesn't mean she'll be ready and waiting when Emma arrives. In fact, Emma told Sarah she'd probably be home in a few minutes, though not to worry if she wasn't. Who knows? Maybe Hannah Byers will see her at the door and invite her in this time. Emma hopes she will — she wants to see Hannah's quilts.

"What Hannah does — or did — is so original," Ruth told Emma the day before, when Emma stopped by the store to buy fat quarters for her lesson with Angie. "She liked traditional blocks, but she liked messing about with them, if you know what I mean. Different from what Gwen Marston does, not liberated exactly, but quite innovative. Amazing use of color, simply amazing."

If Angie's actually waiting for her today, Emma will get her started on a single patch quilt, the simplest quilt in *First-Time Quiltmaking*. She's not allowed herself to think past that, feeling foolish for imagining that Angie will even get as far as sewing two squares together, not to mention the fact that Emma's skills themselves are pretty limited. Can she really teach someone else to quilt after only two months of quilting herself?

She thinks of herself as an advanced beginner, but only because anybody who's made a block more complicated than, say, a five-patch chain practically qualifies for the title. Emma will also admit that while she's not the queen of precision, her mistakes are less glaring than they were at first. It doesn't hurt that she has hours a day to work on quilting, something she feels guilty about when she contemplates that she could be — should be — writing.

"It's four-oh-five, girl!" a gravelly voice calls down to her from the porch. "You're late!"

Waving, Angie Byers struggles to her feet. Emma gives a limp wave back and calls, "Well, hey, there! You ready to quilt?" She's trying to sound cheerful and confident, but she's pretty sure what she really sounds like is an overexcited aerobics instructor.

"Yes, ma'am." Holding tight to the wrought iron railing, Angie makes her way slowly down the porch steps. "I even told Mama about you teaching me, and she gave me all sorts of supplies. I told her I wanted to make a quilt for Ray, so as not to ruin the surprise."

"Did you ask your mother to teach you how to quilt?" Emma says, waiting at the end of the walk. She's a little concerned by how off-balance Angie seems. Was she like this last week, so unsteady?

Angie reaches the sidewalk and grins at Emma. "Oh, at this point I don't think Mama would teach me how to sew if I begged her, considering all the hell I gave her back in the day. Besides, she don't do that anymore — make quilts. She just got bored with it after all those years of doing nothing but."

Emma raises an eyebrow. "I thought you said she had arthritis."

"Well, that, too," Angie says with a shrug. "Between you and me, Mama's arthritis is mostly an excuse not to do much of anything but watch TV."

"She sounds depressed," Emma says, following Angie up the driveway to the carport. "I mean, from what I understand, quilting was a huge part of her life. It seems odd that she would give that up to sit around and watch TV."

Angie shoots her another grin, but this one has an edge to it. "I can tell you're from off the mountain. You know how? You think it's okay to get into other people's business."

When Emma begins to apologize, Angie holds up her hand like a traffic cop. "No, no, that's all right. You can't help how you were raised. But around here we let folks have their privacy."

"Yeah," Emma says, thinking about how many times since she's moved here absolute strangers have commented on the details of her personal life. "I've noticed that."

Angie gives Emma a sour look before leading her into the house through the carport door. Emma doesn't know what to expect. Dark and gloomy? Wood paneling and linoleum floors? The house's idiosyncratic exterior doesn't offer a clue as to what the inside might look like, and Emma fears the worst.

So it's a relief to enter a light and airy kitchen, a hint of citrus in the air, a vase of bright orange tulips on the large wooden table that takes up the center of the room. "Ray sent them over to Mama," Angie tells Emma, pointing at the flowers. "He's trying to win her over. It's a lost cause, but he don't know it or else won't believe it."

"I guess it's nice that he's trying," Emma says, and then thinks it's funny that Angie doesn't even bother to pretend

Emma wouldn't know who Ray is, doesn't know more of Angie's story than any stranger has a right to.

"Are you having a good visit with your in-laws?" Angie asks, taking a glass out the dishwasher and turning toward the sink. "I never had any myself, but I hear they can be a lot of work."

Emma shrugs. "Mine actually are pretty easy. Okay, sometimes they drive me a little crazy; you know, giving advice when I didn't ask for any — "

She stops talking when she realizes Angie has stopped listening.

"You want some water?" Angie asks, holding out the glass. Emma shakes her head no and Angie says, "Okay then, let's get to it."

I am teaching a drug-addict how to quilt, Emma thinks as she follows Angie through the kitchen and into another room. Here's your brain; here's your brain on drugs, here's your brain on drugs using a rotary cutter. Which reminds Emma — she hopes she remembered to pack a glove for Angie to wear while she's cutting fabric.

The odd thing is, Angie doesn't actually strike her as someone dosed up on painkillers; she seems acutely alive. She reminds Emma of the girls she was drawn to in high school, though never really friends with, girls who spent every break in the smoking court out by the bus drop-off, Kools or Salems dangling from their lips, their hair teased and sprayed to improbable heights. There were always one or two Emma could tell were secretly smart underneath their cultivated badness, girls who crammed their A tests into their notebooks before anyone could see. Emma is sure Angie is smart, but it strikes her as a surreptitious kind of intelligence. In the short amount of time they've spent together, Emma senses Angie reading her, and she also senses that Angie is using her somehow, though Emma hasn't the faintest idea to what end.

"Mama said we could set ourselves up in here," Angie says, flipping on a light to reveal a formal, if somewhat battered, table and sideboard. "It's the dining room, but we never used it as such. In fact, we never used this room much at all. Everything always happened in the kitchen."

Emma sets her bag down on the table's scratched surface. "Do you have brothers and sisters, or was it just you growing up?"

"Two brothers," Angie says, pulling out a chair and slowly lowering herself into it. "One of 'em, Cecil, died in Vietnam, and Clyde moved to California. We ain't heard from him in years."

"That must be hard on your mother."

Angie shrugs. "It's a hard life wherever you go."

There's a moment of silence as Emma tries to think of how to respond to that and then realizes she can't. Instead, she pulls out two of the fat quarters she bought from Ruth and sets them on the table. "Today I thought we could just practice a little, and then next time we can go to the Sewing Room or you could order some fabric online — "

"I ain't going to the Sewing Room," Angie interrupts, "and I can't order stuff online 'cause I wore out my credit card. But Mama's got plenty of fabric and she won't mind me using it. In fact, she made me a pile of stuff in the front room. Do you mind grabbing it?"

Angie flashes one of her trademark grins. "Seeing as I just got myself settled and all."

Emma makes her way down the hallway toward the front of the house. She hears the blare of the television but no other sound, and wonders if Mrs. Byers is even here. Maybe Lettie has taken her out to run errands. But when she looks into the room where the sound is coming from, there she is, small and fragile-looking in an overlarge, brown recliner.

"I put the things you need on the couch," Mrs. Byers says without taking her eyes off the television screen. "There's a cutting mat and a tote with my scissors and my rotary cutter and rulers, some thread and stencils and the like. My fabric's upstairs — Angie knows where."

Emma stands in the doorway, waiting for — what? For Hannah Byers to invite her to have a seat on the yellow and brown plaid couch? For Hannah to acknowledge her, as a neighbor, a fellow quilter, someone who has come to help her daughter? Whatever it is that Emma wants from Mrs. Byers, it's clear from the way the old woman keeps her gaze held firmly to the TV she's not going to get it.

"Do you — would you like to join us?" Emma asks, wondering if maybe Mrs. Byers is simply too stubborn to join the party if no one's going to bother to invite her. "I mean, it seems silly for me to be teaching Angie when you're right here in the house. Ruth at the Sewing Room has been telling me all about — "

Mrs. Byers dismisses her with a wave of her hand. "I'm done with all that. My fingers don't work right no more, and I can't hardly see a thing. And all them ladies at Ruth's store, just gossiping the live-long day! Well, I've had my fill. Let's just put it that way — I've had my fill."

Emma nods, then picks up the tote and the cutting board from the couch. "Well, maybe Angie will get the quilting bug and carry on the tradition," she offers lamely, wanting somehow to connect with this woman.

Mrs. Byers gives a slight snort. "I don't know what that girl's up to. Never did know, and I sure don't now. But if you think this quilting idea of hers is going to last … Well, don't get your hopes up is all I'm saying."

Walking back to the dining room, Emma would desperately like to call Holly and get her take on all of this. What's the real story here? Why has Angie Byers suddenly become a presence in her mother's house again? Why has Hannah stopped making quilts and cut herself off from her friends? And why does Emma feel like she's suddenly tangled in their web?

When she reaches the dining room, Angie is back on her feet and pacing around the table. "Started feeling jumpy just sitting there," she says in way of explanation. "Don't know why. I think I'm probably ADD, only when I was a kid, they didn't have ADD. My teachers used to call me 'Little Miss Ants in the Pants.'"

Emma eyes her warily. "Are you sure you feel okay? You look a little pale."

"It hurts if I sit too long," Angie says, giving her hip an exaggerated rub. "My back and all."

Before she can stop herself, Emma says, "You change your story a lot. Two seconds ago, you were ADD. Now your back is bothering you."

"I got a lot going on," Angie says. She sounds nervous to Emma. "It's hard to keep it all straight. Why don't we go ahead and get started?"

"Fine," Emma says, ready to get this over with. "Let's get started."

As Emma explains how to use rulers to straighten the fabric, Angie seems agitated, but when she finally has the rotary cutter in her hand and begins to cut, she calms down. "I bet I watched Mama do this a thousand times," she says, carefully using a twenty-four inch ruler to measure out a two-and-a-half inch strip. "Well, when I was little, she used scissors and these shapes that she'd cut out of cereal boxes. I remember that real well. But then she brought home one of these" — Angie holds up the rotary cutter — "and, honey, it was a whole new ballgame."

Emma looks around the room and realizes one important item is missing. "Did you say your mother has a sewing machine you can use?"

"Lettie said she brought it down," Angie says, not bothering to look up as she measures another strip. "Check under the table, why don't you?"

Emma bends down and there it is: a Bernina 1030, same as hers. She hoists it up on the table. "Oh, good, it's got a quarter-inch foot on it," she tells Angie as she examines the machine. "We should still check it to make sure we're getting accurate quarter-inch seams, and then we can start sewing some strips together."

"I ain't never used that thing before, in case you were wondering," Angie informs her. "I was always scared I'd get my finger stuck in it. I mean, sort of like on purpose."

Emma just nods as she puts a spool of thread on the machine's spindle and then sits down in front of the sewing machine. "I think everyone has moments like that. Like, 'What if I drove my car into oncoming traffic? What's stopping me?'"

Angie stares at her. "You? You'd do something like that?"

"No, that's not it at all," Emma says. "I'm just saying everyone has those bizarre kind of impulses."

"Sometimes I think my whole life is a bizarre impulse," Angie tells her. She stretches her neck right, then left, then reaches her hands upwards. There's something methodical in the way she stretches, as though this is a ritual, a way of re-centering. "But I promise if you show me how to use this sewing machine, I will do my best not to sew any of my body parts to the fabric."

Emma laughs. "Okay. Well, let's start with sewing a straight line. You take my seat, and I'll walk you through it."

For the next few minutes, Emma explains to Angie how to use the sewing machine, and then she brings over two strips of fabric and a container of flat-head pins and demonstrates how to pin the fabric right sides together.

"And now you're ready to sew," she says after the fabric is pinned. "All you have to do is lift the needle, and place the fabric under it so the right edge is right against the metal guide, but not bunched up or pushed up against it."

Angie nods, puts the pinned strips on the metal plate, drops the needle, and gingerly pushes the foot pedal. "Should I go faster than this?"

"Um, yeah, if you want to have those strips sewn together before dinner."

Angie looks up at her and smiles. "I like you, you know that? You're all right."

"I'm a saint," Emma replies, oddly pleased by Angie's declaration. "Now get sewing."

Angie pushes down the pedal with a little more force, but not too much, and lets out a laugh of delight as the pinned strips start moving along the feed dogs. "This is cool!"

Emma feels ridiculously ebullient. One eight-year-old could have taught another eight-year-old what she's taught Angie. It's not a big deal. And yet, somehow it feels like one. Maybe that's what happens when you have such drastically low expectations, Emma thinks. She'd never thought she'd actually see Angie sitting at a sewing machine, sewing.

"You're doing great," she says, and then she turns around to see Hannah Byers watching from the doorway. From the expression on Hannah's face, Emma can tell she never thought she'd see this day, either.

18.

"**I bet she's going** through detox," Holly says Friday night when Emma calls to ask her what she thinks is up with Angie Byers. "That's why she's so agitated. It's a classic symptom of opioid withdrawal. That and nausea and body aches, vomiting … it's not much fun, from what I hear."

Emma considers this. "So Angie's trying to detox from painkillers and at the same time learn how to quilt?"

"Maybe it's a distraction for her," Holly suggests. "Something to keep the mind off how her body's feeling. Something she can do in a safe place — the house she grew up in."

The more Emma thinks about this, the more it makes sense. She and Angie worked together for a little over an hour and a half on Friday. During that time Angie took several breaks — to get a drink of water, to go to the bathroom, to smoke — and when she returned she'd had a hard time settling back into what she'd been doing before she left. Whether it was rotary cutting or sewing or pinning, it didn't matter, it still seemed to take her a moment or two to remember exactly what she was trying to accomplish.

"Her mother stood there for twenty minutes without saying a thing," Emma tells Holly now as she pulls a bowl of grapes from the refrigerator. "It started to really get to me. Here she is, this practically world-famous quilter watching me, a total amateur, teach her daughter how to quilt. I kept waiting for Hannah to say, 'You don't have any idea what you're doing, do you?' Completely unnerving."

"I doubt she was paying any attention to you," Holly says. "Her daughter — her only daughter, right? — is finally learning how to quilt. How profound is that?"

"I guess," Emma agrees reluctantly. She munches thoughtfully on a grape, picturing Hannah in the dining room doorway, never uttering a word. "I wonder if Sarah will ever want to make quilts. She doesn't seem that interested in it right now, but maybe later?"

"Maybe," Holly agrees. "Although you have to admit, neither of us have ever gotten into needlepoint, and we're pretty old."

"But Mom never tried to teach us. I asked her once, but she said it would be a waste of time, that little girls didn't really like needlepoint."

Holly laughs. "I think she just wanted some time alone. If we learned how to do needlepoint, maybe we would've bugged her all the time, you know, asking her to help us find the needle we just dropped in the carpet. Not much fun."

Emma can't argue with that. She feels like she should be encouraging Sarah to sew — to make handbags and totes, if not quilts — but the selfish fact of the matter is that she doesn't want to share her sewing machine.

I am a terrible mother, she tells herself after hanging up with Holly. A terrible, selfish mother. Thank goodness for her in-laws, who are paying her children the attention they deserve. She can hear Linda and Sarah having a conversation about horses in the living room and thinks about how good it's been for Sarah to have her grandmother around while she's going through such a tough time at school. Sarah's actually been happy this week, baking cookies with Linda and going for walks around town with her grandfather. "This girl should be a tour guide when she grows up!" Mike exclaimed yesterday when the two of them returned from their hike. "Or a writer. She has amazing powers of description!" Sarah had beamed, and Emma immediately forgave Mike for waking her up at 5:30 every morning this week to ask her to show him how to work the coffeemaker again.

What's going to happen when Linda and Mike leave tomorrow? Emma wishes she knew how to help Sarah get through all of this — well, girl stuff. But what can she do? She remembers all too well the girl wars of her own late elementary school years, the nasty notes, the betrayals, the silent treatment. Oh, good grief, the silent treatment. Suzie Harris, the queen bee of their second-tier group — they were the smart girls, the good girls, the sort of cute girls — was always giving someone the silent treatment, and naturally everyone else fell in line behind her. Emma remembers the first time she'd been on the receiving end. No one talked to her for a week, and every night she lay in bed sure that the silent treatment would kill her, that she would die of sheer loneliness and humiliation.

Did her mother even know it was happening? Emma couldn't remember. Emma wouldn't have told her, that was for sure — it was too awful to actually talk about. Big Ed must have sensed something was going on, though. He'd stop by her room at night while she was doing her homework and say, "A real friend is the one who walks in when the other walks out," or "Strangers are just friends waiting to happen. Why don't you call up somebody in your class you'd like to get to know better?"

But her mother? After years of being a homemaker, Janice was just starting a new job that year as an office manager, and she'd come home after work exhausted although clearly thrilled to be spending her days outside of the house. On Saturdays she was taking a continuing ed class at the community college, learning how to use computers, which were so new back then that no one was sure they'd actually catch on.

So, no, Janice probably hadn't known what Emma was going through. But Emma certainly is aware of Sarah's situation, and she wishes she knew what to do. She doesn't know how people deal with problems like this in Sweet Anne's Gap. In Chapel Hill, Emma could have called a few parents and there'd be school assemblies on bullying and mediation sessions with the parents of the girls and then mediation sessions with the girls themselves … but this isn't Chapel Hill. Who can Emma call?

She glances at the school calendar held to the refrigerator with a sea turtle magnet. Mrs. Lange, the guidance counselor? She's a lovely woman with snow-white hair and an ample bosom, but the one time Emma went to talk to her — about some medical records the school needed to have on file for the children — she'd been asleep at her desk, her whistling snores filling the overheated office.

And then she thinks: Charlotte Stengle. Didn't Ruth say that Charlotte knew everything about everyone? If that's the case, then maybe she might have some ideas about what Sarah can do to make friends — real friends, friends who won't make her life miserable.

"Those are some powerful girls," Charlotte says when Emma arrives in her office on Monday morning. Charlotte is sitting behind her desk, her green eyeglasses perched on top of her head. The desk gives Charlotte an authority she doesn't usually possess, and Emma, who spent the whole weekend worrying about how to help Sarah, relaxes, as though surely Charlotte has the answer in an envelope hidden in her top drawer.

"I was hoping it would be different here," Emma says, taking a seat in the rickety plastic chair across the desk from Charlotte. "That there wouldn't be so much mean girl stuff. Stupid, huh?"

Charlotte smiles wryly. "Overly-hopeful, that's for sure. As far as I can tell, it's universal." She points to a catalog on her desk, *Simon & Schuster Fall Children's Books*. "Every new publishing season, there's at least fifty new books about bullies and cliques — novels, graphic novels, nonfiction. The kids eat it up. It's practically their whole world in fifth and sixth grade, but it starts dying down in seventh grade for the most part."

"I'm not sure Sarah's going to make it to seventh grade, the way things are going," Emma says. "She keeps talking about moving to Australia — by herself."

A tow-headed boy sticks his head in the door. "Miss Stengle, I can't make the computer check out my book."

"Is the barcode scanner turned on?" Charlotte asks him. "We turn it off overnight."

The boy's face lights up. "That's a great idea, Miss Stengle! Thanks!"

Charlotte looks at Emma and shakes her head. "Sometimes they make you feel like you're a genius. It's the great thing about working with elementary school kids." She pauses, tilts her head to one side. "You know, I just thought of something. There's a real nice fourth grade girl, Carter Lowell, who Sarah might like. She and Sarah check out a lot of the same books, and they're both going through a horse-y phase. Do you think Sarah would mind being friends with a younger girl?"

Emma shrugs. "She might not mind. But it would need to be somehow — orchestrated, you know? Because if I suggest it, forget it. All my ideas are the worst ideas in the world."

"Yeah, what do our moms know, right?" Charlotte laughs as she picks up a pencil and starts tapping it against her desk. "The other thing I was wondering — well, maybe if Sarah got involved in some kind of project? Like the displays we're doing for the centennial. We're working on several about the history of Sweet Anne's Gap and one about the school, in the front hallway and in the library. And there will be a big presentation of the projects in the auditorium for the community. Maybe Sarah could think of some way to contribute to that? It might make her seem like less of an outsider."

Emma wonders if that's what it really is. After all, what's to dislike about Sarah? She's funny, she's always ready to try new things, and in preschool it was noted that she was an excellent sharer. But one thing's for sure: she's not from here.

"Do you have any ideas about what Sarah could for a project?" Emma asks Charlotte. "What do you think might appeal to the other kids?"

Charlotte thinks for a moment, and then her expression brightens. "Remember those dolls you told me about? The ones you found in your attic?"

Emma nods. How could she ever forget Sunny and Tuesday?

"Maybe you could look around your house, see if there are any other old toys up in the attic," Charlotte suggests. "In my experience, when it comes to history, kids are really interested in other kids. Like what sort of clothes children used to wear, and what they played with. If Sarah finds some interesting things, she could talk about them at the centennial assembly. She could show everyone those dolls. It might help her connect with some of the other children."

"Miss Stengle!" a voice calls from the main room of the library. "Saunders just spilled!"

"Duty calls," Charlotte says to Emma, rising from her seat. "Now where did I put the paper towels?"

Walking home, Emma mulls over Charlotte's suggestion. What could the unopened trunks contain that would make Sarah a star? Money? Diamonds? Old comic books? It's funny how little thought Emma's given those trunks in the last couple of months, although now she realizes that they've always been there at the edge of her mind, a mystery she's wanted to hold onto for as long as possible. She wonders if Angie has hidden stolen goods in those trunks, too, and if so, what?

She supposes the real question should be *why*? Emma knows who Dallas McKinney is now, has seen him smoking outside of the bank on Oak Street, where he works as an assistant manager, and quite frankly he doesn't strike her as Angie's type, or at least what she imagines Angie's type would be. He's pleasant enough looking, a little paunchy around the middle, his hair thin on top, but he must be, what? Sixty at least. He doesn't look too bad for sixty, but he also doesn't look — well, interesting. Or dangerous, or the least bit edgy, traits Emma thinks Angie would find desirable. A man who dresses in short-sleeved shirts and navy blue ties? What in the world could Angie see in him? Emma decides Angie would have told her if she'd deposited any more stolen property in the attic. No, probably all the trunks contain is old clothes and knickknacks, nothing to get excited about. In fact, as soon as Emma gets through her front door, the idea of searching the trunks falls to the bottom of her list of things that need doing. She should take Homer on a walk, clean the kitchen, make lunch. But first — check email. She goes into her study and powers on her laptop, and then looks around, pleased as always with the little world she's made here. She catches the eye of the girl on the mantel, the McKinney girl, as Emma has come to think of her.

"Who are you?" Emma asks out loud. "And why do you keep looking at me like that?"

Later, Emma will deny this to herself, will have all sorts of explanations — she's tired, she's feeling overwhelmed by all the work she has to do for the quilt show, she possibly has a touch of the flu — but nothing can change the fact that she could swear the girl in the picture is leaning toward her, is whispering, "Why don't you look in the trunks and find out?"

19.

Emma thinks about waiting until Sarah gets home to open the trunks. It might take her mind off the fact that her grandparents have gone home. Emma and Sarah could pretend they're real-life Nancy Drews, investigating the Mystery of the Girl in the Picture. This is something she and her daughter could share, Emma thinks — the history of the house they live in, the discovery of its secrets, how it all connects them to Sweet Anne's Gap.

On the other hand, Sarah might not have any interest in the trunks at all. After all, a trunk isn't a horse, nor is it likely to contain a horse. Emma went through an equine phase, too, when she was Sarah's age, and she remembers how for almost two years she and her friends lived and breathed anything that had to do with horses. In fact, she's just emailed her mother to ask her to ship what remains of her once extensive collection of horse figurines. She wonders if Sarah's newfound love of all things horsey is a reaction to her loss of popularity at John D. Coe Elementary. Maybe she's thinking who needs friends when you have the Black Stallion and Misty of Chincoteague?

No, it's unlikely Sarah will care about what the trunks contain. And that's okay — it's not like Emma needs Sarah to make the trunks meaningful. What Emma hates is when she gets excited about something and her children stomp all over her enthusiasm. "Let's build Hogwarts out of Legos!" she said one recent gray Saturday afternoon. Sarah had rolled her eyes, and Ben had said, "Uh, Mom? They make a kit for that. If you want to get the kit, then sure."

Emma did not want to get the kit. She wanted to sit at the kitchen table with her kids and make something up. Well, what she'd really wanted to do was work on a quilt, but in the name of good mothering she'd come up with this wonderful idea for family togetherness, only to have it squashed like a bug. This never happened in the pages of *Family Fun* magazine. All the children pictured in *Family Fun* were wildly appreciative of every effort their parents made.

No, Emma decides. She won't wait for Sarah.

Mounting the stairs to the attic, she imagines that she's following the McKinney girl. One thing she's learned about the McKinneys is that they were town folk. The mica mine was founded in 1889 by Lorenzo McKinney, and Emma wonders if he was the McKinney girl's father. That would explain the fine dress and the studio photograph, maybe even the sour expression. Maybe she was a poor little rich girl, neglected by her socialite parents.

She might not be a McKinney at all, Emma reminds herself. If she was Lydia McKinney's mother or grandmother, her surname most likely wasn't McKinney. Emma really needs to go to Town Hall and see if she can find any family records.

Why hasn't she done that?

Yes, she imagines the McKinney girl asking, why haven't you?

I've been a little busy, Emma imagines replying.

The attic is cool, as though the winter air has found a nice place to hang out until it's forced to make room for spring. Emma shivers a bit, but more from excitement than from the chill. She spies the two trunks against the wall and wonders if they've been waiting for this moment, too. Silly thought, she knows, but she can't help but feeling that this house has secrets it desperately wants to tell her.

The keys are where she left them, on the nail at the back of the post in the corner. Emma twirls them on her finger as she walks over to the trunks, as though this is a casual perusal and she has no expectation of treasure.

She slips a key into the first trunk, but it doesn't do anything, so she tries another. This time the lock clicks, and Emma braces for the champagne pop of the lid, remembering the trunk she opened with Lettie. But this trunk opens without drama. The hinges creak and Emma leans forward to peer inside. She realizes she's squinting, the way she does when she steps on the scale, hoping for good news, preparing for bad.

The scent of mothballs suddenly fills the air, and Emma's eyes widen. Mothballs mean fabric, and sure enough, the first thing she sees is a christening gown, lacy, sepia-stained white, and tiny. She lifts it up to admire, wondering who it belonged to — Miss Lydia? The McKinney girl? She thinks about how many times in the last few months she's read about the importance of labeling quilts, and now she understands. If only there were a label attached to this dress! Well, maybe there's a picture of a baby wearing it, Emma thinks, gently laying the gown on the top of the second trunk.

She reaches back into the open trunk and lets her hands search blindly through its contents. Her fingers touch upon scratchy lace and thick wool and buttons and embroidery. At the very bottom she feels something cool and hard, and pulling it out discovers a silver hand mirror, its glass cracked, but beautiful nonetheless. Emma looks at her jagged reflection, half expecting to see the McKinney girl staring back at her.

Placing the mirror to the side, she rummages through the rest of the trunk's contents, pulling up two dresses, one black with a long skirt and buttons from the waist up to its high neck, the other white and shorter. Maybe the one in the McKinney girl's photograph? Is this the McKinney girl's trunk?

The dresses look like they might fit Sarah. Maybe she could bring them in for the school's centennial display.

Reaching in again, Emma's hand brushes against paper. It's a program of some sort, its pages yellowed and stained brown around the edges. The cover reads "St. Paul's Episcopal School for Girls, Pine City, Commencement, May 15, 1910."

All right then, McKinney Girl, Emma thinks. We're going to figure out what your name really is.

There are fifteen to choose from. There is a McCloud, a MacDougal, a McNair, but no McKinney. Okay, so the McKinney Girl is not the McKinney Girl. Emma can adjust. But who is she?

Emma scans the row of names, hoping one will leap out at her — *Me! Me! Pick me!* — but none does. But there's a splotch of ink bleeding through the paper, and when Emma turns the program over, she sees that it's been signed.

Dear Lillian,

> *When the golden sun is setting*
> *And your mind from care is free*
> *When of others you are thinking*
> *Will you sometimes think of me*

Affectionately, Ethel Beth Tilley.

Emma flips the program to the previous page and looks down the list of names until she finds Lillian A. West. So that's who the McKinney girl is. "Lillian," Emma says, just to hear the roll of the L's. Not a disappointing name at all.

She returns to the trunk, pulling out a woman's dress, a somber black affair, then a caped gray wool coat, and black button-up boots with tiny heels. Miss West's trousseau perhaps. Emma can't believe how well preserved it all is, especially when generations of children have surely gone through this trunk and pulled everything out, tried it on. Here's a small straw hat with a green ribbon for decoration, here's an embroidered handkerchief. How have they survived all of these years?

Emma carefully refolds the dresses and the coat, tucks the boots back into the trunk's bottom corner. She'll take the commencement program downstairs, where she plans to go online and see what she can find out about Lillian. So she wasn't a McKinney, at least not originally, but clearly her family had money. Did they have a house in town? Maybe Lillian wasn't from Sweet Anne's Gap at all; maybe she was a Pine City girl, or from down in Marion, a big city gal.

Emma eyes the remaining trunk. Will its contents be more interesting or less? What if it contains Lillian's diary?

Her letters? Her photo album? Emma reaches into her pocket for the keys. She wants to wait, to draw out her excitement, but she also wants to get the whole thing over with. The first two trunks have been a trove of riches, at least if you're the sort of person who likes old stuff and cracked mirrors and ancient black boots, which Emma is. How could the third possibly measure up?

It takes a moment to tug the third trunk's lid open, and once again, Emma looks through slit eyes. Okay, she tells herself, this is it. She opens her eyes and steps back, sagging a bit with disappointment. Phone books. *Morgan County Phone Directory: Yellow Pages, 1973. Pine City and Surrounding Areas (Sweet Anne's Gap, Bakersville, Cranberry) 1969.*

Well, maybe Sarah could contribute them to the school's centennial display. Maybe they could find an old rotary dial phone and do a communications project. *Talking to Our Neighbors Through the Years.*

Emma leans over the trunk and picks up one of the books, feeling a sneeze build as the mildew and dust meet her nose. It's a floppy, unwieldy thing, and she almost drops it, and then she *does* drop it when she sees what it's been covering up.

Emma takes a deep breath, lets it out. Kneeling in front of the trunk, she removes the remaining phone books and smoothes out the quilt they've been hiding. Only four blocks are visible, but even before Emma lifts the quilt and carefully unfolds it on the attic floor, she knows it's a sampler quilt. The blocks, made from faded blues and reds, tiny florals, paisleys and geometrics, are familiar to Emma from her quilt collecting and research — Flying Geese, Churn Dash, Lady of the Lake, Sawtooth Star. She turns the quilt over, hoping against hope that it will have a label.

No label, but the initials LWM are embroidered in the lower right hand corner. "So you *are* the McKinney girl, sort of," Emma says, thinking of the picture on her mantel. "You became a McKinney girl, anyway. And I bet you're Lydia McKinney's mother. And when Lydia got married, she moved your things here."

And then Emma has the funny feeling she's not alone. The skin on her arms prickles into goose bumps. "Hello?" she calls out.

"We're home!" Ben's voice calls out from the entranceway. "What's for snack?"

Emma shakes her head, laughing at herself. For a second she'd been convinced that the ghost of Lillian McKinney was standing behind her. Silly.

So why is it that she suddenly feels — *feels* — Lillian smile?

"What are you doing up here?" Sarah calls from the attic steps, her voice curious. "Did you find my pink sweatshirt yet?"

"Not yet," Emma calls back. "I wasn't actually looking for it, to be honest."

Sarah has reached the attic door and is now looking at the trunks' contents strewn across the floor. "What's all that stuff? It looks really old."

"It belonged to the family who lived here before we did," Emma explains. "Mostly it's just clothes. But there's a mirror and a quilt, too. Miss Lydia — who we bought the house from? I think all this stuff was her mother's. Lillian's. The girl in the picture on my mantel?"

To Emma's surprise, Sarah looks halfway interested. "So how old do you think it is? Like, from the 1800s?"

"Not that old. But some of it's from the early 1900's."

Sarah walks over to the open trunk. "Can I look?"

"Sure," Emma tells her. "Maybe you'll find something interesting. Some of the things I've found are from when Lillian was a girl about your age. It looks like the clothes would fit you."

Sarah sticks her hands into the trunk and moves them around, reaching, feeling. "It would be cool if we found her diary."

"Very cool," Emma agrees as she holds Lillian's sampler quilt up to the window so she can examine the stitches, which are uniform and tiny. "Or some letters."

"Did you write letters when you were a kid?" Sarah asks. "Because they didn't have email or texting then, right?"

"Right. And yes, I wrote lots of letters. And notes to my friends. I used to leave notes in a secret spot in a tree for my best friend Karen."

"That's awesome. I mean, you can't really leave an email in a tree."

There's something different about Sarah today, Emma realizes. She seems almost — well, happy. "Did you have a good day at school today?" she asks.

"Not really," Sarah replies, still digging around in the trunk, tossing aside handkerchiefs and two pairs of yellowed, elbow-length gloves. "Well, not until the end, anyway. I went to the library right after last period, and there was this girl there who was checking out, like, a hundred *Pony Club* books. Her name's Carter, and she actually *has* a pony. She said I could come over and ride it, but you'd have to say it was okay."

"That sounds like fun," Emma says. "Why don't you ask her to get her mom to call me?"

"I already gave her your phone number. Her mom's going to text you and —" Sarah stops midsentence. "Hey, I found something that isn't clothes!"

She pulls out a crumbling mailer, one of those ancient inner-office envelopes with a red string and a winder closure, and taps her finger against it. "Whatever's inside is sort of hard, like cardboard. Can I look?"

Emma nods, and Sarah carefully opens the envelope and pulls out what in fact looks a lot like a piece of cardboard, but when flipped over reveals itself to be a photograph.

"I can't believe it!" Sarah cries, and turns the photograph around so Emma can see it. "Lillian had a horse! Look what it says — 'Lillian and Silky, May 1909, Pine City, N.C.'"

Emma reaches over and takes the photograph from Sarah. She recognizes Lillian immediately from the picture downstairs on her mantle, although standing next to her horse, Lillian is smiling — no more menacing scowl. She's dressed in a white shirtwaist, her hair pulled up in a bun, Gibson-girl style.

"Do you think she rode Silky wearing a dress?" Sarah, who has come over to stand next to Emma, asks. "I think that would be sort of uncomfortable."

"She probably rode side-saddle. I think most women did back then."

Sarah shakes her head sadly. "Poor Lillian." Then she brightens. "But she did have a horse! Can I have this picture in my room?"

"Sure," Emma says, feeling suddenly light, her daughter's happiness contagious. "And maybe you and I could do some research, find out more about who Lillian was and what she was like?"

Sarah is already heading downstairs. "Okay," she calls over her shoulder. "And maybe Carter could help."

Emma walks over to the stack of boxes where she has carefully laid out Lillian's quilt. Ah, the McKinney girl, she thinks. Good old Lillian.

She smiles, then wonders why she's smiling. It only takes a second to figure it out: She feels like she's made a new friend.

20.

Emma has two weeks to finish the program copy, and her stomach tightens every time she thinks about it. There are only a handful of quilts left to collect, that's true, and she has pages of notes. Mavis has done a fantastic job of taking notes on all the quilts she's delivered to Barbara's office, and Emma will have no problem translating them into copy. So there's absolutely no need to panic —

Except that she also needs to get the press releases out. She's been emailing with an editor at *Carolina Today* magazine who's agreed to run a short piece in the April issue's "Upcoming Events" column, but she also hopes that the big state papers — *The News & Observer* in Raleigh, the *Asheville Citizen-Times*, and *The Charlotte Observer* — will run longer pieces, and she needs to pitch the story to them sooner rather than later.

There's only one thing to do, she realizes Wednesday morning, after a night of feverish dreams in which she kept trying to text Barbara about the show, only her fingers were like sausages and her phone kept losing its charge. She will spend all day at Helen's drinking coffee, eating muffins, and writing. She'll set up camp in a booth and give Cindy twenty bucks to keep the coffee coming and the teeming masses at bay. By the time she needs to be home for the kids, she'll have a draft done, minus a quilt or two, and that's all there is to it.

"You need a blueberry muffin, maybe three — I can tell it from the look on your face," Cindy says when she sees Emma getting settled into a back booth. "And lots of coffee, too, am I right?"

Emma nods. This is no time for moderation. She needs sugar and caffeine on the double.

Okay, laptop opened and powered on. Notes out. They're up to forty-nine quilts, with the expectation of seven more coming in by the end of the week, three of those being quilts that Mavis will collect, and four that Emma and Lettie will pick up on Thursday. Over half the quilts are pre-1900, and most of them have never been displayed in public. This is Emma's hook for publicity, that the show will feature close to thirty never-seen-before historic quilts. She wants to catch the interest of amateur historians and genealogists and Civil War buffs. People who love quilts will show up regardless, she figures, but others can be lured in with the right pitch.

Barbara's husband Ty has photographed all the collected quilts, and Emma's created an online album for easy reference. With the books that Barbara has given her, along with the help of several online sites, the Quilt Index in particular, Emma has been able to name most of the quilt and block patterns or at least been able to make educated guesses, knowing that Barbara will check after her. Robbing Peter to Pay Paul, Drunkard's Path, Tulips in a Basket, Whig Rose, Carolina Lily. Emma loves the names almost as much as she loves the quilts.

What surprises her is how much affection she feels for the quilters themselves. What must it have been like to have lived in such isolation, most of your day spent doing what was necessary to survive. And yet these women found time to create beauty and comfort for themselves and their families. Emma can imagine how much they looked forward to the end of the day, when they would finally have time to sit by the fire and sew. She knows that feeling herself, though she doesn't work a tenth as hard as the quilters who made these quilts. Still, some days while she's busy making dinner and packing the children's lunches, she has the thought that it won't be long before she can sit down at her sewing machine. Just thinking about it, her entire body relaxes.

Some of the quilts show signs of age and use, but many were clearly valued enough to be carefully stored and only brought out for special occasions. The colors are faded, but the technique is sure and the artistry is undeniable. Emma remembers growing up, how boys would say things like "If women are equal to men, where are all the great women artists?" At the time, she hadn't known how to answer that, unfamiliar as she was in elementary school with artists such as Frieda Kahlo, Georgia O'Keefe and Mary Cassatt. Now she'd know to send the boys into their houses to check out the quilts their grandmothers had made, the Double Wedding Rings tucked away in linen closets, the Dresden Plates draped over the backs of their couches.

What she's trying to say in the program — and what has taken her two cinnamon rolls to get at — is that all the quilts in this exhibit, from the Baltimore Album quilt to Louellen Walls' MIA quilt, are connected. They're all part of a project that has spanned centuries, a project in which women sew scraps of fabric together in interesting ways and make art,

art that both comforts and signifies comfort. She thinks about Peggy Weaver, the young woman she and Barbara met the first day they went out to collect quilts. Twenty-six years old with three children under the age of five, Peggy Weaver dyed her own fabric from things she found in the woods around the trailer where she and her family lived, berries and leaves, even insects. From this hand-dyed fabric, Peggy made quilts of such vibrancy the colors practically jumped off the blocks.

The problem is how to say something important about quilts and art and women's lives in five hundred words or less. After two hours of solid writing, Emma looks up from her computer and stretches. It's 11:15 and she's made progress. It's time for a break. She'll go to the bathroom, check her email, maybe order a grilled cheese and fries. And a Coke. The diet will start as soon as she turns in the program copy and sends out the press releases.

When she gets back from the bathroom, her phone buzzes, announcing a text. Emma doesn't recognize the number, but the sender is friendly. *Hi there! I hear Sarah would like to ride Carter's pony. Can she come home with us after school on Friday?*

Carter's mom, I presume? Emma texts back.

Good question! the texter replies. *Yes, I'm Suzanne. Sorry about that! Do you want to grab a cup of coffee and meet? I'm at Helen's this very minute if you're free.*

Not only am I free, I'm here. At Helen's. In the back, with the laptop and the mess.

A woman two booths up from Emma's stands and looks around. When she sees Emma, she asks, "Sarah's mom?"

Emma slides out of the booth, wiping the crumbs from

her pants. "Also known as Emma. I take it that Sarah passed along my phone number, but not my name?"

"Yep. All the note said was 'Mom's number.' Which makes sense, if you think about it. I mean, you're not Emma to her. So can I join you for a minute, or are you too busy?"

Emma waves to say *come on over*, and Suzanne does. "I'm on a bit of a busman's holiday," she says, slipping into the booth. She's tall, attractive, maybe in her late thirties or early forties, with lovely brown eyes and wavy salt and pepper hair held back from her face with a blue batik scarf. "I own a little bakery close to the Penland School. Now I'm thinking about opening a business here. Not a bakery, but an art gallery focused on textiles. That's my background, actually, textiles. Baking came later."

"Do you quilt?" Emma asks eagerly, though she suspects their paths would already have crossed if Suzanne were a quilter.

"Not exactly, but I do work with fabric. Ruth at the Sewing Room orders supplies for me. Every once in awhile I'll quilt a wall-hanging just to keep her happy."

"Ruth isn't happy unless everyone's quilting," Emma says, and they both laugh at the truth of that.

"So I just got an email this morning from Charlotte Stengle — something about our girls doing a project for the school's centennial pageant? I hope Sarah's interested. It's the sort of thing Carter would love to do, but would never do on her own."

"Same for Sarah," Emma says, relief washing over her. At last a friend for Sarah — a real friend it sounds like. She sends up a silent prayer of thanks for Charlotte Stengle and her matchmaking gifts.

Suzanne leans forward and smiles a conspirator's smile "What do you say we have lunch, and what do you say we order desert first?"

"Pie?" Emma asks.

"Yes, pie!"

Ten minutes later, after she takes her last bite, Suzanne sits back and sighs. "Helen's has the best banana cream pie *ever*. Mine can't touch it."

Emma looks around and then whispers across the table, "Have you actually met Helen? Because I've been coming here for months now, and I've never once seen her."

Suzanne grins. "I have news for you. There is no Helen."

Emma sits back, stunned. "What? But everyone talks about her. Cindy even told me about Helen's special home-made cake mix that she bakes her cakes from every day."

"That's Julio," Suzanne informs her, taking a sip of coffee. "And Mario and Juan. And Esteban when he's not back in Mexico City helping out his folks."

"Helen is Julio?"

Suzanne nods. "And Mario and Juan and Esteban. I keep trying to steal them away, but they're loyal to Trace. He was the only person in town willing to hire them when they were trying to get off the migrant farmworker circuit a few years ago.

"Trace Brown?"

"Sure. He owns Helen's, didn't you know?"

Emma shakes her head. "No one told me. Wow, Trace Brown is Helen."

"Well, his mom was," Suzanne says. "Then she died and left him her restaurant."

Emma starts to laugh. Just when she thought she had

this town figured out, some new secret is revealed. When Cindy comes to refill their coffee cups, Emma scowls at her and says, "You made me think Helen was a real person!"

Cindy holds a finger to her lips and looks around the room. "Shush now! That's company policy for folks who might just be passing through. It gives the place a warm, fuzzy feel if you think Helen is back in the kitchen baking up cakes. I would have told you soon enough what the real story is. I tell all the regulars."

So Emma is a regular. She grins as though she's been given a prize.

After they order actual lunch — grilled cheese for Emma and a BLT for Suzanne — Suzanne points to Emma's computer and pile of papers. "So we've yet to discuss what you're working on here. It looks like a big project."

Emma nods. "It is. I'm doing all the publicity and marketing for the centennial quilt show. I now know everything there is to know about quilts and quilting in the southern Appalachian region. Two months ago I knew nothing."

"God bless the Internet," Suzanne says. "So what will you do when the show is over? Do you have more work lined up?"

"Not really," Emma says, realizing that she hasn't thought about her unwritten novel in weeks. Has she given up on it? Should she give up?

Suzanne checks her watch, looks at Emma. "What do you say we eat our sandwiches and walk down to the antiques store on Trade Street? Do you know it — the one that's always closed? The realtor gave me the key so I can have a look-around before I decide if I'm really serious about buying it. The thing is if I do open this gallery, I'll need help — with everything, really, but especially with getting the word out. That sounds like something you might be good at, if you're at all interested in a marketing project. And maybe there would be other things for you to do as well, who knows. It would be fun to have somebody to go with me on curating trips."

"I'm definitely interested," Emma says, ignoring the twinge of guilt she feels about abandoning her novel once again. No, not abandoning — postponing. She'll get to it when it's the right time, remember? "I've always wanted to see the inside of that store."

Suzanne leans out of the booth and waves at Cindy. "Bring us the check with our sandwiches, would you, sweetie?" she calls. Then she turns to Emma and says, "Yeah, I've been dying to see the inside of that store, too. It might not be what I'm looking for, but you never know until you walk through the door, right?"

Which is true for every new adventure, Emma thinks as she starts packing up her things. How can you know what's right until you take a look around?

21.

Monday night's guild meeting is filling up, people greeting each other from opposite ends of the room and exclaiming over the new fabric lines that Ruth has just put on display. Emma has to lean closer to Mavis to make herself heard, even though their chairs are only inches apart. She tells her about Suzanne, about the plans for the gallery, how maybe Mavis's son-in-law Mark could help do some of the work to get the place ready. When Emma finishes her report, Mavis reaches into her purse, pulls out her pinging phone, looks at the screen and mutes it. "That was Sherilyn right now; I'll tell her to tell Mark. I'd like to see something happen with that building," she says. "It was built by Charlie Martin — Shana Martin's daddy — way back in the day. His second wife's the one who opened up the antique store, but it didn't do much business. Her stuff was cheap without being interesting. I already got a garage filled up with junk just like it."

Emma agrees that the contents of the shop are disappointing. After all those weeks of looking in the window and wondering what wonders might be hidden inside, now she knows — lots and lots of plastic ice cube trays and puzzles with "pieces missing" written on the boxes. But the space itself had potential, Suzanne said as they were looking around, and Emma had squinted and hoped she was right.

"I'd love to see a good art gallery in town," Mavis says, whispering now that the meeting is about to begin. "Class up the place a little. You think your girl's gonna buy it?"

"She sounded pretty serious about it. She's got the money."

"And now she's got you," Mavis says, patting Emma on the knee. "A professional writer and publicist."

Emma smiles, pleased by Mavis's support. Really, she's feeling pleased in general. Beneath her chair, her first finished quilt is tucked away in a tote, ready for show-and-tell. She's spent all day admiring it, feeling a little silly in the process, knowing that as quilts go, it's not that much, a pink and gray four-patch with floral borders and a dark gray binding. But it's hers — she made it, she quilted it, she bound it, and last night she watched TV snuggled beneath it on the couch. In a few minutes, she'll parade it across the front of the room. She's already anticipating the warm applause of other quilters, each with her own first quilt memories. She looks around, thinking that she'd like to hug everyone here, she feels that good.

Sure enough, everyone makes a fuss after show-and-tell is over. She's squeezed and patted and generally treated like a beauty pageant winner. Dorothy Brown comes up to her and takes her hand. "I'm so proud of you!" she exclaims. "You've come a long way in very little time."

"And I've got a long way to go," Emma says. "I'm just glad to be on the journey, corny as that sounds."

"Not corny at all," Dorothy assures her. "I know exactly what you mean. Now, I heard you're not just quilting, you're teaching Angie Byers to quilt. I'm glad to hear Angie's finally interested. I suppose you know she's a problem child, but her mother's one of my dearest friends and one of the sweetest women in the world. Have you seen Hannah at all?"

"A couple of times, but she hasn't really said anything. She just stands in the doorway and watches."

Dorothy shakes her head sadly. "I wish like anything we could get her back to quilting. But you keep teaching Angie — I know you're doing her a world of good!"

"You're teaching Angie Byers how to quilt?"

Emma doesn't have to turn around to know that Christine McCrae is standing behind her. She's done her best to avoid Christine — here, at the dollar store, at Helen's — but it's hard to avoid someone when they're standing two feet away from you. So she turns and says, "Yep, I'm teaching Angie Byers how to quilt. Believe me, I'm as surprised as anyone — not only that Angie asked me, but that I have anything to teach her."

Christine winces, as though sympathizing. "Oh, you'll probably get better in time. Of course, if you start hanging around with the likes of Angie Byers, well, you might be taking a wrong turn on that journey you say you're on. Who knows, though? Maybe you two are perfect traveling companions."

Emma, having no idea what to say, sputters, and Dorothy steps in to save her. "Christine, why are you being so ugly? Emma's quilt is real pretty."

"Oh, well, sure," Christine says, sounding like she's trying to be helpful. "It's nice. I made one just like it when I was nine." She turns to Emma. "You know who taught me to make quilts? My granny and my mama. It's kind of a tradition around these parts, quilting. But what do you know about community traditions? You're just one of those newcomers who wants to move in and change everything."

People are starting to gather around. Emma feels hot, feels perspiration on her neck. "I'm not trying to change anything."

"Uh huh," Christine says, clearly unconvinced. "How long before you start going to town council meetings to get the zoning laws changed? Everybody who moves here from off the mountain can't stand the zoning in this town, all those chickens in folks' front yards. I give it a year before you start complaining. And then you'll run for assistant school superintendent, because our schools aren't good enough for your children. That's usually the next step."

Christine looks around at the crowd. "Remember that guy Michael Fortenberry, moved up here from Charlotte and ran for Mayor after living here for a year? Remember his campaign slogan — *Let's find a new way to get things done*? The old ways weren't good enough for him — our ways weren't good enough for him."

To her dismay, Emma sees lots of heads in the crowd bobbing in agreement. People who were applauding for her only moments before seem to be looking at her more critically now. *I'm one of you*, she wants to shout, but who would agree when it seems so obvious now that she's not.

Christine points at Emma. "And now you're running *our* centennial quilt show. You're in charge of quilts that are a part of *our* history. Not your history. Ours. Because you're clearly the best person for the job, right? Worked at a university, big-time professional something or another, of course you should be the one telling us all about our past. Who better than Emma Byrd, whose lived here for what — three months? And been making quilts for what?

Three months? Yes, I can see why you've been selected to tell us all about our quilt heritage."

"You need to shut your mouth, Christine." Mavis has joined the crowd now, and everyone turns to look at her. "Emma's been making a mighty fine effort to fit in around here, a lot more than most newcomers. You need to give her all due respect."

"Why should I respect a woman who hangs out with drug addicts? Or maybe Angie's her newest project. Maybe she's going to save Angie Byers from herself. She's like one of them missionaries who came up in the '20s and '30s. Hillbillies needed to be fixed, right? That's what all outsiders think."

Mavis comes forward and takes Emma by the arm. "You don't have to stand here and listen to all this nonsense. Let me take you home." She turns to the crowd. "Y'all should be ashamed of yourselves. You know exactly why Christine don't like Angie Byers — we all do. But Emma here don't have nothing to do with that. Christine needs to leave her alone."

With that, Mavis pulls Emma out of the store. "Don't take any of that to heart, you hear me? Christine's just bitter about Angie; she always has been. I suppose I don't blame her, but it's not right for her to take it out on you."

"So should I stop helping Angie with her quilt?" Emma asks numbly. She feels as though she's been run over by a herd of galloping horses. She tries to remember why she was feeling good earlier, but now she can't.

"You helping Angie is the right thing to do," Mavis insists. "Will it lose you some friends? Sure, but it'll make you some friends, too. You're doing a good thing. Don't let Christine get inside your head — about any of it."

Emma is still numb when Mavis drops her off at home. The night air is almost warm; the world is tilting toward spring. Emma can smell the narcissus and daffodils that have come up in her front yard. Instead of going inside, she sits on the porch, trying to sort through what just happened, but she can't make her thoughts come together. It reminds her of when she was a kid and had done something wrong. She'd lie on her bed, waiting for her dad to come up and tell her how she would be punished, thinking *I'm in trouble, I'm in trouble, I'm in trouble.*

And that's all she can think now. *I'm in trouble.*

And then, *I thought they liked me.*

Which is when she starts to cry.

22.

Emma had been thinking about taking her quilt over to show Angie, but after Monday night she can't bring herself to look at it. And when she gets to Angie's on Friday for their third lesson, she's glad she didn't bring it. Compared to the quilt Angie's working on, Emma's quilt really does look like something a nine-year-old would make.

"I can't believe how much progress you've made," Emma says, standing in front of the design wall Angie has crafted from a piece of foam board covered in flannel. "You've gone above and beyond what we did last week. How'd you learn to make an Ohio Star block?"

"Internet," Angie says with a shrug. "I couldn't sleep Monday night, so I decided to watch quilting videos on the computer. To be honest, I thought they'd help me doze off, but there's something sort of captivating about watching someone sew. Anyway, this one lady was doing Ohio Stars, so I thought I'd give it a try."

"You don't even need me," Emma says, and although she says it to be encouraging, she suddenly realizes it's true. If Angie can teach herself to quilt from videos, what does she need Emma for?

Angie takes a seat in front of her machine and then leans back to stretch. "Sure I need you. I know you're coming over, so I get the work done. And if it hadn't been for you, I wouldn't have known that there were quilting videos on YouTube."

"Glad to be such a fount of information," Emma says flatly.

"You gotta remember I grew up watching my mama quilt. And my granny, too. Quilting's in my DNA *and* my medial temporal lobe."

Emma stares at her, and Angie laughs. "Yeah, I know what a medial temporal lobe is. Don't look so shocked."

"Well, what do you need my help with today?" Emma asks, sitting down next to Angie at the table. "It seems like you've got your quilt under control."

"What I've got under control is the Ohio Star block. But I need help figuring what other colors to use and how to put the whole thing together. Like should I use that stuff that goes in between the blocks?"

Emma has to think a moment about what Angie might mean, and then she guesses, "Sashing?"

"Sashing! That's it. Sashing and cornerstones. I don't know a thing about either."

Neither does Emma, not really. She appears to have reached her limits as a teacher. Looking at Angie's blocks on the design wall, she wonders if she's reached her limits as a quilter, too. Well, of course, she hasn't. She can learn, as her ability to now make reasonably square half-square triangles proves. But Angie has taught herself to make stars with perfect points, just by watching a video. She's already past Emma in ability and clearly had more talent to begin with.

Emma thinks back to Monday's guild meeting, all the smiles and pats on the back. Was she being patronized? What were people really thinking? Probably the same thing as Christine, that a child could have made Emma's quilt. She almost laughs, remembering all the grandiose ideas she's had about herself and her amazing quilting life over the last few months. It would help if she could actually sew in a straight line. She feels herself blushing. People must think she's an idiot.

When she turns back around, Angie is staring at her. "What's going on in that head of yours? You worried about the show? You said Friday you got all the press releases out, right? And the program to the printer? So you don't have anything to be worried about. Everybody and Aunt Minnie's dog is gonna be there."

"I'm not worried about the show," Emma tells her. "I'm just — I don't know. I think I'm just tired. I've been busy with a lot of different things — the show, helping my daughter get ready for the school pageant, just life in general. And I'm not sure you really need me. I'm glad to give you deadlines if that's helpful, but I don't think I have much to teach you at this point. When you finish the top, I can help you make the binding — but you know what? There are videos for that, too."

"I do need you," Angie insists, and to Emma's surprise there's a current of emotion running through her voice. "I mean it. All you got to do is stay one step ahead of me and we'll be fine."

Emma can't help but smile. "Who could stay one step ahead of you?"

"Only a chosen few, it's true," Angie says. "And I have chosen you. So say you'll still help me, okay?"

"Okay," Emma says, but she says it reluctantly, and Angie picks up on that.

"Come on, girl! I need you all the way in! You know what your problem is?"

Emma would love to hear what Angie Byers thinks her problem is. "Tell me."

"Your problem is you've got the first week of April blues," Angie says, standing. "Your problem is you've finished all your big projects and you ain't got a thing to do. But I know exactly what you need to do. You need to come with me to Helen's this very minute, eat some sugar and plan out your spring garden."

"My what?" Emma asks, but Angie is already at the front door, pulling on her jacket.

"You heard me, your garden. You need a new project, maybe three. So here's how I see it: *one,* you help me make my quilt; *two,* you start a new quilt yourself, and *C,* you plant your garden. It's getting to be about that time."

Emma stands up and grabs her sweater. "What time is that?"

"Garden time!" Angie rolls her eyes. "Have you not been listening?"

Emma follows Angie out the door. The sky is overcast, but the air is warm, and new grass is coming up bright green with its sweet smell of chlorophyll. A garden? She's never had a garden before, although she's always wished she had the time. Of course now she does, and she's got the yard as well. What she doesn't have is the enthusiasm. Going to the trouble of putting in a garden — the tilling, the composting and fertilizing — it just seems like so much work. But it's not the thought of work that makes Emma resist the idea of a garden. It's the thought of literally putting down roots in a place where she doesn't feel all that rooted right now.

She's tried to be a part of things. She volunteers at the school and hangs out at Helen's and — well, she's tried to be a member of the community. But after Monday's guild meeting, she wonders if the community actually wants her membership. Maybe people would be happy for her to go away.

Maybe it doesn't matter. Last week, before the guild meeting, Owen had mentioned there was a job opening up in Raleigh — a step up the career ladder — but he couldn't imagine moving back to an office job, and Emma and the kids seemed to be doing so well here, why mess with a good thing? At the time, Emma had agreed, but now she wonders if she should urge Owen to look into the new job. The fact is, the schools here aren't as good as the Chapel Hill and Raleigh schools, and Emma might or might not have a job here, depending on whether Suzanne decides to open her gallery, and if she's going to be perfectly honest about it, her so-called novel is dead in the water. There are plenty of good reasons to move back, even if Owen has to suffer putting on a tie every day. He'll do it if it's the right thing for the family.

Three months ago, she made a pledge to connect. She's done her part. And a few people have made the effort to connect with her in return. It surprises her that Angie Byers is one of them. Emma sighs. She doesn't want to plant a garden, but she supposes she might as well. Maybe the garden will provide her with a sign, like having exact change when she bought her sewing table. If it thrives, it means she's on the right road here. And if it doesn't?

Then she'll find another road to walk down.

23.

Angie's hands are surprisingly steady on the wheel. No tapping fingers, no cigarette waving, just one hand at ten o'clock and the other at three. Today she's wearing a man's white button-down shirt over tight jeans, her hair held back with a red bandana, no make-up. She looks young, Emma thinks. Or at least younger. Not so hard around the mouth.

"The thing about Howard is you got to haggle with him for a good price," Angie says as they drive out of town on Highway 15 toward Morgan's Garden Supply near Pine City. "Like most folks around here, he's got his snowbird prices and his year-rounder prices. Only the year-rounder prices ain't listed."

"You've got to give him the secret handshake first," Emma says, and Angie nods.

"Something like that," she says. "Now it's a good thing I'm going with you, because Howard ain't gonna try to get anything over on me the way he would with you."

"What was it like here when you were growing up?" Emma asks now as they pass a newly constructed tanning salon-slash-payday loan business. She can't help but wishing that these sort of places didn't exist. They're like so much litter by the side of the road, unsightly and annoying.

"It was boring, just like it is now, only worse," Angie says with a barking laugh. "Hardly anything you see on this road was here. You had to go to Asheville or Marion to buy clothes, and down to Pine City to buy any groceries at all. Now at least you've got the Dollar General if you need milk or bread."

"There was Helen's, right?"

Angie nods. "Helen's was it. You'd go after school and drink Cokes and eat french fries 'til Helen kicked you out for hogging all her tables. If the weather was good, we'd go down to the river and somebody'd turn on their car radio so we could dance. That was a good time. We were so backwards up here, we didn't know a thing about the '60s or hippies or psychedelic rock music. Boys all had crew cuts still."

It's funny to Emma, how much easier it is to imagine Sweet Anne's Gap in 1935 than in 1965. She could believe that the turbulence of the '60s and '70s completely passed over this part of the country, isolated as it was before cable TV and the Internet. But even boys raised in the mountains weren't immune to the draft, and most likely they brought the outside world back with them when they returned home.

"Did anything change up here during the '60s? Or did it just stay like the '50s until you got cable?"

"Things changed, late '60s, early '70s," Angie says, nodding. "The outside world got in little by little. You had your VISTA volunteers coming up, and your folklore-types collecting stories, and people from off the mountain learning how to weave tablecloths over at Penland. The drugs got in with the outsiders and the Vietnam vets, and that changed everything. Changed me, that's for sure."

Emma wants to press in further, but something about Angie's expression warns against it. She looks out the window, hoping her silence will coax Angie to share more of her history, but it doesn't. Still, Angie's hands stay steady.

"Did you quit smoking?" Emma has a sudden realization Angie hasn't lit up once since they left home.

"Yes, ma'am, believe it or not." Angie's grin is of the proverbial cat-that-ate-the-canary variety. "One whole week now. In fact, I'm in need of a piece of Nicorette, if you'd be so kind to grab one out of my purse for me. I'm trying not to get addicted to that, too, but Dallas says better Nicorette than nicotine."

"Dallas? McKinney?"

"The one and only."

Angie states this in a breezy tone that says, *You gonna make a big deal about it? Go ahead and see if I care.*

Emma knows she should probably leave this alone, but instead asks carefully, "You guys have been friends for a long time, huh?"

"Friends," Angie says with a snort. "I guess that's what you'd call it. Or not. But we have been tangled up together for a long time, that's for sure. And now we're sort of at the same place in our lives, so he's someone I can lean on."

"Same place?" Again, careful. Emma does her best to make her tone innocent, as though she has little to no interest in the topic but is trying to make polite conversation.

"Yeah, the same place. Look on the map and find a town called Sobriety. That's where we're both residing these days. Nice not to live there alone. Of course, Dallas has been sober for thirty years, and I'm more of a newcomer. Now if you could get me that gum, I'd surely appreciate it."

Emma picks up Angie's weathered maroon purse from the floorboard and looks inside. Wallet, toothbrush in a clear, plastic holder, small tube of toothpaste, box of Nicorette.

"You have the neatest purse of anyone I've ever met," Emma says, passing the Nicorette box to Angie. "Where are all the receipts and the loose pennies?"

"Part of my program is keeping my life neat and orderly. Avoiding chaos. I decided to start with my purse."

Angie pushes a piece of gum out with one hand and pops it into her mouth. "Good lord, I needed that," she says after several chews, sighing loudly. "Amazing how fast this stuff gets into your bloodstream. I'm a new woman."

"You seem to be," Emma tells her. She wants to ask more about Dallas, but she's not sure she really wants to know if Angie and Dallas are an item. It will not improve Christine McCrae's disposition a bit if they are, and something Emma has learned about small town life is that one person's bad mood can ruin everybody else's day.

Howard Morgan is throwing bags of cow manure into the open trunk of a sagging Impala when Angie and Emma pull into the parking lot of Morgan Garden Supply. He is tall and thin but for a pot belly that makes him look vaguely pregnant. As soon as he spies Angie getting out the truck, he slams the Impala's trunk, knocks on the driver's window to signal he's done, and trots over to greet them.

"Angie-Pangie, you're a sight," he says in a familiar tone that suggests he and Angie go back a long ways. "Never looked better, I'll give you that much. I saw Lettie the other day, and I swear, you two could be sisters."

"Well, I had her when I was twenty-two, so I reckon we almost are," Angie says. "Now Howard, this here is my neighbor, Emma. You might think you're going to rip her off, but you are not. Are we clear on that matter?"

Howard blushes, and Emma feels sorry for him. Who on this earth is a match for Angie Byers, she wonders? Not this man, that's for sure.

Howard turns to Emma. "Now Angie's just teasing. Ain't nobody around got better prices than me, and for a friend of Miss Byers, well, I believe you'll find my prices even more than fair."

"I'm sure I will," Emma tells him, and thinks, *Oh, you poor man.*

Sure enough, Angie puts Howard through his paces. "Now don't go trying to sell her that old, dried up rosemary bush," she scolds as Howard shows them his selection of herbs. "You know she shouldn't plant rosemary 'til the fall. And why are you showing her these plants? Because they cost twenty times the price of seeds, that's why." Angie turns to Emma. "Nothing easier to grow from seeds than herbs. Just buy you a packet of basil, one of oregano, maybe peppermint, only you got to plant that in a container or it'll take over the whole garden."

Angie helps Emma fill several flats worth of peppers, tomatoes, zucchini, yellow squash, marigolds, begonias, and Shasta daisies. "It's too late for peas," she says, slapping away the seed packet Howard tries to put in Emma's basket. "You got to start those in March. How you feel about eggplant?"

Emma closes her eyes at the cash register, scared to see what all this is going to cost her, and is shocked when Howard gives her the final tally, which turns out to be thirty dollars less than she thought it would.

"Call it the Angie Byers discount," Angie says as they pull out of the parking lot, still waving at Howard. "I have spread a lot of happy memories around this town, if you catch my drift, and now it's payback time."

"So why didn't you get anything for yourself?" Emma asks. "The price was definitely right."

"I might be moving soon, and Lettie don't have time to tend a garden."

"Moving? Out of town?"

"Would you miss me?" Angie asks, and even though she's grinning, Emma senses that this is a real question.

"You know, I believe I would. I like having you for a neighbor."

"Well, I wouldn't be moving all that far away," Angie says, sounding pleased by Emma's reply. "I've been looking at a house down near the high school. I used to drive by it every morning and thought it was just the sort of house I'd like to live in. Normal looking, you know? Not like that monstrosity of Mama's."

Angie turns and looks at Emma. "You want to see it? It's only a few minutes out of our way. We could see if the sign's still up."

"Sure," Emma says, "but just for a minute, okay? Ben's baseball game starts at one, and it's the first game of the season, so I can't be late."

"Oh, I'll have you home in plenty of time, don't you worry." Angie presses her foot to the accelerator and the truck lurches forward and then picks up speed. In a few short minutes they're turning right onto Richard Pettit Memorial Road and passing Richard Pettit Memorial High School. "It's just up here on Mountain Home Lane," Angie informs her, pulling onto a small side street. "It's a real pretty little neighborhood."

It is, in fact, the sort of neighborhood that always surprises Emma, because you don't expect its kind in Sweet Anne's Gap, with its sidewalks and quarter-acre lots, the houses a predictable mix of bungalows and small Cape Cods. The yards are neat and clearly tended to, each with a stand of forsythia threatening to bloom at any minute.

"Really nice," Emma tells Angie. "I like it."

"Yeah?" Angie asks, fixing Emma with a doubtful look.

"Really nice," Emma repeats. "Maybe not exactly what I pictured."

"Yeah, I know," Angie says, pulling the truck over to the curb. "You were picturing a trailer park, am I right?" Emma starts to protest, but Angie waves her away. "Don't worry about it. Hell, I look at me and think 'trailer park.'"

"Which house is the one you want?"

Angie points to a house three yards up from where they're parked. "And look, the sign's still up! Let's go see."

The house is a little bungalow with a screened front porch, the rhododendron bushes standing sentry. Emma can see that with a little work, it could be a magazine sort of house, the kind you dream about as you're waiting in the dentist's office, wishing your life was taking place somewhere else.

Except that in the magazine picture, Christine McCrae would not be sitting on the front steps, shaking her head and scowling.

"You just stop right there, Angie Byers," she calls down the sidewalk. "I know what plans you got up your sleeves, and I'm here to tell you, you best stay away from my daddy."

24.

"**How can you know** what plans I've got up my sleeves when I don't have a thing up my sleeves besides my arms?"

Christine snorts. "You know where I saw my daddy this morning? Blue Tree Realty office, is where. I was driving back from dropping Brittney off and got stopped at the light right by that big picture window. Looked in, and there's my daddy talking with Pat Teague. I decided I better go see what was going on, and what was going on was my daddy arranging to see this house."

"Well, what do you know?" Angie says under her breath, and then, louder, "Guess he's getting tired of living with his mama."

"How long before he gets tired of living with you?" Christine asks with a sneer. She stands up and suddenly seems to tower over them. Emma wouldn't be surprised if Christine suddenly sprouted talons and exhaled fire through her nostrils. It's turning out to be that sort of morning.

"Who said anything about us living together?" Angie asks, though the way she grins makes it clear that that's been the plan all along.

"Daddy did. Right there in the middle of Pat Teague's office. It was humiliating. She goes to our church!"

It's only then that Christine seems to notice Emma standing next to Angie. Her face changes, the pinched scowl softening into a smile, her eyes growing brighter, as if she finds something about the sight of Emma especially pleasing. "Oh, hey there!" she calls in a voice so friendly that Emma distrusts it immediately. "How convenient that you're here, too. Saves me a phone call."

Emma takes a step back, wondering if it's too late to run away, but Christine moves in closer as if to hold Emma in her magnetic field. "I stopped by my granny's on Wednesday, just to check in, and I found her fussing and fretting. She said when Mavis Abercrombie picked up some quilts from her last week, she made her sign some sort of agreement. You know about that agreement, right?"

Christine pauses, waiting for Emma's confirmation, and when Emma nods, she continues. "I do, too. I stopped by the church yesterday to see Nancy, the church secretary, and she was nice enough to make me a copy. I was surprised to read that if the quilts get damaged or stolen from the show, that is just too bad. Granny was mighty upset when I called and pointed that out to her."

Emma starts to answer, but Christine holds up a hand to stop her. "Granny's right to worry, don't you reckon? Those are valuable quilts. Folks are going to be in and out the whole weekend of the show, and I think it would be mighty easy to steal a quilt if you put your mind to it. I wanted to tell Barbara what I thought of the agreement, but she's out of town until Tuesday. Gone down the mountain to see a specialist about that ankle of hers. Nancy — we've been good friends since high school — says old Pastor Barbara's been a little depressed about how slow it's been healing. So

I decided I better just collect those quilts and put Granny's mind at ease. And while I was there, I picked up that Birds in the Air quilt, too. Just to be on the safe side."

"Oh, come on Christine," Angie protests. "You're being ridiculous. Ain't nobody gonna steal your damn Birds in the Air quilt."

"You already stole it once," Christine replies. "What's keeping you from stealing it again?"

"Looks like I got your daddy now," Angie says with a wicked glint in her eye. "I don't need his quilt."

Christine chooses to ignore this. Instead she turns to Emma and says, "I suspect a lot of folks signed over their quilts not truly understanding what they were doing. So many valuable quilts, too — Civil War quilts, autograph quilts, just lots of quilts with historical importance. Those are the quilts I'm worried about. I'd tell Pastor Barbara to expect to get some phone calls when she gets back."

"A lot of people are looking forward to that show," Emma points out, speaking in her best grown-up voice, even though she's not feeling very grown-up at this point. In fact, she's feeling like she'd really like to scratch Christine's eyeballs out. "Why try to ruin it?"

"I'm not trying to ruin it," Christine says. "I'm trying protect this community's heritage."

"God, you're an idiot," Angie says. She rattles her keys at Emma. "Could we go now? I've got a life to live and a meeting to attend. And you've got a baseball game, if I recall correctly."

"You're going to lose," Christine hisses after them, and Emma is pretty sure she's not predicting little league outcomes.

In the car, Angie opens her purse and pulls out her Nicorette pack. "When you quit drinking and drugs, they tell you to stay away from imbibers," she says, popping a piece of gum into her mouth. "Easier to avoid temptation than to resist it. The problem when you quit smoking is that it's so friggin' hard to avoid the Christine McCraes of the world. In fact, it's pretty near impossible."

"Thank God for Nicorette, right?" Emma smiles and holds out her hand as if requesting some gum. "Or is it only for smokers?"

"*Ex*-smokers," Angie replies, starting up the car. "And nicotine addicts. I wouldn't recommend being either if you can help it."

"So no gum for me."

"No gum for you, young lady."

They ride in silence for a while. Emma wonders how likely it is that Christine could get people to take their quilts out of the show. Maybe a few of them, she thinks, but most people will be reasonable. And more than that, they'll want their family heirlooms to be admired. They'll want to see their names in the program. Really, Emma convinces herself, there's not much to worry about. Christine is just being her usual, difficult, pig-headed self.

"It's funny to think that Christine and Lettie are half-sisters," she says to Angie, the idea just occurring to her. "They're so different in personality — in their temperaments, really. Lettie is so kind and generous, and Christine is, well, Christine."

Angie glances at Emma suspiciously. "What makes you think they're half-sisters?"

Emma realizes this isn't something she's ever discussed

with Angie, and she feels her cheeks grow hot. "Uh, I guess I thought it was one of those not so well kept secrets," she stammers. "And Lettie mentioned something to me — "

"Yeah, I bet she did." Angie sounds tired all of the sudden. Keeping one hand on the wheel, she reaches blindly for her purse, then grabs the pack of gum and pops out a piece. "For some reason, she's always thought that, even though I've told her a million times it's not the case."

"But she said Dallas was always giving her stuff when she was growing up. She and Christine used to have fights about it at school."

Angie puts the gum in her mouth, chewing hard to incorporate it with the first piece. "Dallas just felt sorry for her, that's why he gave her all that stuff. He's a good man, even if no one but me believes it. Plus, we were together at the time and giving Lettie presents was his way of giving *me* presents, if you get my point."

"So who's Lettie's dad?" Emma asks before she can stop herself. She holds a hand up. "Sorry, I know. None of my business."

Checking the rearview mirror as though she suspects someone is following them, Angie says, "It's not your business, that's for sure. But seeing as we're such good friends I'll tell you, only you can't say anything."

"I won't," Emma promises, feeling nervous. Does she really want to know this?

"Okay, then," Angie says, breathing in deep and then letting out the breath before continuing. "Way back yonder about twenty-seven — no, make that twenty-eight — years ago, I had the strangest one-night stand of my life. Wasn't planning on it, didn't seek it out. If I'd taken better care of my car, it never would have happened. But no, I'd been driving around for weeks with not one, but two red lights blinking on my dashboard. What was I supposed to do? I didn't have any money to pay to have it fixed. So I kept driving, and one night on the way home from work, my car broke down on Highway 15, over in Ledger. I figured I'd have to hoof it home, since it was late and unlikely anyone would be driving by. But I was wrong about that. I'd just gotten out of the car when Trace Brown pulled up in his truck — "

"Trace Brown!" Emma gasps. "But he's an old man!"

"He was a lot younger then, girl, and he was fine-looking. Well, except for them tiny ears. And him and Dorothy were going through a rough patch … that old story, right? One thing led to another, and nine months later I had me a little bundle of joy."

"Did you ever tell anyone who the father was?"

"I told Dallas as soon as I knew I was pregnant. And I told Mama a few years back. She didn't take the news very well."

"Is that why — ?"

Emma doesn't have to finish her sentence before Angie nods. "That's why she stopped quilting. Stopped going down to Ruth's store, quit the guild, quit Dorothy Brown. Couldn't face her."

"But nobody else knew! Dorothy doesn't know, does she?"

They've reached Emma's house, and Angie pulls into the driveway, but leaves the engine running. She turns to look at Emma. "Dorothy Brown's no fool. I think she may have put two and two together at some point. You ever notice Lettie's ears? They're tiny. She's got Trace's eyes, too. The fact is she looks a whole lot like her daddy. Now whether or not Trace knows is anybody's guess. Men can be pretty dense sometimes."

Emma slumps in her seat. She feels exhausted, like she might not have the energy to get out of the car and walk up the front steps to the house. "I don't know what to say."

Angie grins and pats her on the knee. "I wasn't asking for your opinion, honey. It is what it is."

"Are you ever going to tell Lettie?"

"I'm thinking about it. I used to believe I never would, but there's something they say at my meetings — you're only as sick as your secrets. Besides, Lettie deserves to know, I reckon."

"Wait — what about Kenny Brown?" Emma thinks to ask, one hand on the door handle. "I thought — "

"What, that we were close? Yeah, we were. Like family, or at least what passes for family these days. He helped me walk again after I broke my back. Folks read other things into our relationship, if you catch my drift, but it was friendship pure and simple. Now you best scootch, girl, or you're going to be late for that baseball game of yours."

Emma glances at the dashboard clock: she has twenty minutes to get something to eat and head over to the baseball field. Of course one of the benefits of living in a small town is that the baseball field's a five-minute walk from just about anywhere you happen to be.

It isn't until she's in the kitchen making a quick peanut butter sandwich that Emma remembers her garden supplies are still in the back of Angie's truck. She sighs. She's had enough Angie Byers for one day, friend or no. It occurs to her that she won't be able to hang out at Helen's anymore and take innocent delight in the three old men as they perform their parts in the daily town drama. The plot has thickened. Trace Brown is a more complicated figured than he was last week, when he smiled and tipped his hat at Emma on his way out the door with his elderly compadres. What if there's more to his story? Does he know that Lettie is his daughter? Does he know, but choose to ignore the inconvenient fact?

Emma takes a bite of her sandwich, but she doesn't taste it. *You're only as sick as your secrets*, Angie said, and Emma wonders if that counts for the secrets that other people tell you, the ones you wish you'd never been told.

25.

"**Emma? We have** a problem." Emma twists around in her seat and looks at the clock on the wall above the kitchen sink. It's almost 10:30, which means the Log Cabin class she's signed up for at the Sewing Room starts in thirty minutes. She's busy trying to solve her own problems — how to become a better quilter is at the top of today's agenda, followed by helping Sarah find more vintage toys for her centennial pageant presentation — and quite frankly she's not sure she has the time or the energy for anyone else's. Still, she hasn't talked to Barbara in over a week, so she does her best to sound cheerful.

"You're back! How was your visit with the specialist?" Emma rises and takes her coffee cup and the carton of half and half over to the counter, using her shoulder to pin the phone to her ear. "You doing okay?"

"That's not actually the problem I'm talking about," Barbara says, her voice flat, and Emma wonders if Christine's right about Barbara being depressed.

"Please don't tell me you heard from the printer and the program's not going to be ready on time," Emma says with a laugh. "I promise I got everything in under the deadline with at least five minutes to spare."

"It may not matter if the program's back from the printer on time. I had eighteen voicemails on my machine this morning, each one from someone who has a quilt in the show, each one saying they didn't understand the release form they'd signed and now they want their quilts back."

Emma nearly drops her coffee cup. It's been over a week since her run-in with Christine, and she hasn't heard a word until now about anyone taking quilts out of the show. Sitting down at the kitchen table, she realizes she's been an idiot. She'd let herself believe Christine wasn't going to go through with her threat; she should have known the woman was just biding her time. "I know Christine took her family quilts back, and she'd said she might contact a few other folks…"

"Eighteen's more than a few, Emma," Barbara says, sounding — what? Irritated? Were priests allowed to get irritated with people?

"It is," Emma agrees. "But we can get replacements, right? We still have two weeks until the show."

There is an uncomfortable moment of silence. When Barbara speaks again, her voice is gentler, but still strained. "They're all pre-1900 quilts, Emma. They're not replaceable. If you add Christine's quilts, the total is twenty-one. I think you can guess why that's a problem."

Emma doesn't need to guess. "That only leaves us with nine pre-1900 quilts," she says. She stands, suddenly in need of another cup of coffee. "And we're selling the show based on the number of historic quilts we have."

"And selling it quite well, I might add. Also in voice mail this morning I heard from the arts editors at two newspapers. Oh, and did I mention the president of the

Durham-Orange Quilt Guild called? The guild is renting a bus to come up the first morning of the show. She's especially interested in the Civil War-era quilts and also wanted to know the best place in the area to get lunch."

"I hope you told her Helen's," Emma says, trying to inject a note of levity.

Barbara sighs. "Emma, I want to laugh about this, but I can't. And I can't help but notice that sixteen of the people who called are from your contact list. A number of them said that you and Lettie didn't talk to them about the risks of loaning the quilts."

"Lettie said it was best not to worry people," Emma offers lamely. "You know, because the likelihood of a quilt getting stolen is so small."

"It is small, but that's not the point. These people were trusting us with their valuable and much-loved possessions. And now they think we were trying to fool them. So we've done considerable damage to St. Stephen's reputation in this area, not to mention the fact that instead of being a grand celebration of the town's centennial, the show's going to be a perfectly respectable local guild show, the sort you might — *might* — drive thirty minutes out of your way to attend."

Emma leans back against the counter and rubs her forehead. She can feel a headache setting in. "I'm so sorry, Barbara. What can I do?"

"I wish there were something," Barbara says, sounding tired. "But I'm afraid there's not."

"Maybe I could talk to Christine, get her to call everyone back. Because this is really about Christine being mad at me, mostly for moving here, but also for being friends with

Angie Byers. Maybe I could — I don't know — tell her I won't be friends with Angie anymore."

"Whatever motivated Christine to get people to withdraw their quilts, she's no longer a part of this equation. It's now between us and the families loaning us the quilts. They don't trust us to take care of their quilts, and I don't blame them. We haven't proven ourselves trustworthy."

"*I* haven't proven *myself* trustworthy you mean," Emma says.

"Listen Emma, I understand your motivation here — you didn't want people to say no. I get that. To be honest, I blame myself. I asked too much of you. You're a newcomer here, you don't understand how the relationships work. It's all about trust and reputation."

Emma can barely make herself squeeze out her next words. "I'm sorry, Barbara, I really am. Why don't you send me a list of the people who are withdrawing their quilts? At least let me try to get them back."

"You can try, but I don't think it will do much good."

"Fine," Emma says. "Just let me try."

After she hangs up, Emma turns to check the clock; it's 10:45. She thinks about skipping class. She tries to remember who else is signed up. Is someone going to be there that she'd rather not see? But the fact is, if she sits at home, all she'll do is stew. So why not walk over to the Sewing Room, borrow one of Ruth's machines for the class, and get her mind off this mess. On the way out the house, she texts Barbara, *Please send the list ASAP.* When she gets home this afternoon, she'll start making phone calls. Surely a few people will listen to her and change their minds, she thinks as she pulls the door shut behind her.

She's halfway down the street when a familiar voice calls out to her. "Hey, girl, slow down! Where you off to?"

Emma closes her eyes and takes a deep breath. She is not in the mood for Angie right now. She knows the quilt show crisis isn't her fault — not really — but still.

"I've got a class," Emma says when Angie reaches her. She makes herself smile, but she's sure it looks forced. "How about you?"

"I'm meeting Dallas for lunch at Helen's. We got paper-work to go over. We might get into that house by next month, fingers crossed."

They walk a little ways without talking. It's a beautiful morning, Emma finally notices, full-fledged springtime, a chorus of birds in every tree. As they approach Highway 15, she notices how many businesses have put big pots of geraniums outside of their doorways. *Picture-perfect*, she thinks, even though she knows that not every picture tells the real story. In fact, very few of them do.

"So, did I do something wrong?" Angie asks as they're crossing the street. "Because you're acting strange, and I'm known for messing stuff up."

Emma debates whether to say anything about Christine and the quilts. It's not Angie's fault or her problem. On the other hand, Angie can be remarkably clearheaded about things sometimes. Maybe she'll see something that Emma doesn't.

By now, they're standing in front of the cafe. The late morning crowd is dispersing, and Emma can imagine Cindy wiping down the tables and filling up ketchup bottles as she gets ready for lunch. If she didn't have her class, she'd go in and get a cup of coffee, add another inch to her waistline with a piece of coffee cake. But Ruth does not look kindly upon class skippers. The cake will have to wait.

Angie puts her hand on Emma's shoulder. "I wish you'd tell me what's wrong. I'd it hate it if I've done something to screw up our friendship."

Emma smiles, a real smile this time. To her surprise, there are tears in her eyes. "You haven't done anything. It's Christine — she called a bunch of people, got them to take their quilts out of the show."

Angie nods slowly. "Classic Christine. I almost feel sorry for her, you know? But she's got to learn how to deal with her crap without taking it out on other people."

Angie pulls out her phone and checks the time. "Okay, well, I'm late. I sure am sorry about those quilts — or the lack of quilts, I guess I should say. But you know what? I bet things will work out. I really do."

With that, Angie is up the steps and gone. Emma stands on the sidewalk, feeling like she's been slapped. Things will work out? What kind of 12-step nonsense is that? What kind of friend leaves you alone on the sidewalk, nearly in tears, and just walks away? The kind of friend who doesn't know how to be a friend, Emma thinks. The kind of friend who's probably not really a friend after all.

Emma looks at her phone. 11:10. She's late, and she doesn't feel like going to class anyway. She turns, crosses back over Highway 15 and heads for home. She's going to spend her day streaming the Chapel Hill radio station and surfing the web. Maybe she'll look at some real estate sites. She's starting to think that any place is better than here.

26.

On Thursday morning, Emma is lounging on the couch with a Pottery Barn catalog when the doorbell buzzes its imperious buzz. She's made plans to meet her realtor, Shana, at Helen's at eleven; is it possible Shana thinks they're meeting here instead? Emma sighs. She thought she had forty-five minutes before she had to explain how life in the mountains isn't working out for her family, forty-five minutes she planned to spend pretending she could afford sectional sofas that cost as much as a semester at a good state college.

She and Owen have decided not to tell the children they're thinking about moving unless they make a firm decision to put the house on the market. There's a long list of people Emma will wait to tell — Mavis, Suzanne, Angie, Barbara, among others. She wants to make a quick get-away if and when the time comes, and it'll be easier if there's not a long lead-up to their departure. Hopefully the house will sell fast. It's the perfect time to put it on the market; snowbirds are starting to come up from Florida to sniff around for vacation homes. And while Emma hasn't had time to do everything she'd planned, the fact is, the house looks good. The upstairs floors are shed of their shag carpets

213

and have been polished and buffed within an inch of their lives. The living room floor needs to be refinished, but the indoor-outdoor carpet has been replaced with a jute rug, and the scruffy hardwoods seem to be a decorating choice rather than the result of Emma having run out of time.

When was the exact moment that Emma got serious about moving? Was it being abandoned by Angie in front of Helen's? Was it making sixteen phone calls and getting hung up on sixteen times? Or was it when she went to Barbara's office a few days later with her brilliant plan to save the show? She'd searched the folklorists' field reports and made a list of people who owned Civil War era quilts who hadn't responded to Barbara and Ruth's initial queries. What if she and Barbara went door to door and asked for these quilts in person? Emma would even offer to pay the people out of her stipend for the loan of their quilts.

She'd called the printer and they could hold the program job until Monday. So if she and Barbara could get started right away, there was a good chance they could have all the quilts they needed. Emma would pull an all-nighter updating the program copy and the show could go on as planned.

Walking into St. Stephen's, Emma looked forward to giving Barbara this good news and slipping back into their easy friendship. She still felt the shock of Barbara's barely contained anger on the phone, her sharp tone. She wanted the old Barbara back, the funny, slightly goofy, warm Barbara. The Barbara who used to like her.

Instead, what she got was a weary — and wary — Barbara. Sitting at her cluttered desk, a pair of crutches leaning against the wall behind her, Barbara looked as though she'd aged five years, her normally rosy complexion pale, her skin drawn, her hair more gray than blonde. She looked as though she were in pain.

"How's the ankle?" Emma asked as she made a seat for herself on the couch among the piles of books and assorted clutter. "Better, I hope."

"It's better, but still not a hundred percent," Barbara said. "More like seventy-two percent. Maybe seventy-three."

As Emma laid out her plan, she watched Barbara's face, waiting for some light, a spark, something to show that Emma's ideas resonated with her. But Barbara's expression remained static, and when Emma finished, she shook her head, looking even more tired than before.

"I can't do it," she said. "I can barely do the work I need to do here. I'm not mobile enough to go trekking through the hills and hollers. And the fact is, I'm not willing to let you do it by yourself, simply because it would be a waste of time. Believe me, people will have heard about what happened. You'd be lucky if three people opened their doors to hear you out."

"But this time I'd be totally up front with them," Emma insisted. "And we'd explain to them how important their quilts are to our show."

Barbara shook her head. "I'm sorry, Emma, but no. I've already contacted the papers and the printer. This is just going to be a very different show than the one we planned. And that's fine. I've been calling guild members, and we'll have plenty of quilts, beautiful quilts from local quilters. People will enjoy themselves. So I want you to let go now, okay?" She smiled at Emma, and there was at last a hint of her old warmth. "It's really all my fault — I gave you a job you weren't suited for. You're not from here, so of course you were concerned people would be suspicious of you. I should have anticipated that would be a problem."

Leaving Barbara's office, Emma felt — what? Did she feel anything? Deflated, she supposed, flat, the gray sky overhead a perfect complement to her thoughts. How many times did people have to tell her that she wasn't from here, didn't fit in here, didn't belong here, before she got the message?

Really, it was her fault. She'd bought into a fantasy that turned out to be unworkable. A simple life in a small town, a beautiful house, friendly neighbors, a new career as a writer — all you had to do was move in, do a little remodeling, and that life would be yours. Except that it wasn't. Not for years and years, anyway, and suddenly Emma lacked the patience to wait. And the fact was, she'd never really be from Sweet Anne's Gap, would she? Maybe one day the children would be considered locals, but even that was doubtful. No, they'd probably always be that family from off the mountain that lived in Miss Lydia's house. They'd never entirely fit in here.

When Emma got home, she called Shana and made an appointment. And then she called Holly.

"I should have known better," she told her sister as she paced up and down the hallway. "I quit my job, sold my house, moved two hundred miles away from practically everyone I know, thinking I was going to have this great life. The simple life of a writer. And why? Because we found an inexpensive house with gables. What was I thinking?"

"That you were ready for a change? That you wanted to try living your dream?" Holly asked. "And didn't the house with the gables come *after* you made the decision to move?"

"'Living your dream,'" Emma replied in a sing-song voice. "Who comes up with that junk? Oprah?"

"You wanted to try a different life," Holly revised. "And maybe everything hasn't gone your way, but a lot of things have. Don't be hasty, Emma. A little resilience might be in order here."

"I'll never fit in," Emma said flatly. "That's the problem. I thought I could be a part of things here, but I never will."

"You know what Dad would say: If opportunity doesn't knock …"

Emma sighed. "Build a door. I know. But Holly, I don't have any wood."

"Then go cut down a tree."

After she hung up with Holly, she thought about cancelling her appointment with Shana. Maybe Holly was right; maybe she was giving up too soon. But when she thought of the mess she had made of the quilt show, she simply felt too tired to be resilient. Meeting with Shana was the right thing to do.

But she's positive they planned to meet at Helen's, so what's Shana doing here now? Emma puts down her catalog and goes to the front door. When she opens it, Angie Byers is standing on her front landing, wearing ripped jeans and a black leather jacket, in spite of the warm temperature. Her truck is idling in the driveway, Lettie at the wheel.

"Get your purse and get in the car," Angie orders. "We're going for a ride."

"I can't go for a ride," Emma tells her. "I've got an appointment at eleven."

"Well, cancel it, girl, because we've got places to be. Let's move."

Emma shakes her head. "Sorry, I can't cancel. It's important."

"Emma Byrd, you try my patience sometimes. Listen, I've been thinking about that whole mess with the quilts, and when Lettie showed me the list, well, I got to thinking even harder."

Emma's not following. "What list?"

"Of the folks you collected quilts from." Angie leans in, grabs Emma's wrist. "We're gonna get every one of them quilts back, don't you worry. You need to understand something about this place — everybody's had their wild days and their bad times. A lot of 'em have had their wild days and bad times with yours truly by their side. Most of them owe me, and some of them wish they didn't know me. One thing's for sure, though; when I tell 'em we want their quilts for our show, they'll sign whatever form I put in front of their face."

"*Our* show?"

"Yep, the Angie Byers Big-Ass Centennial Quilt Show. That's the new official title. So go get your purse, and let's hit the road."

Thirty minutes later they're sitting around Trudy Nidiffer's kitchen table. Trudy has her arms crossed, and her eyes narrow whenever she glances in Emma's direction. "You really think I'm going to let y'all keep that quilt and hang it in your show? I don't think so. I ain't picked it up from the church yet, but I'm aiming too as soon as Mason gives me a ride."

Angie leans back so that her chair is resting against the wall. She shakes her head, like Trudy just doesn't get it.

"You ain't got any worries about that quilt getting stolen, girl. I got Randy Marcotte and Stewart Partridge on guard Saturday night. You remember them? Old biker buddies of mine from back in the day. They don't ride no more and they don't drink no more, and they don't mind to help a friend out. You might remember how me and Randy were the best of friends at one time during high school."

Trudy cackles. "I remember the two of you getting caught in the girls' locker room senior year. I thought Mrs. Croley was gonna have a fit. I never seen a woman's face so red as when she was dragging you out that door."

"I was just getting a little physical therapy after a particularly rigorous volleyball game," Angie says with a wink.

"You can call it that if you want to," Trudy says. "But your shirt sure was buttoned up funny."

The two women shake their heads and laugh.

"Anyway, Trudy," Angie says once their laughter ebbs. "I ain't gonna let a thing happen to your quilt, and you know Randy ain't. You seen him lately? He's the size of a house and strong as three bears tied together."

"And you say he's guarding things all night?"

"Him and Stewart are camping out in the parking lot. Your quilt's gonna be safe as houses."

Trudy turns to give Emma one more dirty look, then picks up a pen. "I'll sign it 'cause of you, Angie. That's the only reason."

Angie pushes the release form across the table. "That's all the reason you need, girl."

On their way back to the truck, Emma turns to Angie. "Do you really have a couple of bikers lined up to guard the church?"

"You bet. The only question is who's gonna pay 'em the fifty bucks apiece I promised."

At the next house, Angie insists on going in alone. "I know some pretty serious dirt about Debbie Hauser, and I don't think she'd appreciate me sharing it in front of you two. Wait here in the truck — it shouldn't take me but a minute."

"What do you think she knows?" Emma asks as she and Lettie watch Angie walk up to the front porch. "Drugs? Murder? Larceny?"

"Drugs is my guess. She was with Ray for almost three years; she's probably watched a lot of deals go down."

"You must be glad she's not with him anymore."

"I am. I don't know that I'm crazy about the fact that she's with Dallas, although I suppose you could argue it was meant to be, sort of like Prince Charles and that woman — Camilla something-something. If it had turned out that Dallas was my daddy, maybe I'd even be excited. But now that I know he's not, it just seems sort of, I don't know. Tired or something. I can't explain."

"So Angie told you, huh?"

"Yeah, and she told me she told you, too. Which is weird, I mean that she told you first. I don't know, maybe she was practicing for telling me."

"Probably. It's a pretty big secret, and she'd been keeping it from a lot of people for a long time."

"Well, at least it explains Granny's retreat from the world. Mama didn't tell her until three years ago — took her near thirty years to work up the courage. And now I understand why Mama wouldn't tell me for so long. I think it would have been a lot easier for her if it had been Dallas, you know? The real funny thing is — " here Lettie's voice breaks, and it's a moment before she speaks again. "The real funny thing is, I used to wish somebody like Trace Brown had been my daddy. I just thought he was the best, you know? And now that I know he is? It makes me kind of sad, 'cause for him to be my daddy, he had to sleep around on Dorothy. So I guess he's not so great after all."

"He's human," Emma says. "He made a mistake."

Lettie shrugs. "Yeah, I know. But it doesn't matter anyway. It's not like we're gonna have some great father-daughter relationship. It's not like we're even going to talk about it."

"How's your mother-daughter relationship going?"

"It's going all right," Lettie says with a wry smile. "I'm glad Mama's around again, and I'm especially glad she's sober. But to be honest, I won't mind when she moves a few blocks down the road. A little bit of Angie goes a long way."

As if to underscore the point, Angie comes back down the walk, a quilt in her arms, grinning ear to ear. "I got what it takes, girls," she calls. "Yeah, man, I got what it takes!"

By the time they get back to town, they've got six quilts and sixteen signed release forms. Ten of the people they've spoken with today never got around to picking up their quilts from the church. On the one hand, that means they don't have to put any quilts in the truck bed and risk getting them dirty. On the other hand, it means their procession into St. Stephen's is less dramatic than it might have been.

"I hope Barbara's here," Angie says. "If she ain't, we're driving over to her house. I want my pat on the head for a job well done."

As it so happens, Barbara is at the front desk, leaning on her crutches and talking to the church secretary. "Hey,

Reverend Barbara!" Angie calls out. "I could use me some pastoral care."

Barbara turns carefully, her eyes widening when she sees the trio of women carrying two bulging bags apiece. "Are those what I think they are?" she asks, and Angie nods.

"Brought you back some of your quilts," she says. "We thought they might come in handy for that quilt show of yours."

"But how — ?

Angie holds up a hand. "Let's put it this way — people know I'm crazy, but they also know if I say nothing bad's gonna happen to their quilts, then nothing will. Now, no need to thank me, just get me in good with Jesus and send me down the righteous path."

Barbara swings her way over to where Angie, Lettie and Emma are standing. She places her hand on Angie's head. "May the Lord bless you and keep you, Angie Byers. Peace be with you."

"And also with you, honey," Angie responds, and Emma thinks the smile on her face could only be described as beatific.

27.

Emma has known a lot of mean girls, and the funny thing is, Christine McCrae is not the meanest girl on her list. That honor would most likely go to Stephanie Scopes in seventh grade, who regularly threatened to make Emma drink toilet water if she didn't let Stephanie copy her homework. Most of the mean girls Emma has known over the years never resorted to threats of physical violence. They preferred to tear you apart emotionally, usually on the sly, passing around slam books and starting whispering campaigns about how you desperately needed to use deodorant. On the whole, she preferred Stephanie's tactics, which were honest and straightforward, even if they made Emma's stomach hurt.

Now, looking at Christine over her cup of coffee, Emma wonders how mean she really is. Mean girls are after power, but Christine seems to want something else. Vengeance? Well, sure, there's that. But maybe more to the point, she seems to want justice. If Emma looks at things from her side, she can see why. If she were Christine, she'd think it was unfair her father loved Angie Byers all those years and not her mother. Unfair that he humiliated Christine and her mom in front of the entire community when he finally left the family. And she'd think it was really unfair how he's humiliating them even more by moving in with Angie now.

So she's quite willing to concede that Christine McCrae has cause for complaint. Life hasn't been particularly good to her, at least when it comes to fathers. And she's also willing to concede that Christine was right when she questioned the advisability of a newcomer to the community being put in charge of the quilt show. The fact is, Emma screwed it up. So when she looks across the table at Christine, she forces herself to see a woman with real grievances and a legitimate point of view. She's not a monster, just someone Emma's not all that crazy about.

"So why are we here again?" Christine asks, squeezing a lemon slice over her tea. "Because I've got to be back at work in thirty-five minutes."

"Where do you work?" Emma asks, surprised she doesn't know, given that everyone knows everything about everybody in this town. "Around here?"

"At McCauley & Weems? The law office two doors down across the street?" Christine's voice drips with disbelief, like, how could Emma not know such a basic thing?

"That must be interesting," Emma says. "Are you the receptionist?"

"I am a paralegal," Christine replies through clenched teeth.

Emma sighs. "I'm sorry. I don't know why I assumed . . ."

"You assumed I was a receptionist because you're a snob," Christine tells her. "You probably think someone who grew up here couldn't possibly be smart enough to do anything but answer phones and make appointments."

"I don't think that," Emma protests, but she wonders if

Christine might be right. Is Emma a snob? She doesn't think so, but maybe that's the sort of thing you'd never think about yourself. Someone else has to point it out to you.

"You do," Christine says flatly. "Maybe not about everyone who grew up here, but you surely think it about me."

"To be honest, Christine, I've never actually thought about you that much," Emma says, surprising herself because it's true and she's just realized it. "I mean, I've thought about how much you hate me, but as far as who you actually are, or what you're really like? I haven't had the time to think about those things. I've been too busy trying to jump over all the hurdles you put in my way."

"I don't put hurdles in your way," Christine mutters, dabbing at a spot of water on the table with her napkin. "I don't know what you're talking about."

"I'm talking about you telling your daughter not to be friends with my daughter. I'm talking about you trying to ruin the quilt show I've worked so hard on. Maybe I wasn't the right person to be in charge of the show, but I bet if I weren't friends with Angie, you might have tried to help me out instead of trying to mess things up."

Now Christine is looking Emma straight in the eye. "That's my point! Who would be friends with Angie Byers? She's a drug addict — okay, okay, a *former* drug addict who sleeps with anybody she wants to, even if they're married. Who would be friends with someone like that?"

"She asked for my help, I gave it to her, and we became friends. That's the only way I know how to explain it. By the way, if I'm such a snob, how did I end up being friends with someone like Angie Byers, huh?" Emma asks, sounding all of ten years old. "Tell me that."

"So you're a snob with bad taste," Christine says, and then she looks away as if she doesn't want Emma to see the expression on her face. But Emma does see it. Christine McCrae is obviously tickled by her own remark and is trying hard not to smile.

"I see you smiling," Emma reports. "So maybe you have a sense of humor after all."

The smile immediately disappears. "So tell me again — why are we here?"

"I want the Birds in the Air quilt in the show," Emma says, and Christine starts shaking her head, *no way*. "No, listen — hear me out. The fact is, we don't need it; we've gotten most of the people who took their quilts back to change their mind. But this quilt — it means something to me. It's what got me down to the Sewing Room. It delivered me into Ruth's hands and made me a quilter. You're right — I'm not that much of a quilter, but I love making quilts. So I want that quilt in the show. If you do that for me, I'll do something for you."

"What on earth could you do for me? I'd really like to hear that."

Emma leans in. "I'll go to church with you."

"You'll what?" Christine leans back. "You'll do what with me?"

"Go to church. The first time we met, you were very concerned because my family doesn't go to church. Well, I've been thinking about that, and I've decided it's time."

"You want to go to church with me?" Christine asks, and Emma nods.

"Yep, I want to see what all the fuss is about."

Christine looks out the window. She massages the index

finger of her left hand with the thumb of her right. "The thing is," she says finally, "I'm not really going to church much these days. It's a little bit embarrassing when your daddy has an affair with the church secretary, and then dumps the church secretary for his long-time girlfriend."

Emma takes a sip of her coffee. "I can see how that might be hard."

"You don't know a thing about it," Christine replies, but to Emma's surprise there's no venom in her voice. She just sounds tired.

Cindy comes by with a pot of coffee, tilting her head and raising an eyebrow as if to ask, *do you want a refill?* Emma nods, and she and Christine watch as Cindy expertly fills her cup.

"I never did like coffee," Christine says after Cindy leaves. "My husband, Wade, he drinks it by the gallon. But the few times I've tried it, it made me too jittery."

"I learned to drink it in college," Emma says, peeling open the creamer. "All those late night study sessions."

Christine takes a sip of her tea and Emma blows on her coffee. The silence between them stretches out. Christine starts tapping her fingers on the table, like she's waiting for something that's taking too long to arrive. Finally she leans toward Emma and says, "I think if you really knew Angie Byers, you wouldn't be friends with her."

Emma considers this. She knows enough about Angie to know that while she likes her a lot, there are things that make her uncomfortable. She hasn't given a lot of thought to Angie's relationship with Dallas. Looking across the table at Christine, she wonders if the reason she hasn't is because it would make her sympathetic to this woman who's done so much to make her life miserable.

"Listen," she says finally, "just because Angie's my friend doesn't mean I don't — that I don't get it. If I were you, I'd be furious. I would be. From what I know about it, Angie has done real harm to you and your family. But at the same time she's been making some pretty serious changes in her life. She's sober, she's trying to make amends. Maybe one day she'll make amends to you. I hope so. My point is, I'm not going to stop being her friend, but that doesn't mean I don't see things. That I don't think you have a reason to be angry."

Christine seems to think about this and nods. "I appreciate that."

"Anyway, about church," Emma forges on. "We could try a new church, see how we like it. We could go to St. Stephen's and see if they really believe in Jesus or if it's all about the communion wine."

Christine shakes her head. "My granddaddy would roll over in his grave if he saw me listening to a woman preacher. Baptists don't do women preachers, in case you weren't aware. Of course, the exercise might be good for him — it might open his mind a little."

Emma laughs. "So have we got a deal? You let us hang Birds in the Air in the show, and I give you the opportunity to turn me into a God-fearing Christian?"

"Well, if you put it that way, how can I refuse?" Christine doesn't smile, but her voice is slightly warmer now, almost halfway friendly.

Emma shrugs. "You can't. So you'll do it?"

"I'll get the quilt from Granny and drop it off." Christine checks her watch. "I guess I need to head on back to work."

She waves to Cindy for the check, but Emma stops her. "I've got it, don't worry. But there's one more thing I wanted to ask you."

The suspicious look returns to Christine's eyes. "What now?"

"Do you want to meet me at the church tonight and help hang the show?"

Christine looks around as though searching for an answer. After a moment, she nods.

"Yeah," she says. "I'd love to."

28.

There is something about waiting for one of her children to perform that completely unnerves Emma. Other parents jiggle in their seats and whisper excitedly as their child mounts the stage or the pitcher's mound, whereas Emma holds tight to her armrest or her water bottle and closes her eyes, mouthing the universal mother's prayer, "Please be okay, please be okay." Sarah has a tendency to lose her focus on stage, wandering off her mark or absentmindedly chewing her cuticles, while Ben freezes up if too many eyes are upon him (his outings as a pitcher have not been overwhelmingly successful, though he does fine at shortstop).

This afternoon, at the centennial pageant, attended by not only the entire student body of John D. Coe Elementary, but by parents and town luminaries as well, Emma feels especially jittery. It's not that she expects Sarah to do a bad job. In fact, given how many times Sarah and Carter have rehearsed their presentation on early 20th century toys and clothes, she's likely to give the performance of a lifetime. It's more that Emma feels like this is it — the moment where the citizens of Sweet Anne's Gap give the Byrds a thumbs up or the boot. Emma has decided to stay, but will they have her?

She figures people will either embrace Sarah as the worthy inheritor of Lillian McKinney's wardrobe or whisper among themselves that Lillian's dress really ought to be passed over to Brittany McCrae or another McKinney descendant.

Emma searches the audience for Christine McCrae and finds her seated in the second row next to the school principal and the president of the PTA. When people had called Christine difficult, Emma assumed that meant that she was unpopular. Rookie mistake, she thinks now.

"What are you smiling at?" Owen asks from the seat next to her. He has taken the afternoon off from work, Sarah threatening to disown him if he didn't.

"Oh, I was just thinking about how much fun it was last night, hanging the quilt show," she says, not wanting to bore Owen with more Christine McCrae drama. "It reminded me of getting the gym ready for prom."

"Is there going to be dancing tomorrow? Because if there's dancing, I'm not going."

"No dancing, I promise." Emma pats Owen's hand. "But you'd have to go either way. We set up a loafers' corner for people just like you."

Owen grins. "Sounds like my kind of quilt show."

Emma hopes that it will be everyone's kind of quilt show. It will be big enough to satisfy even the greediest quilt viewer — they're up to 67 quilts now and the show has spilled over into the sanctuary, where they have draped the smaller quilts over the backs of the pews. Emma thinks she might like that way of displaying quilts even more than hanging them. There's a homey feeling to the sanctuary now, as though this is how St. Stephen's does church on Sundays, with quilts for everyone to wrap themselves up in.

Ten women showed up the night before to hang the quilts, including Mavis, Ruth, Dorothy Brown, Christine, and Charlotte Stengle. Ruth helped Barbara set out a spread of goodies — brownies and pound cake, coffee and wine — and after they'd gotten half the show hung, Dorothy Brown said, "I don't know about the rest of y'all, but I could use me a drink for medicinal purposes." As it turned out, so could everyone else. Emma was surprised to see the locals imbibe — it was a dry county after all — and especially Christine, whom she assumed would be teetotaler. But no, Christine held out her glass to Barbara and said, "Pour it to the top; I mean, when in Rome, right?" Barbara, leaning on her crutches, laughed so hard she started snorting and thumping her chest with her hand.

The ice was officially broken after that. Dorothy and Mavis took charge, and they immediately began to revise Barbara and Emma's careful plans. "You cannot hang Courtney Jones' quilt next to Lucinda Petry's!" Dorothy exclaimed, and Mavis had agreed, saying, "Not unless you want to start World War III right here in your prayer center, you don't."

"What would be a peaceful and Christ-like solution?" Barbara asked, and the two women pondered this.

"Put Courtney next to Annie Cook," Dorothy decided. "They're cousins, and they always got along real good."

"And you can't hang Hilda Mason's quilt next to Bertina Mason's," Mavis said, pointing to the plans spread out on the conference room table.

"Why not?" Emma asked her. "They're both samplers from around the same period."

"Yeah, but Hilda was Walter Mason's first wife," Mavis

explained. "And Bertina was his second. The grandchildren still don't get along."

On and on it went — Mavis and Dorothy rearranging the show to make sure nobody's feelings got hurt or feathers got ruffled, that all family allegiances and feuds were noted and dealt with. They worked until 10:30, with plans to reconvene Friday night for final touches.

Now Emma feels eager to get back over to the church and finish the job. She peeks in her purse at the program she took with her from Barbara's office; she hopes people who come to the show will be as pleased with it as she is. She hopes they'll think she's done a good job writing this community's history through quilts.

The curtain rises and the children of John D. Coe Elementary parade onto the stage. Emma searches for Sarah and finds her in the back next to Carter, the two of them in their long dresses and braids looking as though they've traveled a hundred years to get here. There is an opening song about someone named Anne McIlveen, the sweetest ol' gal you ever done seen, and then the stage goes dark but for a single spotlight. Sarah and Carter come forward as a stagehand brings out a large wooden box, which he sets next to Sarah.

Emma reaches over and squeezes Owen's hand, and Owen squeezes back. He of course has utter faith that all will go as planned. Lines have been learned, stage blocking has been memorized. What could go wrong? Emma tries not to refer to the long list she's composed over the last few nights, her mind racing with one worry after another as sleep eludes her.

"She's going to do great," Owen whispers. "And even if she doesn't, so what?"

Emma refuses to let herself answer that question. She takes a deep breath and decides that best course of action is to pretend the child on the stage is not her child, but some young stranger who she has absolutely no emotional investment in.

"Imagine a hundred years ago," Sarah begins, her voice projecting across the audience, "before TV and cell phones …"

"Before the Internet and video games!" Carter adds, and then they're off, pulling toys from the box, explaining how the children of Sweet Anne's Gap lived and played a hundred years ago. Although Emma knows, from having repeatedly timed it, that their presentation is three minutes and twenty-five seconds, it seems to be over in a flash, the audience applauding warmly when the girls finish.

"I'm so glad they went first," she tells Owen, relaxing into her seat. "Now I can enjoy the show."

"*Enjoy* might be a strong word," Owen says. "But okay, sure."

The assembly goes on for forty-five minutes, and by the end, Emma feels like she knows more about mica mining, planting by the moon and building a railroad through the mountains than any woman has a right to. Ben was in the train presentation, dressed up like a junior engineer, and Emma enjoyed watching him doing nothing more than walk across the stage behind the window of a cardboard train on wheels.

There is loud, extended applause as the curtain goes down after one last bow from all of the children. As Emma and Owen make their way to the cafeteria for a punch-and-cookies reception, people lean over and pat them on the shoulder, say "Sarah was absolutely wonderful!" and "Your girl did a mighty fine job up there." By the time she reaches the punch bowl, Emma is glowing. People know her, and they know that Sarah is her daughter. How funny that the drawback and benefit of living in a small town are virtually one and the same — everybody knows you. Of course, Emma's not fooling herself. She knows that one great elementary school performance by Sarah doesn't automatically mean the Byrds will now be accepted, but it does mean that they've added a thread to the fabric that makes up Sweet Anne's Gap daily life. They've entered into the story.

Emma suddenly feels too exhausted for small talk, even if she is the mother of a celebrity, so when Suzanne finds her it's next to a poster on fire safety near the emergency exit. "Ah, so this is where the Introverts Anonymous meeting is. Our girls did good, don't you think?"

"They did great," Emma says. "I don't think Sarah's going to be coming off cloud nine any time soon, that's for sure."

Suzanne smiles. "Carter, too. In fact, the girls are asking for a sleepover at our place tonight, so they can celebrate their brilliant performances all night long and then ride the pony in the morning. You okay with that?"

"Sure, I'll get Owen to pick her up Saturday before lunch. I'll be at the quilt show all day."

"That's right!" Suzanne exclaims. "It's the big show! How about I bring Sarah and Carter over to St. Stephen's after lunch to see the quilts? I'm sure they'll have expert opinions on all the historical stuff. And then how about I have you over for brunch on Sunday to celebrate?"

"That sounds — oh, wait!" Emma shakes her head like she can't believe she's forgotten this. "I have to go to church on Sunday."

"You *have* to?"

Emma nods. "I told Christine McCrae I would. We're going to St. Stephen's, which ought to be interesting."

"Well, maybe I'll see you there," Suzanne says. "I like to pop in from time to time. And maybe we could do lunch afterwards?"

"Perfect. By then, I'll definitely need to process."

What she needs right now, Emma realizes, is a nap. After dinner, she's back to work on the show, and then she'll be busy all day tomorrow. Really, she probably should have declined Suzanne's lunch invitation — will she even be able to sit up at that point? — but if she's learned anything these past few months, it's that you don't turn down offers of friendship. Emma needs all the friends she can get.

After she and Owen collect the children, they walk back home, Sarah and Ben still in their costumes. As they near the house, Emma sees someone on the steps. Angie?

"Is that somebody's grandma on our porch?" Ben asks as they get closer, and Emma sees that whoever's on the steps is too old to be Angie Byers and too bent over to be Ruth or Dorothy Brown. So who is it?

The snow-white hair should have tipped her off. Hannah Byers, of course. Well, not of course. In fact, Emma has absolutely no idea why her neighbor has finally come over for a visit. Does she have a complaint? Does she want Emma to discourage Angie from moving in with Dallas McKinney (as though anyone could stop Angie from doing anything)? Is she hoping Emma might teach Lettie to quilt, since she's done such a bang-up job with her daughter?

They're close enough to the house that she can see Hannah has a cardboard box next to her — Angie must have finally finished her quilt and wants to put it in the show. She missed the deadline, but maybe she thought Emma would take a late quilt if her mother brought it over. Maybe she thought Emma would take any quilt, given the recent crisis.

"Hello, Mrs. Byers!" Emma calls. "How nice to see you! You missed an awfully good pageant at the elementary school just now."

Hannah Byers slowly rises to her feet, then bends to pick up her box. Emma's a little concerned she's going to topple over, but the old woman grabs the rail with her free hand and steadies herself.

"Hey, there, honey" she calls when Emma reaches the front walk. "I was hoping we could talk."

29.

Emma stands in front of Lillian McKinney's sampler quilt and squints. The stitches are so tiny, she can barely make them out, and she marvels at the patience it must have taken to piece each of the twelve blocks. Ohio Star, Old Maid's Puzzle, she recites under her breath. Bear's Paw, Lady of the Lake, Birds in the Air. The colors are faded, but Emma would guess the reds in the quilt are Congo Red and the blues are Cadet Blue. Barbara has been teaching her the history of fabric dyes, although honestly Emma doesn't know how interested she is. She'd rather focus on the names of blocks and patterns. She likes it that she can name almost all of the blocks in Lillian's sampler. She thinks Lillian would be proud of her.

When she steps back, she can view Lillian's quilt and her own, her four-patch simple-as-can-be home-quilted quilt. Unlike Lillian's, Emma's stitches are not always uniform and not always evenly spaced; sometimes she gets carried away pushing down the pedal and the stitches become tiny and cramped and almost impossible to rip out if she makes a mistake. She's working on this.

It was Barbara's idea to hang the two quilts side by side. "You made one quilt in your house and found the other one there, right? In a way, Lillian McKinney is sort of like your patron saint of quilting. The two of you belong together."

Yes, Emma thinks now, nodding. We do.

"I can't tell you how impressed I am with your quilt," Barbara says, coming up beside her. "You've been quilting such a short time, and you made this. Fantastic!"

"It's not much, but it's what I've got," Emma says, knowing it's true, but also aware that at home on her table are four blocks of a modern Dresden plate quilt that's going to knock everybody's socks off. Okay, that will knock her own socks off. The point is, she's making progress.

Barbara nods at the wisdom of this. "We start where we start, and then we keep going. I predict great things from you as a quilter."

"I'm not sure I'm intended for quilting greatness," Emma says. "But I'm okay with quilting goodness. I think that's a fair enough goal."

The exhibit in the prayer room has four focal points among the masses of quilts on display: a selection of Civil War-era quilts near the entrance, a display of quilts from the Great Depression on the other end of the room, another of Baltimore Album and autograph quilts in front of the eastern window and, lastly, in the area created the night before — a circle in the center of the room — five quilts by Hannah Byers.

"Angie told me what happened, and I felt awful bad about it," Mrs. Byers told Emma last night, the two of them sitting in rocking chairs on the front porch. "I know Christine has cause for grievance, but she shouldn't take it out on you. It ain't your fault what Angie done."

Or yours, Emma wanted to say, but doesn't. "Christine has come around," she tells Mrs. Byers. "She's still upset, but she knows how important this show is to the community."

Mrs. Byers nodded vigorously. "It *is* important. Why, everybody in these parts makes quilts — we ought to celebrate that. Dorothy Brown come over to my house just yesterday to show me her Dear Jane quilt. Law, I ain't never seen anything so pretty in my life."

"Dorothy came over?" Emma asked, wanting to add, *and you answered the door?*

"Yeah, me and her been friends for a long time, you know. There's a little water under that bridge, but I think we got everything cleared up. Did you know she did the long-arming on Angie's quilt, the one she's giving me for my birthday?"

Emma rocked back so hard she thought she might flip over. "How did that happen? I didn't even know Dorothy had a long-arm machine."

"Oh, she don't, but Angie called her up and asked if she knowed who'd do the best job on the quilt she was making for me, and Dorothy told her, 'let's go rent a machine down in Marion and I'll show you how it's done.' I didn't know there was a machine down in Marion to rent, but apparently they've opened up a new shop down there."

Emma smiled and shook her head. Sounded like Angie Byers had been trying to make amends — to Dorothy and to her mother. If Dorothy was willing to help Angie with her quilting, which is to say, forgive her, then Hannah was free to be friends with Dorothy again. Tangled webs — wasn't that what small town life was all about?

"Anyway, when I heard what Dorothy done, I just had to call and thank her, and she said, 'Won't you let me come over and visit,' and I said 'Why, I wish you would.' And when she come she said, 'Now Hannah Byers, you have got to hang some of your quilts in this show they're doing at the Episcopal church. I told her I'd think about it, and I've thought about it, and here they are." Mrs. Byers pointed to the box at her feet. "There's five of them. The Houston quilt's in there, and the Best in Show from Lancaster back in, oh, I don't know. It was a while ago. And Angie's quilt is in there, too, if you'll have it. She says it ain't no good, but she's wrong about that. You done a good job teaching her how to make a quilt. Better than I ever could."

"Only because you're her mother," Emma said. "Sometimes our mothers are the last people we want to learn from."

"Yes, ma'am, I know that to be the truth."

In the short period of time that Emma's been quilting, she's become familiar with the debate over whether quilting is an art, a craft or a hobby. Most quilters seem to rule out *hobby* immediately. They're not collecting bottle caps, after all, or building model cars in the basement. But the vast majority seem uncomfortable calling what they do art. *Craft* is the comfortable middle ground, as far as Emma has been able to ascertain.

There's something honorable and workman-like about calling what you do a craft. Calling it an art seems to be overstepping, practically bragging.

Be that as it may, Emma looks around the exhibit and sees countless works of art, and none more deserving of that title than Hannah Byers' quilts. They're nothing short of astonishing. And not at all what you might expect from a woman who has spent her life in an isolated town tucked away in the Blue Ridge Mountains. The quilts are composed primarily of traditional blocks — or what Emma might call tradition-al-*ish* blocks — in hues that remind her of Chagall's palette, the intense blues and bright reds, glowing oranges, vibrant greens. They're poised somewhere on the spectrum between traditional and modern, several of the quilts making interesting use of negative space, others appearing at first glance to meet a traditional aesthetic — blocks set in rows, sashing, cornerstones — only to reveal on closer examination that several of the blocks have tiny differences, a pair of flying geese flying in a different direction from all of the others, for instance, or a star with one point a different color from the rest. The quilts take tradition and freshen it up a bit, make it a little surprising.

The artist herself is standing beside her quilts, holding hands with Dorothy Brown. They are both crying, Emma sees, and the people around them are discreetly giving them some space, a few of them dabbing at their own eyes with tissues. Oh, Angie Byers, you're not so bad after all, Emma thinks, not if you made this happen.

"Excuse me, but can we talk?"

Emma turns around to find Christine McCrae standing behind her and sighs. Good grief, what is it now?

"Walk over to the church with me, why don't you?" Christine says, her voice neutral. "There's something we need to discuss."

Emma takes a deep breath and follows Christine. "Is something wrong? I thought we were good. Or as good as we're going to get."

"Oh, you did, did you?" Christine doesn't bother turning around. "Pretty presumptuous of you, I'd say."

Emma feels like a child being led to the principal's office.

Why is she in trouble? Why can't Christine McCrae stop making her life miserable?

Christine pushes through the door to the garden that occupies the space between the prayer room and the sanctuary. There is a sea of tulips, red, yellow and blue. Emma would like to dive into all that color and hide, but she follows Christine into the sanctuary, which is swarming with people admiring the quilts. Ruth and Mavis run back and forth with white-gloved hands, lifting a corner of a quilt here, turning another one over there. They've posted signs every ten feet politely asking viewers to refrain from touching the quilts, and from what Emma can see, people are keeping a respectful distance. There does seem to be a large crowd hovering awfully close to the McKinney quilts display — maybe that's Christine's complaint; everyone's breathing on her family's quilts, or talking too loud in their presence. Whatever, Emma thinks. Let's get this over with.

"Look at that." Christine points to the crowd in the front. "It's been like that all morning, everybody telling stories. I'm actually learning things I didn't know. Did you know my great-great granny was a nurse in the Civil War? She's the one who made Birds in the Air. I knew about her before today — I mean, I knew she existed and I knew she made that quilt, but I didn't know she'd been a nurse. The thing is, I always wanted to be a nurse, but somehow I never could make my way to nursing school. Anyway, Granny was here a little bit ago, and she said I could have that quilt if I wanted."

Emma takes a hard look at Christine. Is she actually enthusiastic about this? Maybe even happy?

"It's a nice quilt," she says. "I can see why Angie stole it."

Christine looks at her, eyebrow raised. "You are just barely in my good graces, Emma Byrd. Don't push your luck."

"You're Emma Byrd?"

A man has come up behind Christine and now holds out his hand. "I'm Glenn Ledford, and I run the historical society here in town. You've probably heard of me."

Emma hasn't, but she shakes his hand enthusiastically to make up for it. "So nice to meet you!"

"Well, I've been wanting to meet you ever since I saw Lillian McKinney's sampler quilt hung up next to your quilt in the exhibit this morning. Christine here tells me that you're the current owner of Lillian's quilt."

"I am," Emma says. "I found it in a trunk in my attic."

Mr. Ledford nods. "In the old Buchanan place. I know it well. And I know all about Lillian McKinney. I wonder if you'd like to hear about the murder sometime?"

Emma's eyebrows shoot straight up. "Murder? Who was murdered?"

"Why, Lillian McKinney of course!" Mr. Ledford sounds like he can't believe Emma doesn't know this, and given how fast gossip spreads in this town, Emma can't blame him. "Back before the war. I've got three files on the case, which has never been solved, by the way. Quite a mystery, though I have my suspicions about who did it. Most folks do."

Emma feels the need to sit down. Lillian was murdered? Is dead? Of course, she was born in the late 1800s; it wasn't like she'd be alive today one way or another. Still, Emma feels like she's been run over. "I can't believe she was murdered."

"Why don't you come to my office next week and I can show you my files? It was the biggest news story of the time, at least until the war came along. I'm amazed no one has written a book about it. Come by my office on Monday and I'll tell you all sorts of things about Lillian West McKinney. I open at ten sharp."

"I'll be there at 9:55," Emma says.

And then she pulls out her phone and texts Holly. *I found my story*, she writes.

It was only a matter of time, her sister replies two seconds later. *Can't wait to read the first chapter!*

"Emma! Emma!" Suzanne is waving to her from the back of the room. "What a marvelous show! You should be so proud!"

It's almost lunch, but the crowd seems to be growing instead of thinning. Emma pushes through the mass of bodies and meets Suzanne in a middle pew with only a few quilts on display. Suzanne gives Emma a quick hug and says, "I mean it — what a marvelous job you and Barbara have done! And look at all these people! Did you see there are Tennessee license plates in the parking lot? "

Emma plops down onto an empty spot. She'll need a few minutes to recover from the news about Lillian McKinney. "Do you mind?" she asks Suzanne. "The day is only halfway done, and I have no idea how I'm going to make it till five."

Suzanne takes the seat next to her. "You must be exhausted. And you know what? You're going to be too worn out for lunch tomorrow. I don't know what I was thinking. Besides, I have a better idea — let's have lunch at Helen's on Monday and discuss the contract I'm about to sign."

Emma stares at her. "You bought the store?"

"Honey, I bought the building," Suzanne says. "Are you ready to go to work?"

Just as Emma's about to reply, her back pocket buzzes. *Can you take over the front desk in 5?* Barbara has texted, and Emma texts back *K*. Two seconds later, Barbara replies *Is that K as in OK or K as in que as in "what"?*

Be there in 5, Emma taps back. She turns to Suzanne and says, "Duty calls. But I can't wait to talk more about this. Only I'd probably only be able to work part-time. I've just decided to take on a new project."

"Great! A part-time employee is exactly what I can afford," Suzanne says. "You're hired!"

Emma walks back through the garden on her way to the prayer room, smiling at the thought of how much money she'll spend if she takes a job in a gallery two doors down from the Sewing Room. She wonders if she should invest in Suzanne's shop, even if it's a small investment. Emma likes the idea of having a real stake. And she likes the idea of being somebody with an actual place in the community. It's occurred to her that she knows all kinds of people in town who aren't local, but who feel local because they each have a specific role. Ruth is the quilt shop owner and Charlotte is the school librarian and Barbara is the Episcopal minister. Of course, all of them are quilters, and that gives them another way in. It has given Emma a way in, too. *A way into a cult*, she can just hear Mavis saying with a laugh. Well, sure, there's that. But also: into friendship and creativity and good work. Totally worth the money, Emma thinks with a smile.

"You sure look like a happy camper, and I don't blame you."

Angie Byers is sitting on a stone bench, smoking a cigarette.

"But you quit!" Emma cries. "You were doing so well, too."

Angie pats the space next to her on the bench. "Have a sit-down, if you don't mind second-hand smoke. And you're right, I did quit, and I did pretty good at quitting, at least for a while. I think the problem is that I quit too many things at one time. I can't fight all my battles at once."

Emma nods, feeling disappointed. She liked the idea of a one hundred percent reformed Angie Byers. Besides, if Angie starts backsliding in one area, what's to keep her from backsliding in others?

"I'm not going to start taking painkillers again," Angie says, as though reading Emma's mind. "That was a one-time thing that just happened to last three years. Now take a load off, why don't you?"

"I'd love to, but I have to take over the front desk for Barbara," Emma says. "But tell me what you think of the show before I go."

"I think it's added twenty years to my mama's life and taken another twenty off of her face."

"You did that," Emma says. "You know that, right?"

Angie nods. "Yes ma'am. I did it with your help, and I thank you for it."

"But did you know from the start that you'd ask for Dorothy's help, too?"

"That idea come to me about half-way through," Angie says, dropping her cigarette and stomping it into the path's white gravel. "It broke my heart that Mama gave up her quilting, but more than that, that she gave up her friends. I figured that if Dorothy did me a favor, it would show Mama that all was forgiven."

"If Dorothy even knew what there was to forgive," Emma points out.

Angie looks at Emma like she's crazy. "Who are we kidding? Of course Dorothy knew. The woman's not an idiot. Took her thirty years to forgive me, and she didn't have to, but she did."

"Did you ask her to?"

"I begged." Angie stands and stretches, as though she's had a long morning, too. "I begged her for Mama's sake and I begged her for my own. God, I was stupid. Can you believe how stupid I was back then?"

"Not really," Emma says, trying to sound supportive, and then admits, "Okay, yeah, I can believe it."

Angie barks out a ragged laugh and pulls Emma into a half-hug. "I always did like you, you know that, right? You keep it real."

The two women make their way to the prayer room. When they get inside, Angie tugs at Emma's elbow. "Did I show you my favorite quilt in the entire show? It's right over there." Angie points across the room and says, "That one over there. Simple, but colorful. Deceptively primitive, I think you'd call it."

She's pointing to her own quilt, tucked away in a corner, the only space left by the time they got around to hanging it the night before. "Don't you think that quilt is something else?"

"It's beautiful," Emma agrees. "I love it."

"Me, too," Angie says. "I finally done something I'm proud of through and through, no regrets. Well, that quilt and Lettie."

"Come sit with me at the front desk," Emma says. "We can talk about our next quilts. Maybe Lettie could make one, too."

"Sounds like a plan," Angie says, and she follows Emma through the room, past Hannah's quilts, past Lillian McKinney's. Past her own.

"They just hang there like stars, don't they?" Angie asks, and Emma nods. Like stars in the sky, she thinks. Like birds in the air.

Acknowledgments

So many people to thank! First and foremost,
my editors, Kristin Esser and Sandy Hasenauer, who
helped me shape a big mess of a story into the novel
you have in your hands. Thanks to early readers
Barbara Atkins, Marianne Fons, Jaye Lapachet and
Annie Smith, for their feedback and kind words.

Thanks to the listeners of THE OFF-KILTER QUILT
podcast and to my online quilting posse, the TWILTERS.
Your support, friendship and enthusiasm for this
project have meant the world to me.

I owe a great debt to my longtime editor, Caitlyn Dlouhy
at Atheneum Books for Young Readers, who
pretty much taught me how to write a story and
was excited when I told her about this one,
even though it's not for children.

Finally, I want to thank Clifton, Jack, Will and Travis
(the dog), for being the nicest family a girl could have.